LIVE FAST, SPY HARD

A John Sand Thriller

MAX ALLAN COLLINS

WITH

MATTHEW V. CLEMENS

WOLFPACK
PUBLISHING
— EST 2013 —

WOLFPACK
PUBLISHING
— EST 2013 —

Live Fast, Spy Hard

Paperback Edition
Copyright © 2021 Max Allan Collins

Wolfpack Publishing
6032 Wheat Penny Avenue
Las Vegas, NV 89122

wolfpackpublishing.com

Paperback ISBN: 978-1-64734-995-0
eBook ISBN: 978-1-64734-994-3
LCCN 2021931559

LIVE FAST, SPY HARD

For
Paul Bishop
who put Humpty Dumpty
back together

*Bond reflected that good Americans
were fine people and that most of them
seemed to come from Texas.*

—Ian Fleming

ONE

YOU ONLY DIE ONCE
MARCH 1959

CHAPTER ONE
I GOTTA CROW

When John Sand came awake, finding a pounding head awaiting him, he did not open his eyes.

Call it a skill, call it a strategy, but he had learned long ago that when he went to sleep somewhere other than a cozy bed – specifically when that sleep came suddenly in a tense situation – he had best maintain the semblance of a lack of consciousness until he could take inventory.

Beyond a goose egg throbbing at the back of his skull, his tally included having his hands bound behind his back, calves lashed to the legs of a straight-back chair, and his head slumped forward, chin touching chest. Allowing his eyes slits through which to view, he found himself still wearing his gray suit, a now sweat-blotched white shirt, his navy blue tie properly knotted at his throat. Running his fingers over his left wrist, he realized that the Vertex Breguet watch, freshly requisitioned to him by the R & D Branch for this mission, was M.I.A.

Not only did that mean he could not push the stem twice, activating the tiny high speed metal wheel that popped out to cut bonds in such circumstances, he would likely have his payroll packet garnished to cover the loss of equipment.

The Research and Development Branch was, after all, the tightest of sectors when it came to enforcing its budget, the quartermaster himself a stern (and stingy) taskmaster. For the moment, at least, Sand had slightly more pressing problems. Without the quartermaster's gadget, he was back to relying on his wits.

Satisfied he was not seriously injured, Sand lifted his chin and slowly opened his eyes, only to be blinded by bright light, prompting him to squeeze the lids shut again. The fraction of a second after the blinding effect had been enough to chart two other men in the room, one on either side (and just in front) of him. The one to his right appeared to be in his late twenties, had an anchor tattooed on the back of his left hand, and sported the Aryan good looks that might just hint at a past in the Hitler Youth. The one at left was slightly older, thicker, and shifted from one foot to the other, warding off the chill of the apparently unheated room. Both men wore dark pea coats, the one on the left sporting a black flat newsboy cap.

That's all the fraction of a second had got him.

Opening his eyes again but unable to focus his vision adequately, Sand relied on his other senses, noting that the room smelled musty with a secondary aroma of something else - petrol. As he avoided the light aimed directly at his face, he listened sharp. Beyond the high intensity lamp in the darkness, at least two more men spoke in hushed tones. So the odds were four to one, anyway. Things could be worse – could be five of them. Or six.

What an optimist I am, he thought. *Some would say the room is half-empty, others that it's half-full.*

The bright light was a high-intensity, gooseneck desk lamp, resting on an old wood table, which would have been out of his reach even if his hands weren't bound. This was the sole illumination in a cement-block, windowless chamber of indeterminate size.

The blond man at right had a surprisingly deep voice, really wrong for his youthful face. "*Das britische spiona- geschwein ist wach.*"

British spy pig? That was uncalled for, and such poor syntax. Sand would dispatch this illiterate lout first.

The hushed voices beyond the light halted, and feet scraped on cement as the men walked closer to the lamp. Sand could now make out their silhouettes, one on the lamp's either side, but still behind it.

Lumbering around the spotlight, coming to a stop in front of him, almost blotting out the light at first, was a towering, broad-shouldered man with coal-color hair that hung past his shoulders. He smiled, revealing two rows of big white teeth contrasting with flesh of a shade near polished cherry wood. The rangy American Indian wore jeans, a black turtleneck, and a gray blazer that might have served as a tarp on a truck bed. His ensemble was set off by black combat boots.

"Crow," Sand said by way of acknowledgment, and his voice was raspy in his ears.

The Indian's grin became a smirk. "John Sand, pride of MI6, licensed to liquidate without prejudice."

"Also *with* prejudice," Sand noted.

Crow huffed a laugh; it seemed forced to the prisoner.

The Indian said, "All it took was baiting the trap with a bosomy blonde...so predictable. And now here you are – trussed up like a Thanksgiving turkey."

"I'm afraid we don't celebrate Thanksgiving in En- gland." Sand summoned a grin. "Didn't work out so well for your people ultimately, either, and here you'd been thoughtful enough to bring the corn."

"If you think we're in England," Crow said, "I must have hit you harder than I thought."

Sand glanced around at nothing but darkness, though his night vision had kicked in enough to sketch in the more immediate area. "I assume we're still in Germany. And where *is* the lovely Miss Fluss? I'd love to pay her my regards."

The man called Crow leaned closer, but not near enough for Sand to head butt him, the assassin no fool. The Indian held up Sand's Walther P38, made to look small by the large hand. "You have your tools of the trade, and we have ours."

"Like Miss Fluss."

"Like Miss Fluss. When we're done with a job, we consign the likes of her to a toolbox till we need her wares again."

Of course Sand had known the almost ridiculously sensual, bouffant blonde Kyla Fluss, all lipstick and mascara and cleavage, worked for the same masters as Crow. He had known the vixen was leading him into a trap, part of the plan to get close enough to Crow to find out what the assassin's bosses were up to in Berlin. He hadn't counted on Crow having a dozen gunmen with him.

That room had definitely *not* been half-full....

Setting Sand's Walther on the table next to the lamp, Crow demanded, "What do you know of our business here?"

Nothing. Learning something was what Sand had been sent to Berlin to do.

Sand said, "That's the wrong question."

"How so?"

"The question is, have I passed along my information to my people, and have your efforts been exposed?"

Crow merely smiled, a tight crooked line in the craggy face, big teeth tucked away. From a jacket pocket the Indian withdraw a pack of Pall Malls, shook a smoke out, then fished around in the pocket again, this time coming back with a matchbook. He lit the cigarette, leaned a bit closer, and sent the smoke into Sand's face.

His head withdrawing before Sand might finally head-butt him, Crow said, "You blow smoke, *I* blow smoke."

"Aren't smoke signals a little passé?"

The thick-set guard in the flat newsboy's cap had been inspired to take out his own pack of cigarettes, Karos, a strong cheap brand common in Germany that Sand wouldn't have smoked in his most nicotine-desperate hour. The guard motioned for a light, and Crow tossed him the matchbook. When Newsboy Cap caught it, his wrist extended from his coat sleeve, and Sand glimpsed a familiar Vertex Breguet wristwatch.

Good to know – now he could get his watch back while he was escaping.

Crow came closer, the tip of the cigarette in his hand glowing red hot as it neared Sand's eye.

"If I put this out in your pupil, would you talk, I wonder?"

"Is that a rhetorical question? Of course I wouldn't talk. I'd pass out from the pain, you putz."

Crow's brown eyes showed not a glimmer of empathy, but – to his credit – no anger, either. "You would suffer pain and disfigurement for Queen and Country?" The big head wagged. "The *bullshit* you Brits believe."

Sand kept his shrug to a minimum, as the hands tied behind him were working methodically at the knots. "Call me old-fashioned. Or perhaps unimaginative."

With a sigh that began down in the tips of those combat

boots, Crow took a step back, returning the cigarette to his lips. He checked his watch, shook his head again. "Much as I would like to stay and deal with you personally, Agent 777, I'm afraid I have a previous appointment."

"Pity," Sand said. "I was looking forward to getting everything you know out of you before leaving you lot in a pile for the *Bundespolizei*."

The blond and Newsboy Cap laughed a little at that – Crow was their superior and, Sand knew, it was always fun to see your boss get a hard time. But what Sand drew from that was realizing they all apparently spoke some level of English.

Crow remained straight-faced, too cool to take umbrage, then – after a last drag on his Pall Mall – dropped it to the floor and ground it out under his boot.

"I would like to have seen you make the attempt, Mr. Sand, taking us all on." His grin had more teeth in it than seemed possible. "I really would have liked to've seen that."

Turning to his cohorts, barely audible, Crow said in German, "Question him for an hour or so – use your pliers to pry out his fingernails, toenails, squeeze his ball sack just short of popping. Cigarette burns. You won't likely get anywhere, but who knows? And his suffering will entertain. Meanwhile, it will give me time to get to the airport and be seen doing so."

His men nodded.

The Indian withdrew an envelope from his jacket's inside pocket, gestured another of the men on the other side of the bright light – this one dark blond with a hawk nose, high cheekbones, and the bearing of an army officer, who accepted the envelope.

Again in German, the assassin said, "Heinrich, pay

your men when their work is done – hold back half till the body has been disposed of. I will contact you before we begin the next phase."

Heinrich clutched the envelope to his chest, and nodded. His reply, in German, was: "I will be waiting for your call, Herr Crow."

"Make sure no one ever finds his body – *verstehen*? Vanish him from the earth."

Sand, who'd filled much of that in with lip reading, was impressed – Crow's German was excellent. Well, the man had gone from a reservation school to a top college on a football scholarship. Not *real* football, though – rather, that ridiculous American mayhem fest.

More pertinent to the situation, however, was that in giving the order to eliminate Sand after questioning, Crow had provided key information.

Berlin sat squarely in East Germany, with three air corridors that fed three airports: Tegel to the north, Gatow to the southwest, Tempelhof the most central. Each corridor was only twenty miles wide, so there was little margin for error. Which airport Crow was using narrowed the possible destinations, and also gave Sand a shot at triangulating his own current location.

He asked, "Back to the States, Crow?"

The Indian, almost out the door and letting in some light, stopped, looked back with a frown.

"Tegel, then," Sand said.

For the first time genuine irritation put a sneer on the big face. "Where I'm flying out of is none of your bloody business, Triple Seven. What does it matter where I'm going? You're already in Hell!"

"Rather cold for Hell," Sand said, and mock-shivered. "Least you could do for your boys is provide a heater during their hard work. And I don't mean the pistol variety."

Sand's mocking tone apparently got the best of the big man at last – Crow came over and slapped him so hard the chair wobbled. Pain shot through Sand's skull, and his lip split like a teenage boy popping a pimple.

The big Indian gave Sand a final smirk and a farewell in English. "Will it give you satisfaction, Triple Seven? To serve Queen and Country in death as in life?"

As the assassin strode out of the room, laughter rose from his massive chest and echoed off the concrete walls. Why did these damn villains feel an evil laugh was *de rigueur*? Crow may have schooling, Sand thought, but being first in your class didn't mean you had any.

Once the door shut behind the big man, the other three henchmen gathered in a semicircle around Heinrich, just beyond the hot spotlight, divvying up their pay, leaving Sand alone to sit in its glare, blood trickling from his split lip.

Sand had very little time, he knew, perhaps mere seconds before they came back to begin their interrogation. Struggling against the ropes was not necessary – he worked quickly, nimbly, with long, lithe fingers, loosening the knot at his wrists. As soon as he'd come to, Sand had started running his fingers over the ropes, and fairly early in his conversation with Crow had recognized a sailor's knot, the bowline on a bight.

When Sand had been unconscious, one of Crow's flunkeys – likely the sailor with the anchor tattoo – tied this simple sturdy knot to bind their prisoner to the chair. The sailor probably had no idea that Sand would have the time to figure out the knot's configuration, recognize it, and then have the patience to pick it like a lock. After all, they intended to kill and dispose of Sand once Crow was done with him, so they'd not bothered to get too complex in the bindings.

Slipping free of the bonds on his arms, Sand kept his hands behind his back, eyes on the circle of men in the shadows. They were still gathered around Heinrich, their shares being doled out, huddled like sportsmen discussing their next play.

Sand slumped in the chair, and – moving slowly yet precisely – used both hands behind him to work on the single knot of the loop of rope that held his calves to the chair legs. This was another sailor's knot, a more careless job of it than the binding of his wrists.

Free now, he straightened in the chair then stayed motionless, hoping the sudden slackening of the ropes, which no longer bound him, would go unnoticed long enough for him to take command of the situation. How exactly he would do that he was still working on....

To rush the quartet when they were well away from him would be risky if not suicidal, even with surprise on his side. Any overt attempt to draw them closer would make them suspicious, unless they were utter fools. No, Sand needed to keep them thinking they had him completely under their control. Surprise wasn't a significant tactical advantage here.

He would have to wait for them to make their move. They seemed in no hurry to start their interrogation by torture – for a good ten minutes they'd counted their money, smoked cigarettes, and alternated taking long gulps from a bottle of Schnapps, its sweet peppermint aroma joining the other far less pleasant smells of the featureless chamber.

By now Sand's eyes had long since adjusted to the bright light and the near darkness to take stock of the room and decide this was an empty warehouse, though the lack of windows and stale atmosphere led him to believe they were underground. He wondered if they might not be somewhere within the tunnel-and-warehouse system Hitler had built under the capital.

In that case, they were likely on the Allied side of Berlin, though he wasn't certain the tunnels didn't now extend into the Russian Zone of East Berlin, as well. But Crow's non-hurried movements before his departure gave Sand the impression they were still in the West. The enthusiasm his bully boys showed in counting their bounty indicated whichever zone they were in, these were certainly budding capitalists.

When the guard wearing Sand's watch skirted the spotlight and came toward him, the prisoner tensed; but then the man slipped by, disappearing into the darkness, paying no attention to him, probably headed for the loo. Endless receding footsteps seemed confirmation that this was a warehouse.

Sand considered rushing the remaining thugs, with their numbers temporarily reduced by one. But that, too, risked suicide. If even just one of them had a gun, Sand would be cut down before he reached the trio. His Walther was on the table, but that table was far enough out of reach that diving for it would itself invite gunfire.

Of course he might take the loo visitor by surprise when the man returned, making of him an instant hostage. But the three remaining guards could easily kill both of them, then divvy up their comrade's share of the payout. Thugs were thugs, in any country, and a third of a wad of cash was better than a fourth – even these fools could do that math.

So he waited.

Sand didn't know what lay beyond this space within this chamber, but subduing these men wouldn't happen silently. If more of Crow's cronies were somewhere beyond the door the Indian had exited, or past the darkness the guard had disappeared into, Sand would be a man without a plan, much less a gun.

At last the missing henchman returned. The guards were getting tipsy by now, and Heinrich looked at his watch as the straggler approached out of the dark. They would soon begin their interrogation, and drunken louts with pliers were never any fun at all....

The straggler was coming up behind him, off to Sand's left a ways; but the man froze, looked at the ropes, pointed at them like he'd seen a nest of snakes. His eyes wide with shock, he blurted, "*Der gefangene ist losgebunden!*"

The prisoner is untied!

Before that could even register, Sand was on his feet and swinging the chair like a club, smashing it down over the guard's head, sending him to the concrete floor, unconscious. The other three, just tipsy enough to be sluggish, were trying to figure what to make of this when Sand sprang forward, sweeping the lamp off the table, and snatching up his Walther in his other hand.

As the lamp crashed to the floor, the bulb shattering like brittle rain, the room pitched into utter darkness, the table banging over onto its side, gunshots from the trio flying wildly toward where Sand had clubbed the guard, but he had already gone, sliding to his right into comforting black.

A guard fired another round, and Sand aimed toward the muzzle flash, fired, then immediately dove back left, hugging the floor. He shot was rewarded with a grunt, a whimper, the clatter of a gun dropping to concrete, then the thump of a body.

The other two guards fired into the darkness at Sand's muzzle flash, but Sand rolled away, shooting toward the orange-blue reports, earning a shout of surprised pain and another *whump* of a body hitting hard.

The remaining thug didn't fire so blindly.

Both Sand and his final captor were moving as silently as possible in the pitch black, listening hard for the other to give his position away. On his feet now but crouching, Sand figured his adversary would be working his way toward a light switch, and when the man got there, that switch would flip on and Sand would make an immediate, easy target.

Where in this vast undefined space was *that switch?*

Then he knew, or thought he did – it would be by that door through which Crow had exited! He could head that way, of course, but the guard was already closer to it, and would know exactly where it was.

So Sand moved back to where they'd held him, nearly in the center of the room, felt for and found the upended table, then crouched behind it, facing where he knew that door must be...*hoped* it would be....

When the lights came on, Heinrich hesitated, obviously not seeing Sand, but figuring his captive must be behind that table. He fired a shot that smacked into and through the wood. Sand was flat on the floor behind the table now; he rolled and shot twice.

Both rounds struck Heinrich in the chest, the bullets punching through and sending streamers of scarlet enlivening the otherwise drab surroundings. Heinrich, wearing an expression of disappointment more than anything, dropped dead to the cement.

Sand got back behind the table, gun trained on the door for the better part of a minute before he decided no one was out there to come investigate the noise. Then he stood, legs surprisingly steady under him, and his eyes were still on the door when he felt, more than heard, movement behind him.

The agent ducked and pivoted away from the table as the thug he'd cracked with the chair swung a hunting knife in a long loop, missing Sand, the attacker nearly losing his balance as Sand brought his pistol up. The thug turned and raised his blade again.

Both men froze.

In German, Sand said, "You don't have to die."

Answering in the same tongue, the thug said, "If you don't kill me, Crow will."

"Cooperate, and you will be protected while I stop Crow." He repeated: "You do *not* have to die."

"Perhaps you could best Crow," the thug said in English, almost casually conversational for a man with a knife raised to strike. "But his master, *der Holländer?* I think maybe not."

"The Dutchman?" Sand frowned. "Who is the Dutchman?"

"Pray you never find out."

With that, the man's eyes narrowed and he came alive, diving at Sand with the knife swinging in a deadly arc. Sand shot him in the forehead and the thug's knife clattered to the floor as its wielder fell on his back, staring up at nothing, skull cracked like a bloody egg.

"Who is the Dutchman?" Sand asked the corpse.

That was a question Sand filed away. Right now he was in a room filled with fresh corpses, his nostrils twitching with the smells of men who'd evacuated at death, the coppery bouquet of blood adding to petrol and other fragrances in this horrific concrete killing ground.

Quickly, methodically, he searched all four bodies. He came away with two thousand Deutsche marks, which would convert to a little less than a thousand pounds, a damned low bounty for his life. He also snugged his watch back on his wrist – the dead guard didn't need it anymore – and collected a matchbook, the one tossed to Newsboy Cap by Crow.

On the matchbook cover was an oil well gushing crude, and on the back were the words:

BOLDT-LONESTARR OIL
Houston, Texas.

Not a big clue, perhaps, but somewhere to start.

Taking that last bully boy out with a head shot meant the dead man hadn't bled all over his pea coat, which was a plus. Sand slipped it off the body and threw it on, knowing that the last of the winter chill awaited him out in the world, where it would be even colder than this concrete chamber.

He didn't know where he was for sure, but Hitler's tunnels ran beneath Tiergarten Park, which meant Sand was almost certainly on home ground of sorts. The park rested entirely within the confines of the British controlled sector of West Berlin.

Killing the agent here, so close to his own people, would have been an insulting joke Crow could hardly resist indulging in. Sand's mind replayed what the Indian had said – "Will it give you satisfaction, Triple Seven? To serve Queen and Country in death as in life?"

Indeed. Sand would track the Indian down "for Queen and Country," and for his own satisfaction. Throwing on the coat, and walking away from the carnage, he thought, *Even if takes going to hell and Texas to do it.*

CHAPTER TWO

THE SPIES OF TEXAS ARE UPON YOU

Two days later, back in London, John Sand made his way to the Broadway Buildings, entering #54, whose brass plate announced it as home to the Minimax Fire Extinguisher Corporation. After unlocking an inner door with a key that changed on a monthly basis, he traversed a claustrophobic unfurnished lobby to ride the rattletrap lift to the top floor. There he entered the drab outer office of his supervisor, Lord Malcolm Marbury – referred to by Sand and the other MI6 agents as Double M, although not to the distinguished gentleman's face.

In an increasingly bothersome series of novels by a former colleague, loosely based on Sand's real-life exploits, the secret agent had begun to experience the sort of publicity an undercover operative could hardly relish. His friend had taken certain liberties, of course, including depicting a desirable private secretary who carried a torch for the hero.

This was a whimsical inside joke on his friend's part, as Lord Marbury's assistant was a stern, steely-eyed matron with the somewhat unlikely name of Kitty Cash. Mrs.

Cash would more likely prefer seeing Sand set afire with a torch than to carry one for him. A veteran of this office since long before Sand had arrived, she guarded Double M with the tenacity of a pit bull, if blessed with a less genial personality than typical of the breed.

Everything about Mrs. Cash was severe, from the perfect silver bun at the back of her head to her black square-toed shoes. (Sand's author friend had based a character directly upon the woman, disguising her as a Russian spy with a poison spike in the toe of a similar shoe.) Even as he sat on a wooden straight-backed chair, not unlike the one he had cracked over the head of a German thug recently, Sand received only the acknowledgment of a contemptuous glance.

Today, as on every visit here, Sand had greeted her with, "And how are we today, Mrs. Cash?"

"'We' are busy, Agent 777," she'd replied as always. "Have a seat."

"Thank you, Mrs. Cash."

He suspected her attitude toward him reflected her access to the reports of his activities in the field, which included Top Secret (if tasteful) accounts of sexual episodes in the line of duty and carnage in service of Her Majesty.

The walls of this compact outer area had once been white, but were now a yellowed eggshell thanks to decades of cigar and cigarette smoke, some of it due to Mrs. Cash herself, whose teeth were of a similar shade. The furniture seemed rescued from a secondhand shop, and the office always reeked of a mixture of Mrs. Cash's too-strong perfume mixed with the tobacco smoke of herself and others.

Sand did not remember ever seeing the woman in a standing position. Instead she camped behind her desk, constantly typing, her eyes occasionally darting to the telephone/intercom system on her left. Finally, a little light flickered on and she leveled her gaze at him. "You may go in now."

Rising, Sand said, "Thank you, Mrs. Cash," wondering if he might not prefer simply fighting his way through a second cadre of German henchmen to see Double M rather than face such a withering glare.

Walking from Mrs. Cash's outer office through double doors into Double M's ornate inner office was like stepping from Whitechapel to Knightsbridge without crossing the city to get there. Where the outer office was as dreary as a London rain, Double M's oak-paneled inner sanctum – with its bookshelves, United Kingdom/European wall map, and array of citations, awards, and photos with the Queen and Winston Churchill – defined the decidedly upperclass gentleman who occupied it.

Behind a desk suitable for landing small planes, Lord Malcolm Marbury sat reading a report by the light of a green-shaded desk lamp. In a blue suit as crisp as today's chill March air, his white shirt so flawlessly pressed and starched he might have been sewn into it, Double M effortlessly bore the air of the lord he was. His gold cufflinks held the Eton emblem of his private school, his navy blue tie perfectly knotted, his dark hair receding as if trying to avoid the glare of the lamp.

"You made a pig's ear out of that mission's potential silk purse, John," he said, without looking up from the report.

"Yes, sir," Sand said, standing before the desk like a recalcitrant student before the principal. He knew better than to debate the issue.

Double M looked up over the top of the report, his eyes as pleasantly blue as a spring sky. "Did you accomplish anything of use from your encounter? Other than ridding the world of a few miscreants?"

Sand plucked the oil company matchbook from his pocket, stepped forward, and tossed it on his superior's blotter as if it were nothing at all. Picking the matchbook up the same way, Lord Marbury examined it skeptically, then tossed it back to Sand.

"Not exactly weighty evidence of a sinister international plot, is it, Triple Seven?"

"No, sir, but it *is* a place to start."

Marbury rocked back in his chair. "What do you know of Boldt-Lonestarr Oil?"

Sand's near photographic memory enabled him to bring up the information he had gathered both before and after his mission. But it didn't amount to much.

"Began as a small independent company twenty-seven years ago," Sand said. "In the Americas they're known as 'wildcatters.' They've experienced steady growth, becoming something of a major player stateside, jockeying to gain footing in the international market."

"Ownership?"

"According to public records, the main shareholders are two men – their names represented on this matchbook cover. Noah Boldt and Jake Lonestarr are both natives of the state of Texas, and well-known there."

"And you think your matchbook is connected to the activities of the American Indian assassin and the Fluss woman in Germany?"

"I took it from a dead German thug, but he got it from Crow, who is himself from Texas originally. It may be thin, but it's all we have."

That rated a nod from Double M. "Do you really believe this enough to connect Crow to Boldt-Lonestarr?"

"Certainly a possibility...not management, except perhaps in a security division. We are talking about a major American oil company making a move into international territories. If they are employing the likes of Crow, we should look at them hard."

"Still...as you say...it's thin. A lot to build on a single matchbook. Do we have anything else to go on?"

Sand shrugged. "I told the last of the Germans that I could stop Crow. Before leaving this world, he said perhaps I could, but not 'der Holländer.'"

"The Dutchman?"

"Translated. Yes."

Marbury's frown was thoughtful. "Less than an alias. Perhaps more than a sobriquet. You've checked with Records Branch, I assume? Anything come up there?"

"Nothing, sir."

Marbury sighed. "Did you learn anything more substantial at all about Boldt and Lonestarr, before or after the mission?"

Sand shook his head. "The public records I've accessed were very light on ownership details, beyond what I mentioned. All we really know is that those two are the main stockholders. Boldt appears to control more shares, but not by much. Neither is exactly low-profile – in their home state, they both have generated considerable publicity."

Marbury made a face. "And you are in a position to know of such things."

Sand moved past that embarrassing topic quickly. "They are both active in the Houston community. Charities. Political contributors. Supporters of local colleges and the arts. Solid citizens."

"With a notorious assassin in their apparent employ."

"So it would seem." Marbury paused, mulling it. "As

you know, we've had unusual reports about abnormal activities in the world oil market. Someone may be working toward cornering that market, and employing strongarm techniques, even terrorist techniques, to do so."

"That could fit in here."

Double M looked past Sand. As his superior mused, the agent waited, until Marbury said softly, "I met Noah Boldt once."

"Did you, sir?"

"In Washington, DC, at a Presidential affair. Friendly. Public-spirited. He told me, Triple Seven, that he would like me to call him what all of his friends call him..."

"Sir?"

"...'Dutch.'"

Sand slowly nodded. "Shall I book the next flight to Houston, sir?"

"Mrs. Cash will do that for you. Use the David Sterling alias."

Sand's nod came quick this time.

"I'll have the Home Secretary arrange something, so you'll be expected. Might make the entrance a little easier. In the meantime, go home and pack. A deeper dossier will be sent round to you with more detailed background."

"Thank you, sir." Sand began to go, but Lord Marbury's voice turned him around.

"And, John?"

"Sir?"

"Let's try to accomplish more this time than simply littering the landscape with dead nobodies, shall we?"

"Do my best, sir."

But no promises, Sand thought.

******

The next morning, Sand caught a plane to New York, then a connecting flight to Houston. While he was in the air, he managed not to flirt with assorted attractive young stewardesses, instead keeping his nose buried in the Boldt-Lonestarr Oil dossier that Double M had dispatched via messenger.

Not much was available about the two men's younger days, prior to pursuing a partnership as wildcatters during the Great Depression. They had built their company from nothing at all into not very much, constantly on the brink of bankruptcy until the late Thirties when they made a major oil strike. Soon they were selling crude to gasoline companies and then directly to the United States government, when during World War II their two man-operation burgeoned into an empire. They now controlled oil from the ground to the gas pump with franchised gas stations in all forty-eight states. That was their collective breath Standard Oil felt on the back of its neck.

Boldt was the oil man, Lonestarr the salesman. While Dutch found the oil and supervised the drilling operation, Jake had sold options, bringing in investors who kept them afloat. Together the pair oversaw the galloping growth of their company into the industry titan it was today.

Sand was impressed. These were men to be reckoned with. Though the dossier indicated nothing specific, he knew Boldt and Lonestarr were the kind of entrepreneurs who would almost certainly have a degree of ruthlessness in their approach.

But ruthless enough to take on the likes of Crow?

David Sterling, his cover, was an up-and-coming (non-existent) young executive, a vice president already with a small American company, Campbell Oil, actually a CIA front, providing MI6 with the business cards, pens, and other small tokens that would prove Sterling was exactly who he said he was. The CIA had also provided a rock-solid back story, and even a phone line that could be used to prove his point should Boldt and/or Lonestarr need convincing.

When he stepped off the plane in Houston, the temperature difference from London to Texas slapped him like an unruly child. When he'd left home, the UK capital had been cool with a sharp breeze. Now, bright sun beating on him as he took portable stairs down to the runway, he was almost uncomfortably warm in his gray woolen Savile Row suit.

Strolling into the airport, briefcase in hand, suit bag over a shoulder, he was prepared to hail a taxi until he noticed, near Baggage Claim, a broad-shouldered Hispanic individual – pockmarked, dour, with a droopy black bandito mustache, in the improbable formal livery of a chauffeur. The man held up a sign saying *David Sterling*, and his expression said that if you weren't David Sterling, you best move along. Perhaps four inches shorter than Sand's six-foot-one, and probably weighing close to Sand's twelve stones, he had piercing dark eyes and black hair so long it was tied back in a ponytail.

If this was someone only posing as a chauffeur, John Sand was about to take an interesting ride. Of course his Walther was in his briefcase, relatively handy. What the hell.

"That's me," Sand said, with a nod at the sign.

The man's mouth twitched in something that might have been a smile, then he lowered the placard and nodded respectfully.

"Welcome to Houston, Mr. Sterling." The voice was a warm baritone with a cool edge and only a hint of

Mexican accent. "Mr. Boldt hoped you might stay with him at his home."

"Mr. Boldt is a gracious man."

A Muzak version of "Yellow Rose of Texas" accompanied their conversation.

"Mr. Boldt believes good business associations require a personal touch. He would like you to be his guest."

"Well, let's not disappoint him, then."

They began to walk toward the exits.

The chauffeur asked, "Do you have any other luggage?"

"No."

"Would you like me to carry your suit bag, Mr. Sterling?"

Sand ignored the question, offering the man half a smile. "You know my name. Might I know yours?"

"Cuchillo," the driver said, showing a quarter-inch of his upper teeth, which apparently was a grin.

"As in knife?"

"As in knife." Big shoulders shrugged. "Is that any stranger than being named for your country's currency, Mr. Sterling?"

"Good point, Mr. Cuchillo."

"Just 'Cuchillo,' please. Allow me."

The driver took the suit bag and they walked out of the airport, back into warm buttery sun. He already liked this obviously tough little man. But Cuchillo's presence only confirmed the notion that the likes of Crow might also be in Boldt's employ.

He followed the driver to a big black Cadillac in the parking lot where Cuchillo opened the trunk and deposited the suit bag while Sand held onto the briefcase. Cuchillo opened a rear door but Sand shook his head and helped himself to the front rider's seat.

Settled within, the two men exchanged nods and smiles that were small in fact and large in meaning.

As Cuchillo drove them past the edge of the city, Sand watched the exchange of green grass for concrete, grazing cows for people, and serene countryside for the bustle of city. Did Dutch Boldt dislike city life, or simply prefer privacy? Self-made men of business often had a tendency toward keeping outsiders from poking in their business, after all.

And yet David Sterling, a stranger, had been invited into Boldt's home.

Perhaps the oil man wanted "Sterling" as his guest to keep an easier eye on his caller's movements; or maybe his host liked to size up a potential business associate in more depth than a few meetings might provide. Could be Boldt was just a sociable type.

Certainly the ride out to Boldt's estate might tend to calm guests, slow their lives down, make them feel at ease. The effect was the opposite on Sand, however, sending alarm bells going off, like a submarine making a deep dive. He knew very well that one reason to put people at their ease was to lull them into letting down their guard.

And John Sand wasn't about to let that happen.

They took a left onto a private drive and had gone some way before Cuchillo said, "Here's the house."

The "house"?

Well, that was certainly an understatement. Sitting nearly half a kilometer back from the road, the Boldt "house" rose like an ivory castle from the flat Texas prairie, high and grand and yet somehow not pretentious, not exactly. Two alabaster turrets capped the roof, one flying the flag of the United States, the other the one-star red-white-and-blue state banner of Texas. The mansion somehow seemed a two-story Americanized variation on Buckingham Palace; but instead of sitting behind a spiked wrought-iron barrier, the Boldt spread rested beyond a pole-and-rail fence as white as the structure it surrounded.

"Cozy cottage," Sand said off-handedly as Cuchillo drove past the home and around to a gated driveway.

"We like it," the chauffeur agreed.

Cuchillo used a remote control and the gates swung open as they neared; then they were passing below a sign that straddled the driveway and read *Plata Luna* – Silver Moon. Sand liked the music of that.

As the car followed the long winding drive up to the house, two men and a woman walked out and stood near where the driveway circled in front. The female was young, shapely, her auburn hair brushing her shoulders, some of it drifting on the breeze, as if she were riding on horseback. She wore a short-sleeved pink sweater and a straight black skirt with black heels, simple attire she made stunning.

This was the kind of woman who could make a man like Sand swear off stewardesses altogether.

She stood between the two men. Towering over her, at her right, was a rangy man of about sixty, silver sideburns extending beneath the wide brim of his Stetson. Sand knew the man from the dossier – Noah Boldt, "Dutch." His tan suit had a western cut, his brown string tie an arrowhead choker, and he wore intricately tooled brown-and-red cowboy boots.

On the other side of the woman stood a skinnier man with similar Stetson and an overwhelming silver mustache, fidgeting a little; he was probably three-and-a-half stones lighter than Boldt, and two or three inches shorter, yet could still be called tall. This (Sand also knew from the dossier) was Boldt's partner, Jake Lonestarr. Like

Boldt, Lonestarr wore a western-cut suit, but his was gray, with a turquoise-stone bolo tie, his cowboy boots black with white tooling.

As the car eased to a stop before them, Boldt opened the rider's door for Sand, who stepped out, taking his briefcase along.

Even though Boldt squinted against the afternoon sun, he gave Sand a big wide grin and extended a paw slightly smaller than a frying pan.

"Welcome, Mr. Sterling. Noah Boldt, but call me Dutch."

Sand took the man's hand and they shook, firmly.

"Thank you for your hospitality," Sand said. "We won't talk business until you deem it appropriate."

Boldt gave him a crooked grin that could have meant damn near anything, then turned to the elaborately mustached man and said, "This is my partner, Jake Lonestarr. We only go back a thousand years or so."

Sand shook hands with the lanky man, who also had a firm grip, and a wide smile beneath the big silver mustache. Both the mustache and the smile struck Sand as working too hard.

Lonestarr said, "We're happy you're here, Mr. Sterling. We'll be very interested hearin' what you have to say."

Sand gave Lonestarr a deferential nod, then turned to the auburn-haired beauty. Her lovely green eyes were the highlight of her warm expression.

Boldt said, "This is my daughter, Stacey. She'll be your liaison. She's the vice president of my company."

She stepped forward, shook his hand. Warm and firm. "A pleasure to meet you, Mr. Sterling."

Sand said, "So you're part of the family business?"

She didn't seem to like the question and those eyes

turned icy. "Does that surprise you, Mr. Sterling?"

"If so, it's a pleasant one, Miss Boldt. Nepotism doesn't generally manifest itself in so agreeable a manner."

She didn't seem to know whether to be amused or insulted by that. But the ice in her eyes did recede somewhat. "I'm relieved to hear it."

Her father seemed amused by the exchange, and he waved around at the ranch, saying, "Mr. Sterling, someday this will all belong to Stacey...so yes, she has a right to her position with the company, but she's also earned it."

"No offense meant," Sand said. "It's a welcome change to see a beautiful young woman in a position of authority."

Biting off the words, Stacey said, "Doesn't a *queen* rule your country?"

"Constitutional monarchies have their limitations," Sand said. "The line of succession here sounds more meaningful. Anyway, with no offense to Her Majesty... she doesn't have your substantial charms."

He gave her the full wattage of the smile that had melted many a female heart the world over.

She laughed in his face, green eyes dancing, sun catching her hair. "Does that kind of B.S. normally work for you, Mr. Sterling?"

"Now and then," he said, with a chagrined grin and a shrug.

A laugh came bubbling out of her like freshly uncorked champagne. "Well, that kind of bull doesn't go very far in Texas, Mr. Sterling."

Before this, her accent had been almost unnoticeable; but now it caressed each phrase.

"I'm immune to flattery," she went on, "and I have had every cowboy, oilman, and salesman in Texas try, hopin' for a shot at me and the Boldt family fortune...and many of them have done a whole hell of a lot better than you just did now."

Turning on her heels, she strode into the house. Sand watched her go, and it wasn't a bad view at all.

Boldt chuckled. "You'll have to forgive Stacey, Mr. Sterling. She takes after her late mama – that woman couldn't take a damn compliment either. But the child's smart and well-educated...Rice University...and she's got a fine head for business. I'm sure the two of you will be able to work together. She's just...independent-minded."

Lonestarr muttered, "More like headstrong."

But Boldt ignored his partner and slipped an arm around his guest's shoulders. "Cuchillo will bring your bag and show you to your room. Take your time, get yourself cleaned up, and Stacey will come fetch you before dinner. If she bites your head off, not to worry – she'll spit it out soon enough."

"A relief to know."

Boldt's grin was as big as Texas. "Hope you're ready for a real lone-star state barbecue, Mr. Sterling, 'cause that's what we've got planned for you."

"Do you?"

"We do. Just us and a few of our closest friends. I'm sure you'll have a hell of a time."

"Well, thank you, Mr. Boldt."

He squeezed Sand's shoulder. "I told you before, call me Dutch. And this is Jake."

"And I'm David," Sand said.

"Well, Davey, you get settled in, and we'll treat you right good. Tomorrow, we'll see if we can get some business done. But for tonight, you're our guest. Dress is casual."

Sand gestured to his gray suit and said, "In London,

this *is* casual."

Boldt guffawed. "Afraid you'll have to do better than that, son."

The two Texans accompanied him into the mansion, Cuchillo bringing up the rear with Sand's suit bag. Once inside, the guest paused for a moment to marvel at the grand foyer and massive crystal chandelier, then the chauffeur led him up the marble stairs to one of the bedrooms at the far end of the hallway.

Cuchillo hung the suit bag in the closet.

"Thanks, Cuchillo. I suppose a tip is out of the question."

"Did you want me to cut you?"

"Not particularly."

Moments later, Cuchillo – half-way out the door – said, "Miss Boldt likes you."

"You could have fooled me."

The chauffeur shrugged. "You didn't get slapped."

Alone, Sand surveyed the room. Queen-sized bed, nightstand with a lamp on either side. A dresser, a chest of drawers, spacious closet, door to an adjoining bath.

A large window overlooked a giant stone patio, with a swimming pool beyond that, and – off to one side – a barbecue pit with what appeared to be most of a cow on the spit. A few men in white were attending the meat like surgeons, while several other white-coated workers set out silverware and plates on a round table next to a line of long banquet tables home to enough different dishes to feed most of Houston. At the end of the food lines was another group of banquet tables with beverages that included coffee, iced tea, lemonade, and at one end, a keg of beer.

Nothing appeared amiss either outside or in his room. Not so much as a wrinkle in the bedspread. Just the sort of perfection to make Sand suspicious. He thoroughly combed the room for bugs, finding nothing. He had been at it for the better part of an hour, barely having found time to clean up a little and replace his white shirt and tie with a black Ban-Lon under his gray suit coat, when he looked out the window to learn Dutch Boldt's idea of "a few close friends" was at least fifty people.

They all appeared to be well-heeled, most of the men in western wear and cowboy hats, most of the women in dresses or skirts with silk blouses covered in fringe. To Sand it looked like an American western movie, maybe an old one starring Gene Autry, come to life. The only thing missing was the Indians. Then, back near the barbecue pit, he spotted Crow.

He might have been gut-punched.

If Crow saw him, the game would be up. He jammed himself against the wall next to the window, adjusting the curtains slightly so he could peek between their outside edge and stay hidden. Looking again toward the barbecue pit, he saw Crow talking to both Boldt and Lonestarr...

...then realized he *wasn't* looking at Crow.

This Indian, in jeans and a tan-trimmed-brown western-style shirt, looked like Crow, same cherry-wood skin tone, same long black hair; but while Crow was bigger than Boldt, this creature was not – larger than Lonestarr, but smaller than Boldt. Crow's brother, maybe? A cousin? Despite certain racial cliches common in the USA, not all Indians looked alike, even those of the same tribal heritage.

Had the two oil men spoken about "David Sterling" to this Indian? If they had, would it have meant anything to Crow's *near* doppelganger?

The matchbook might not have been much in the way of evidence, but it had led him here, and John Sand now knew this was right where he needed to be.

CHAPTER THREE
STABLE MATES
——

A knock at the door drew Sand away from the guest room window. After a glance at the dresser mirror assured him the shoulder-holstered Walther didn't protrude under the gray suitcoat, he went to the closed door and said, "Yes?"

"Stacey Boldt, Mr. Sterling."

Then she was standing before him in a tan-and-white cowgirl outfit with white fringe and matching boots, her green eyes alive and her mouth bestowing him a small smile, her lipstick red and glistening. This may have been Texas, but the effect was sheer Hollywood, and he took the risk of smiling back at her.

"I would comment on how lovely you look," he said, "but I try to learn from my mistakes. So let's leave it at, 'Good evening, Miss Boldt.'"

Her smile lingered. "My father thinks I owe you an apology."

"And do you always do what your father thinks you should?"

"When it comes to business, usually, but perhaps that's because we tend to see things eye-to-eye in that department."

"And in other departments?"

"Let's just say Dutch Boldt has no concept of how difficult he's made it, giving his little girl a big job in the oil business."

He joined her in the hall, shutting the door behind him. "Traditionally a man's game."

She shrugged. "Times are changing."

"Slowly, but they are. Still, if any apology is owed, it's mine to give."

Her head cocked and she might have been deciding whether that struck her as patronizing or not. But then her eyes met his. "Let's skip the apologies altogether and go downstairs and join the party."

"Splendid idea," he said, and offered her his arm. Another risk, but one worth taking, he thought.

She accepted the offer; they exchanged half-smiles that added up to a whole one, and they (he believed the term was) "moseyed" down the stairs, which were wide enough for their side-by-side descent. Soon she was leading him down a hallway toward the back of the house.

As they went, he said, "Looking out my window, it appears half the population of Texas is in attendance."

"Not quite," she said. "It's a big state, remember."

"And all on my account?"

The bubbling laugh came again. "Did Daddy lead you to believe that? No, this shindig's been on the docket for weeks."

Of course, among the attendees was that American Indian who looked disturbingly like Crow; but even if some familial connection existed between the two, why should the near-double know anything about Sand, much less recognize him?

The pair strolled through sliding glass doors out onto the patio. Dusk was settling into darkness and gas lamps on polished steel poles, defining the party area, were already burning. A small country-and-western band was set up on a portable stage at the far end of the festivities, their tune carrying over to the house.

"'You ought to see my Blue-Eyed Sally,'" the leader was singing over fiddles and guitars. "'She lives way down on Shinbone Alley.'"

Stacey was still holding onto his arm. She sang lightly along, "'Stay a little longer'...." Leaning close, she said, "I know it's heresy, but I must admit I don't usually care for country music."

"Nor do I. But that's country swing, which is a different breed entirely. Bob Wills and his Texas Playboys?"

She gazed at him with new respect. Her increased interest was lost on him, however, because his eyes were on the barbecue pit where the Indian was still in conference with Jake Lonestarr. Dutch Boldt was no longer chatting with them, off to one side having a word with Cuchillo, who had traded his chauffeur's livery for a western shirt and jeans.

"Who's that with Lonestarr?" Sand asked, keeping it casual.

Stacey had to look around to find them, then her voice dropped a little. "That roughneck? Raven Nocona. He works security for the company. Kind of a... troubleshooter."

"Why do I get the feeling he's not your favorite employee?"

She shrugged. "He and his brother Crow joined the company when I was in college."

One mystery solved, he thought.

She was saying, "Whether I like them or not, and I

don't, is not an issue – I don't deal with them. They report to my father and Jake."

Then she was leading him over to talk to her father, who was now with a different group of guests. Sand couldn't help but wonder - if Dutch Boldt was indeed behind the efforts to corner the world oil market, was his longtime partner an accomplice in the plot? That would stand to reason. Perhaps Jake Lonestarr was as much a player in this game as Boldt.

If indeed a game was being played. After all, this speculation was a built on the back of a matchbook....

Dutch Boldt grinned and wrenched himself free of the group of guests, coming over with arms spread wide in welcome.

"Davey boy," he said. "Accommodations up to London standards? You get yourself settled in all right?"

"I only wish London's standards were up to yours, Mr. Boldt."

His host lifted a correcting forefinger. "Dutch."

"Dutch."

All around, people were chatting, drinking, smoking (most men with cigars), and a few guests had started to get in line over by the banquet tables as caterers brought over platters of meat cut freshly off the roasted steer. The aroma wafting toward them reminded Sand that the last time he had eaten was on the flight from London to New York. As if remembering a habit he'd once had, it occurred to him he was famished.

Past the serving tables, closer to the pool, Sand saw three teenage boys bending over as if in a dice game; but then came a brief flash of flame and one of the boys tossed something. It flew skyward about ten feet and exploded – an M-80 firecracker. The boys were laughing, having made more than a few adults jump.

Cuchillo seemed to materialize at his employer's side. Boldt nodded toward the troublesome boys, and his man went over, held out his hand, and accepted the remaining firecrackers from the teens, whose expressions said they knew not to argue.

Throwing an arm around Sand's shoulder, the big man said, "Davey, boy, you know what the best thing is about being guest of honor at a shindig like this?"

"You get to dance with the prettiest girl, even if she's the host's daughter?"

Boldt bellowed a laugh. "Damn, Stacey, I *told* you this fella was okay!"

Stacey blushed, which surprised Sand "a mite," as he didn't figure her to be easily embarrassed.

"You not only get to dance with the prettiest girl," Boldt was saying, "who as it happens *is* my daughter...you get to sashay with me right up to the front of the food line."

"In Texas as in the British isles," Sand said, "rank does have its privileges."

"Davey, doesn't it just?"

Was the man really as good-natured as this? Or was there something sinister edging all that hee-haw?

Sand followed his host to the front of the line, and of course no one did anything but smile and shout greetings. They might have been waiting for the grand marshal to arrive and lead the parade down the banquet table. Servers in white jackets and black pants attended each steaming tray, but Boldt did his own serving.

In fact, Boldt put as much if not more food on Sand's plate as he did his own. Each time, the big Texan would grin and say, "Davey boy, you have simply *got* to try this."

When they got to the last platter, Boldt asked, "Davey,

now do you like it rare or charred or in between?"

"Good and bloody rare," Sand said.

"Personally I take it charred. But you Brits – everything is 'bloody' this and 'bloody' that."

Then, on top of everything already piled there, Boldt laid a steak nearly as large as the plate itself.

"Prepare yourself, son, for the best beef on the face of God's good earth."

By the time they reached the end of the line, Sand was carrying a tray with food enough for three and a pilsner-style glass of beer to wash it down. Boldt led Sand and Stacey to one of the picnic tables scattered around the backyard.

They ate mostly in silence. Stacey, who had served herself perhaps a third as much as what her father had layered on his guest's plate, ate as slowly as her parent did not. Starved though he'd been, Sand was defeated half-way through the delicious, down-home meal, although some slimy thing he was told was "fried okra" had not rated a second bite.

Dutch asked, "How do you like that steak, Davey? Bloody enough for you?"

"Still wriggling," Sand said, "and excellent."

"Best you ever ate?"

Since mentioning the roast beef at Simpson's-in-the-Strand would have been rude, Sand nodded his agreement.

For several hours, the secret agent got Dutch talking about himself, and heard the story of the climb from nothing to everything that Boldt and his partner had made. For a while Stacey went off to talk with some girlfriends and Sand heard from the father about her mother, who had been a benevolent queen of Houston society, a strong woman who in other times would have been a captain of industry herself.

Rose Boldt had died young and Dutch had never thought about remarrying. He paid her memory tribute by granting his daughter's wish to go into the family business. The only thing he and Rose had ever disagreed about was Jake Lonestarr. She had never liked the man.

"For no good reason, really," Dutch said.

For more than an hour, Sand and Stacey danced to the country swing band. She was delighted by how well he could handle the fast tunes, and they fell naturally into each other's arms on the slow ones. They worked up a considerable thirst and joined her father back at the picnic table for another round of beers.

As the three sat chatting, Sand noticed Jake Lonestarr and Raven in an intense private confab off to one side. Now that dusk had turned to dark, the pair was too far away for lip-reading. He would have to get closer.

Picking up his pilsner of beer, he chugged it down. A mediocre lager, but he said, "This is cracking good."

"That's Lone Star," Boldt said. "Finest brew in the state. Made down San Antonio way."

Rising quickly, Sand said, "Another seems called for."

Boldt said, "Davey, one of the servers will refill your glass..."

But Sand was already heading toward the beverage table. As he waited his turn, he glanced back to see Boldt and Stacey chatting pleasantly, clearly not at all suspicious of his departure. He returned his attention to Lonestarr and Raven only to see them walking away from the party and into the darkness.

The black young man in white who was tending the keg refilled Sand's glass. Taking it, gesturing with his free hand, Sand asked, "Any idea what's back that way?"

"That would be the stable, sir."

Sand nodded his thanks and, seeing Boldt and Stacey engaged with another guest, moved to the edge of the festivities. Discreetly, he poured the mediocre brew into a trash bin, then slipped the glass into his suitcoat pocket.

Then he headed toward where he'd seen Lonestarr and Raven heading.

He kept his distance; night had fallen fast and hard over the Texas prairie, and behind him party lights and those gas lamps burned. The laughter and conversation of the gathering quickly diminished, even the country-swing band fading to minor noise. He was having trouble picking out the two figures moving ahead in the darkness; but his twitching nostrils informed him that the young man at the keg had been right about the stables being in this direction.

Even on a moonless night indifferent with stars, the white stable rose distinctly from the dark; typically for a horse farm, half a dozen stalls were on either side, back-to-back with stall doors facing outside. Still, he couldn't see the two men he was tracking, though he could hear their voices now, even if he couldn't make out the words. He edged closer.

From the corner of the building, with the two men standing midway outside of it, Sand could hear them clearly.

"We'll need a few minutes, Raven," Lonestarr said. "Wait here – make damn sure nobody interrupts us."

Raven grunted his understanding.

Sand peeked around the corner of the structure to see Lonestarr walking off down its south side, heading into a stall toward the far end. The Indian lit up a cigarette, the smoke wafting toward Sand, as if tracking him. The agent ducked back and loped off to make his way round the building on the opposite side from the sentry. He was half-way down the east side of the stable when a horse popped its head through the open upper half of the stall door and nickered.

Startled, Sand gave the animal a look.

Pressing himself against the wall into the shadows, he listened intently, heard no one coming, then drew closer to the restless horse, whispering, "Easy, easy." A feed bag hung on the wall next to the stall, and Sand silently pulled it off, the horse bowing its head so the feed bag could be slipped into place.

As the horse chowed happily down, Sand made sure none of this had attracted unwanted attention, then – sensing no threat – moved on. He stopped at the empty stall opposite the one Lonestarr had entered, finding it freshly layered with straw and happily absent of manure.

He opened the half door so slowly its hinges didn't have the chance to squeak. Within the stall, pulling the partial door closed, he paused for his eyes to adjust to a near complete darkness.

At the back wall of the stall, shared with its neighbor just beyond, he knelt down, found a hole between two boards, and peeked through. The other stall was dark, too, though two shadowy shapes could be barely made out, belonging to Lonestarr and someone else, though he couldn't see who that might be. But he could hear their muffled voices.

Lonestarr said, "If your charms aren't enough to convince your latest conquest to cooperate, tell him the Dutchman will send someone less cuddly...Raven, perhaps, or that nasty brother of his you enjoy working with so much."

The response, from a female, was largely inaudible.

Pulling the pilsner from his pocket, Sand pressed the open end of the glass to the wall and listened again.

The voice not only belonged to a female, it was a familiar voice with an unmistakable Germanic accent: "Does that fool Boldt have any *idea* what's in the offing? That when all is said and done he will be left in the frame?"

Kyla Fluss!

That beautiful blonde who managed to be cheap and expensive at the same time, the would-be temptress who Sand had allowed to lead him into Crow's trap back in Berlin.

He smiled, ear to the glass. The girl did get around....

Lonestarr barked a laugh. "My old dear friend is so busy with the mining side of the business that he has no idea what's going on anywhere else, much less in his own backyard."

Then they were laughing together, and Sand realized two things: first, Dutch Boldt had nothing to do with the energy power grab currently under way, and was merely Lonestarr's high-level pawn. Second, two evil laughs at the same time were a bit much.

Still pressing the glass to the wall, and his ear to the glass, he heard Lonestarr add, "Once you get Jacobs, and then Mid-States, we'll be big enough to go toe-to-toe with Standard Oil. King Rockefeller will kneel before *us* when we control all the world's oil."

No laughter now, evil or otherwise – Lonestarr was dead serious. The lanky egomaniac intended to corner the oil market and perhaps rule the world itself – not so crazy a thought, if he controlled its chief fuel supply.

Lonestarr said, "That's just two things you need to take care of, darlin'...and then you can leave the rest to me. I intend to make a very wealthy one-man woman out of you...when your work is done."

"There's already only one man in my life," Kyla said.

"The biggest man in the state of Texas...."

The sound Sand heard next was a zipper. Whether Kyla's or Jake's, the eavesdropper couldn't venture a guess; but the slurping and nuzzling and moaning and groaning that followed were something of a chore to sit through. He had hoped that perhaps pillow talk – or more accurately whispered nothings – might disclose more details about the oil man's scheme. But the only thing he learned was that – despite her assertions to the tall Texan with taller ambitions – the woman's enthusiasm level seemed less convincing here than in Berlin.

Hell, he thought. *They aren't even scaring the horses.*

After the panting ceased, followed by the rustle of clothing, Lonestarr said, "You best scoot, darlin'...before anybody from the get-together sees *us* together...."

"My flight's in less two hours. I should 'scoot' indeed, *liebling.* But one last thing..."

"Yes, darlin'?"

"When Dutch Boldt realizes what you have done to him, he won't go gently. He'll fight back. He may have been a fool because of your friendship...but what an enemy he will make."

"Actually, when things come to light...about how ol' Dutch made mistakes that cost him his share of the company...I feel fairly certain he'll be compelled...saddens me to say...to end it all."

A pause was followed by more mutual laughter. And this time nothing about the dual evil laugh amused Sand at all.

The poisonous pair exited the stall, the half-door closing behind them with a near slam, as if lending a period to the death sentence.

Sand got to his feet, brushing himself off as he wondered if his best option would be to follow Kyla and disrupt

her efforts, and possibly turn her – after all, once she knew
MI6 was onto her, she might cooperate.

Might.

But the better if not wiser route seemed to be warning
Boldt that his best friend and longtime partner was in the
process of betraying him – even plotting his demise. While
the outlines of Lonestarr's scheme remained sketchy, the
man clearly intended to bilk Boldt while setting him up to
take the fall, should things go awry.

Still within the stall, Sand peeked out. Kyla, in a black
leather pants suit that was as subtle as a heart attack, was
walking away, blending into the night but for her shock of
blonde hair. Must have been a road back there, a car waiting.

He exited the structure and came around the east end
carefully, where he could see Lonestarr and Raven heading
back toward the lights of the party. Relieved, he began
retracing his steps when Stacey Boldt came walking in
his direction. Ducking back into his stall, Sand waited,
frowning in thought.

Not that any thoughts were forming....

She must have come out here via a different route than
he had, else Raven was slacking on the job, not spotting
her. With that tan-and-white cowgirl outfit, she practically
glowed even under a less than starry sky.

He was crouched below the half-door as Stacey's
soft voice came, "Gypsy, how'd you get your feedbag
on, you clever girl?"

Worried that her voice would carry at night, Sand
silently slipped out of the stall, Stacey's attention on
removing the horse's feedbag next door. He eased up
behind her as she rehung the feedbag on its nail. Even
Gypsy stayed calm as Sand neared.

He was less than a step from her when Stacey turned.

She gave a little start, her mouth a startled O; but she remained calm as she said, "David...I came looking for you. Someone saw you heading – "

Not wanting her to continue, as Lonestarr and Raven might still be near enough to hear, Sand did the only thing he could think of to silence her. He put his arms around the young woman and kissed her.

She squirmed for just a moment, then she returned his tender kiss with rather more fervor.

Their lips parted, faces inches away, his arms around her and, now, hers around his.

"You've found me," he said. "What now?"

Her answer was to kiss him again. This time she provided a tender kiss, which he built upon. He led her gently into the empty stall and they stood there kissing for some time, until they were sitting and then reclining, finding themselves in a pile of hay, her on her back, him looming.

"Lovely," he said. "So very lovely..."

"Shut-up," she said, "and do something about it."

She began to unbutton her fringed blouse, the bra underneath a flimsy thing her nipples showed through. He got out of the suitcoat and then the shoulder sling with the Walther was exposed.

Her eyes widened.

"When in Texas," he said, and that seemed explanation enough.

He removed the sling and the weapon and pulled off the Ban-Lon. This time he knew exactly from whence the zipper sound emanated. He got out of his shoes and trousers, and from his billfold in the latter he removed a packaged item.

She shook her head. "No...it's all right. I'm safe."

He shook his head. "I might not be."

When the time came, she guided him in and, as he entered her, her soft moan was music and her legs wrapped around him in wonderful embrace. Their passion burned hot and fast, the two of them reaching climax quickly, then they lay in each other's arms, covered in perspiration.

"Well," she whispered.

"Well indeed," he agreed. "We should get dressed."

She studied him as she propped herself on an elbow. "You were in hurry getting me out of my clothes. Now you're in a hurry to get me back into them. Don't you do *anything* slow?"

"We'll get around to that. But I need to talk to your father."

She grinned at him mischievously. "One little fling and you're talking marriage?"

"That *would* be premature. It's business."

"Are all Brits like you? A little Lady Chatterley roll-in-the-hay, then talk business with her daddy in the middle of the night?"

"Get. Dressed." He already was doing so.

She began reassembling herself as well. "I swear, you are the strangest man, David Sterling."

That she knew him only by his cover name disturbed him somehow, though he'd been with many woman while pretending to be many men. But this was different. Something had changed tonight. Jesus, he wasn't falling in love, was he? He couldn't help himself - he grinned.

"What's so funny?"

"Not you, Stacey, most assuredly not you. But I was just struck by a notion I find...unlikely and odd. First things first, though – we need to find your father."

As they walked back toward the party, Sand noticed the silence. The barbecue was over, the guests gone. The band had packed up and left, the caterers and servants having cleaned up and torn down. That was fine with Sand. What he had to say to Dutch Boldt couldn't be overheard by just anyone.

Dutch was sitting at their picnic table, his fingers drumming. He did not look happy. Cuchillo was over by the barbecue pit nearby, stirring the fire with a poker. He did not look happy, either.

Dutch glared at his daughter and her escort. "You two want to tell me where just the hell you've been? I like to maintain a certain air of respectability in my own house."

Stacey sat next to her father and said, "Daddy, we just went for a little walk."

Sand took a seat across from his host. "No time for preliminaries or recriminations either, sir. My name, my *real* name is Sand, John Sand...I'm an MI6 agent sent here to investigate you."

Boldt's eyes and nostrils flared. "Investigate me!"

Stacey was staring at Sand in sudden wide-eyed anger.

"Yes," Sand said, "and you passed with flying colors. But *someone* didn't. Sir, we need to talk."

A voice in the darkness said, "The limey's right, Dutch – we *do* need to talk."

Jake Lonestarr strolled up, a six-shooter-style .45 pointed lazily at them from about waist level. At his side, Raven carried a double-barreled shotgun, which was not pointed lazily at all.

Getting to his feet, Dutch demanded, "What the hell *is* this, Jake?"

"Afraid it's a hostile takeover, ol' pard." Lonestarr's smile was an awful thing, on loan from a skeleton. He gestured with the barrel of the pistol for Boldt to sit. "*Very* hostile takeover."

CHAPTER FOUR
LONESTARR-CROSSED

The romantic interlude with Stacey had come out of a desire to protect the young woman from Lonestarr and Raven; but Sand's passion had soon overridden his mission. And in the process, Sand had lost track entirely of Boldt's partner and Crow's brother.

Now the treacherous Texan was standing before Sand, Stacey and Boldt as the trio sat at the picnic table in a terrible parody of a casual gathering, that six-shooter in a bony hand. His nasty smile was almost as wide as the mustache that surrounded it.

Lonestarr said, "Let's get right to what you get out of our new arrangement, Dutch."

Despite the surprise of this moment, and the cold rage it had summoned in him, Boldt managed to say, "I am listening...old friend."

"Good. Because what I have for you is this – do as I suggest and both you and your spoiled-brat daughter can still be breathin' when the sun comes up."

Right now the night was almost stygian, though the flames of the gas lamps on their poles licked at the darkness, flickering, snapping, whipping.

"I said I was listening," Boldt said. The oil man's big hands had become massive vein-roped fists, resting on the table as if he might pound them.

Raven and Lonestarr had their backs to Cuchillo at the barbecue pit, Sand realized – was it possible they hadn't noticed the Mexican's presence? The pit was back a ways, after all. Also noted was Sand's absence from the deal in the offing that granted life to Dutch and his daughter.

Lonestarr's pistol bobbed up and then back down a bit. "Recognize the weapon, pard?"

"Yes," Boldt said. Nothing in his voice. "It's mine. A gift from you many years ago, when our first big gusher came in."

"That's right. And you've kept it well-oiled and on display in your study. You always did have a sentimental streak, a trait that never dogged me. Pistol's rarely been fired, but tonight we'll put 'er to the test."

"Will we."

Lonestarr nodded. "I intend to shoot this limey prick with your .45. Then you and your little girl and I will go out on my yacht and see to gettin' rid of the remains. I'll hold onto the weapon, of course, for safekeeping."

"Making us your accomplices?"

"That's a crude way of lookin' at it, 'old friend.' While you've been keeping your eye off the ball, I've been ma-kin' strides in the oil market. Ah! That gets your attention, doesn't it?"

Indeed Boldt's eyes had widened, even as Stacey's narrowed.

Lonestarr went on: "I don't really relish havin' to remove my oldest, dearest friend from God's good earth, as you'd put it. And you *are* a popular fella, Dutch –

you'll make a good face to put on certain efforts of mine that some might otherwise frown upon."

Sand said, "Surely, Jake, you don't think I'm the only agent MI6 has to muzzle your maniacal tendencies. Or that the federal authorities of the USA won't be far behind?"

Lonestarr turned his head slowly, like a boat changing course. "You best pipe down, Mr. Sand. You are not part of this negotiation." He chuckled, shook his head. "You really are too well-known at this point to be tryin' to get away with undercover ops. And who is to say your absence on the world stage will be laid on our doorstep, Johnny? You have far more enemies than friends, after all. Now you keep still."

Boldt huffed a harsh laugh. "Using *my* gun is your leverage, Jake? A body dumped at sea will keep its secrets. But then you were always were weak at details. You see the big picture, but not the small things it takes to really succeed."

Lonestarr waved that off. "I have people working *with* and *for* me, palamino. I don't have to sweat the small stuff, 'cause the big stuff's fallin' into place. The question for you is – do you want to be part of this unprecedented expansion, or would you rather join this Brit twit here at the bottom of the Gulf?"

Neither Lonestarr nor his thug had thought to search Sand, probably not figuring the agent would arm himself in such friendly circumstances. But with a .45 in Jake's hand, and a double-barreled shotgun in his bully boy's grasp, could Sand go for the Walther under his buttoned suitcoat, and take both of these bastards out without getting some combination of Stacey, her father and himself slaughtered?

"It's a simple enough business proposition, Dutch," Lonestarr was saying. "Help dispose of the bodies and, yes, that will brand you my accomplices...and I include you, Miss Boldt...but, Dutch – we will still be partners. And we'll all have as much to lose, but also to *win*, when we corner this planet's energy market."

Somewhere in the night, mockingbirds chirped. Sand knew an irony was in there somewhere, but wasn't sure just who was being mocked.

Boldt sighed – it sounded like the wind coming up. Then he slowly shook his head. "We aren't about to kill this fellow for you, Jake. Him or anybody."

Lonestarr shrugged sadly. "Pains me to have it go with this way, palamino," he said, and the .45 came up and leveled at Boldt. Raven's shotgun remained trained on Sand, across from Stacey, next to her father.

Time to make his move. He glanced at Cuchillo, who had slipped into the shadows – Boldt's man had something in his hand, something white...a wadded-up napkin? Seeing Sand's eyes on him, Cuchillo nodded.

Then tossed the white ball into the fire.

As the napkin arced, Sand somehow knew that Cuchillo had bundled up the M-80s confiscated from the boys earlier. What followed might provide just enough distraction....

When the first M-80 exploded, Lonestarr and Raven turned toward the *pop*, probably misreading it as a gunshot, and more *pops* followed, as Sand flung himself across the table, getting the Walther out, taking Boldt down as Lonestarr's shot rang out though his bullet whizzed overhead. All but simultaneously, Raven blasted at Sand, aiming where the agent had been, not where he was, hugging Boldt and rolling on the ground. Stacey slid off her bench, taking cover underneath the table.

Smart girl, Sand thought.

Lonestarr was shooting toward the fire pit and Raven

the same now, his shotgun bearing a magazine tube, blasting away, not having to reload yet. Sand, on his side on the ground with Boldt prone behind them, took aim at Lonestarr, but, damnit! The lanky figure crouched at the picnic table and when he came up held Stacey as a human shield.

Firing as they went, Lonestarr and Raven withdrew with their prisoner into the darkness, in the direction of the stable, soon beyond the flapping flames of the oil lamps and swallowed by darkness.

Cuchillo came out of the shadows, but a blast came from Raven's shotgun, a starburst of orange and blue in the black. The chauffeur went down. Sand started to help Boldt up, but the oil man pushed away the aid.

"I'm fine," he growled, getting himself to his feet.

Sand sprinted to Cuchillo who lay in the grass cursing in Spanish.

"Where are you hit?" Sand asked.

The chauffeur indicated his right arm. "Just a couple pellets because I ducked too slow."

"They're headed for the stable," Sand said. "There's a road back there, right?"

Rising to one knee, Cuchillo nodded. "But also a garage past the training area beyond the stable. That's where Lonestarr parks."

Boldt came over to check on Cuchillo, kneeling, putting a supportive hand on his man's shoulder.

Sand said, "Get him patched up," then left them to it and took off in pursuit. As he darted across the field into the dark, he hoped he didn't get tripped up by a concavity or, even more disconcerting, Raven popping up with that damned shotgun.

He didn't slow until he got to the stable, staying as low

to the ground as he could while doing so. It was risky – the building could provide cover not just for him but for Lonestarr and Raven; they could certainly be waiting here to pick him off.

But he made it to the rear side wall, then peeked around the corner just as Raven lurched out with the shotgun at the opposite end. Sand drew back as the Indian's blast roared past. He waited a few seconds, then stayed low and moved around the opposite side of the building, ready to take the Indian out from behind.

But Raven was already on the run.

Sand charged after him, even as the Indian hugged the edge of the training area. Then Raven, hunkering as he ran, entered the high beams of a waiting vehicle, a big red Chrysler, pulled up just beyond the fencing. The car's back door was open, Raven throwing himself in the backseat, Lonestarr in the driver's seat reaching behind him to shut the door. The dome light had been on just long enough to reveal Stacey in the rider's seat, looking back at Sand wide-eyed, as Lonestarr held the pistol on her.

The vehicle pulled away as Sand came to a stop and jammed another clip into the Walther, racked the slide, and brought the pistol up...

...but he couldn't fire. Not with Stacey in that car.

The big red sedan sped off into the night.

Back at the site of a party that had definitely lost its glow, Boldt was pacing by the picnic table where Cuchillo sat, morose, the right sleeve of his western shirt torn away and in use as a makeshift bandage.

As Sand approached, Boldt bellowed like a dying animal: "Where's my baby?"

"Lonestarr has her."

He made Boldt sit down at the table and did so himself,

reporting quickly, though the details of his failed pursuit hardly mattered now.

Boldt's blue eyes were wild. "Is the man out of his mind? Cornering the worldwide oil market? Is he god-damn insane?"

"Probably, but there's been a method to that madness for some time now," Sand said, "while you were just go-ing about your business. He has both Nocona brothers for strongarm duties and a woman named Kyla Fluss to work the bedroom side of things, and God knows how many others. Meanwhile, he's been setting you up, in case he needs...what's the American expression? A fall guy."

"You must have bought that bullshit yourself, Sanders, if you came here to poke in my business."

"It's Sand. John Sand. I was indeed investigating you, Dutch. But tonight, in your stable, I overheard Lonestarr and Miss Fluss enjoying a little rendezvous. In and around the rumpy-pumpy, the name Jacobs was mentioned, and Mid-States Oil. They discussed framing you for various of their own malfeasances, should you become troublesome."

Boldt shook one of those big fists. "I don't give a good goddamn about *any* of that now, Sand. I just want my daughter back. I lost her mother a very long time ago and it *still* hurts to the bone. I am not about to lose that child."

"I'm not about to let you."

The desperate father came out, leaving the betrayed businessman in the dust. "What do we *do?* Call the FBI? Hell, it's a *kidnapping,* isn't it?"

Sand held up a calming hand. "Lonestarr's been your partner longer than you've been alive, Dutch. You know him like nobody else. Where would he take your daughter?"

"Well, hell, there's a potful of possibilities. He has houses, a cottage here, a lodge there, keeps a suite in the city. Shit, I don't know."

"What about this yacht he wanted to take me on, on a one-way cruise?"

Cuchillo stopped being a statue long enough to say, "*El Cuba Libre.*"

Boldt's eyes tightened. "That's as good a bet as any."

Sand thought about it. "We have options. We *can* call the FBI. But even with MI6 part of this, they'll shut us out. You're on solid terms with the local law, I assume?"

"Oh my yes. They had to name the policeman's ball after me, I was so good to them. But that's no help."

"Why"

"If Jake smells the boys in blue, he won't hesitate to hurt Stacey. He's a ruthless S.O.B."

Sand cocked an eyebrow. "And yet he was your 'palomino.'"

Boldt looked sour and vaguely ashamed. "Somebody ruthless in business can be useful to have around, when they're on your side."

"You may have noticed, Dutch, he's not on your side anymore. Point me in the direction of that yacht – the marina where he keeps it. And I'll take it from there."

Boldt glanced at Cuchillo, who nodded. "We'll take it together, Mr. Sand."

Sand gave him a hard look. "You need to let me handle this, sir. This calls for a professional approach. And I do this kind of thing for a living."

Boldt held up a big hand. "I don't give two shits about who you are and what you do, Sand. She's my daughter. We're *all* going. We're gonna get her back. And we're gonna kill some people."

Sand thought about that. Then he nodded. "All right. But I should make a call."

"There's a phone in my car. Do it from there."

Soon they were in Boldt's big black Cadillac, Cuchillo behind the wheel, Boldt and Sand in back, the vehicle thrusting itself into the night.

"Do you have something in mind?" Sand asked.

Boldt said, "Jake's not the only one with a boat. The *Texas Rose* isn't a yacht, but she's sure as hell faster than the *Cuba Libre*."

"You're willing to put all your chips down on that bet?"

His nod was slightly compromised by a sigh. "We can catch her if they don't get past Galveston Bay. If the bastard gets her out to open sea, we may never see her again."

The car phone was mounted on the back of the front rider's seat. "I need to make my call," Sand said.

"Who to, son?"

"I'm going to get the Coast Guard into this."

Boldt shook his head. "I *told* you – if Jake sees law, Stacey'll be the first casualty."

"The Coast Guard can shadow them and, without getting too close, tell us where they are. Then *we* take them out. Rescue your girl."

"Coast Guard'll cooperate?"

"They will."

"You sound sure of yourself."

"I am."

"Why?"

"I know someone."

Sand got the phone, dialed a familiar D.C. number. On the fourth ring, a sleepy voice said, "Hello?"

"Phillip, I need a favor."

"John," CIA operative Phillip Lyman said, sounding completely awake now. "What do you need?"

Sand explained the situation and what he wanted from

the Coast Guard.

Lyman asked, "What's the name of the boat?"

"The *Cuba Libre*."

"Let me make a couple calls. Give me your number."

"It will be easier for me to call you back. How long do you need?"

"Fifteen minutes."

With a hand over the receiver, Sand asked Boldt, "How long till we arrive at the marina?"

Boldt said, "Twenty minutes."

Sand told Lyman, "Call you in twenty."

But with Cuchillo pushing the speed limit, they pulled up to the Sunset Marina sixteen minutes later. The trio walked the dock. Dozens of high-priced yachts, catamarans, and sailboats bobbed in the warm Gulf water, but the *Cuba Libre* was not in its slip or anywhere in sight on this dark night with its modest marina lighting.

Returning to the car, Sand called the D.C. number.

Lyman said, "The Coast Guard cutter *Sebago* is now trailing your target. You can reach her on this frequency."

As the CIA agent told him the details, Sand committed them to memory, then thanked his friend and colleague.

"I'll do something for you someday," he told the CIA man.

"You certainly will," Lyman said, and hung up.

Sand hustled back to the empty slip where Boldt and Cuchillo were waiting for him.

"Ready to set sail, Mr. Sand?" The big man was already moving along with Cuchillo next to him.

Sand fell in behind the other two as they passed three more yachts, then they got aboard the next one, a sleek Owens Flagship cabin cruiser. Thirty-five feet and constructed of Honduran mahogany, the *Texas Rose* was a thing of beauty, even in scant lighting.

As he climbed aboard, Sand asked, "Engine?"

Boldt, already on deck, said, "Two-hundred-seventy cubic inch Chrysler marine hemi. She goes like hell, and then she goes a little faster. Before I bought it, this baby was a rum runner."

When the cruiser was untied, and everyone was set, Cuchillo fired up the engine and eased the boat out of its slip. Once they were clear of the marina, the chauffeur gunned it and the cruiser raced across Galveston Bay, Sand hanging onto his seat. The boat was fast, all right. Before long they were in the Gulf itself.

While still inside the twelve-mile limit of United States coastal waters, they pulled up beside the Coast Guard cutter *Sebago*, where a couple of seamen tied off their boat. Boldt had broken out two rifles he kept aboard his cruiser, and he and Sand each carried one as they spoke to the ship's commander, Captain Caleb Garver.

Blandly blond and blue-eyed handsome in a recruiting poster sort of way, Garver was irritated to be caught up in something he did not understand.

"I've been ordered to help you, Mr. Sand," Garver said as they shook hands, something the captain did with no enthusiasm, "but I don't much relish mysterious directives from undefined on-high."

"Your displeasure is noted," Sand said, "and I don't blame you. But this mission will not involve you any more than strictly necessary."

"Tell me this much, Mr. Sand. Will you be putting my crew at risk?"

"Just the opposite, Captain. If we can borrow your launch, and you can point us in the right direction, we'll pester you no further and take care of matters personally."

Garver took that stonily. "The yacht we're tracking for you is two miles that way," he said, pointing southwest. "I'm confident they don't know we're here."

"Thank you, sir."

Soon Sand and his two companions were getting into the launch, bobbing in the water. Cuchillo manned the outboard, Sand and Boldt taking seats toward the bow, rifles across their knees. They set out into increasing dark, the Coast Guard cutter and its lights receding behind them.

Sand asked, "Does Lonestarr have a crew on his boat?"

Boldt nodded. "Could be as many as half a dozen. Certainly three or four for sure – Jake couldn't sail a rubber duck in his goddamn bathtub."

"Roughnecks?"

"Let's say he believes in security."

The outboard's whirring carried in the moonless night, so as soon as they spotted the *Cuba Libre* – which took only a few minutes – Cuchillo cut the motor, and they paddled the rest of the way. As they drew near the yacht, only the bridge lights were on. This appeared to be a sleeping ship.

His whisper barely audible over water stroking the sides of the small vessel, Sand said to Cuchillo, "Stay here, and stay ready. We may be leaving in a hurry."

Cuchillo looked to his employer, who nodded, then added, "If we're two against eight, we may need to skedaddle. Best you be ready right here, *amigo.*"

The chauffeur obviously didn't like any of that, but said nothing.

The motor yacht was a sleek sixty-eight-footer with a modest swim platform at the stern. The latter was their point of entry. As Sand and Cuchillo rowed up, Boldt grabbed the edge of the platform to steady their launch. Sand climbed on, then held the launch steady while Boldt joined him. Cuchillo handed Boldt his rifle, then tried to give the other one to Sand, but the agent shook his head.

"You keep it. You need to cover us, and I have this." Sand slipped his Walther P38 from its sheath.

Cuchillo nodded.

Sand went up the stern ladder first, stepping onto the shallow, quiet deck – perhaps, as they said in the cinema, *too* quiet. Boldt came up next, and when both were standing there, bright lights came on like a sudden sunrise, blinding them.

"*Down!*" Sand yelled, but it was too late.

Lonestarr came from somewhere behind the lights, machine gun in his hands.

He fired a rapid fusillade that stitched a path across Boldt's chest, sending him flailing back over the stern and down onto the swim platform with a *whump*.

Sand fired two rounds from his Walther. Both struck Lonestarr in the chest, the machine gun clattering to the deck as the lunatic lost his balance and careened, pitching over the side into the Gulf.

Hearing a mad scream, Sand turned just as Raven smashed into him, carrying both of them onto the deck, landing hard, Sand's Walther spinning away on polished wood as the breath was knocked out of him.

On top of Sand now, Raven drove a granite right hand into the agent's kidney, then a diamond-hard left to his jaw, leaving Sand groggy, fingers scrabbling over the deck for his gun or any damn thing to use as a weapon. His fingers landed on something cold and metallic, then gripped – a glance told him he'd scored a steel gaff hook. As blows continued to rain down on him, Sand swung the tool and raked the hook across Raven's face.

The big Indian howled and fell away, clutching at his cheek, blood oozing from between his fingers. Sand got to his feet and brought the two-foot steel hook down onto Raven's head once, twice, three times, clubbing him, as if driving a nail. That left Raven unconscious, twitching and bloody on the deck, freeing Sand to recover his Walther and go into the bridge. At first, he saw no one, but when he glanced down into the forward cabin, a shot was fired up at him.

He ducked back, dropped to his belly, and fired two rounds down into the cabin. He heard a grunt, a pistol clatter to the deck, then a thud, as the gunman fell.

From below, a voice snarled, "Get off this boat or the woman dies!"

"We're leaving!" Sand called. "We're leaving..."

He withdrew to the stern, and looked down. Cuchillo had pulled Boldt into the launch with him.

Sand signaled for him to pull away.

Understanding the tactic immediately, Cuchillo fired up the outboard, revving the engine. At the same time, Sand reached up, grabbed the roof of the bridge and pulled himself on top. He flattened himself there and waited.

Before long two crewmen came on deck to watch the launch pulling away. Sand didn't hesitate. He leapt down, immediately knocking one overboard, the other serving as his landing pad. Sand rolled off, bounced up, and fired a single shot. The crewman stared at him with eyes just as sightless as the hole punched in his forehead, then pitched back over the side with a lazy splash.

Sand looked down into the water to see the man he'd knocked overboard swimming away as fast as he could manage. Twelve miles was a long trip, but the crewman might make it. Meanwhile, Cuchillo was already turning back. Sand holstered his Walther, grabbed up the machine gun, and got back onto the bridge. He went down the short flight of steps into the cabin, moving quickly but carefully, in case there were any stray Lonestarr gunmen left alive.

There weren't.

The sole occupant was a drugged, groggy Stacey at the far end of the cabin on a built-in couch. He swooped her up into his arms, as if to carry her over a bridal threshold, and made it quickly back to the stern, where Cuchillo helped lower her into the launch next to her father.

Heading back into the cabin, Sand acquired two bottles of vodka and efficiently, quickly, fashioned them into Molotov cocktails. Then he returned to the stern and, just before going down the ladder and his ride, he lit a bottle and threw it into the bridge, the glass exploding. Flames danced everywhere, having a splendid time.

He went down the ladder, joined the others in the launch, then lit and threw the second cocktail onto the bow as they circled the boat, and soon new flames were enthusiastically seeking out the others.

As they sped back toward the Coast Guard cutter, Sand cradled Stacey with his left arm, his Walther still in his right hand.

Turning to the family retainer, keeping his voice low, Sand asked, "How is he?"

Cuchillo's eyes were wet but no tears fell. He shook his head.

Leaning close to the oil man, Sand said, "We got her back safely. She's fine."

Boldt's eyes flickered and he glanced at his daughter, who was huddled close to Sand. Five bullet holes were apparent in the man's chest – it was dark, so there might have been more. By all rights, Dutch Boldt should have been dead back on deck. But the tough old bird had hung on until he knew his daughter was all right.

"Stacey," he whispered, using all his strength to touch her auburn hair.

"Daddy," she said, still groggy.

He managed a weak smile, said, "I'll remember you to your mama."

Then he was gone.

TWO

THRILLING CITIES
MAY 1962

CHAPTER FIVE

THE SPY WHO KNEW ME

John and Stacey Sand were in their living room at the Boldt mansion near the brown leather sofa that perched on a Native American area rug near the rustic fieldstone fireplace. The furniture seemed to look on patiently in the dimly lit room as the couple, on the parquet floor by the wet bar, danced to Del Shannon's "Runaway" as it played on the Motorola hi-fi near the window.

The fast tune ended and the couple paused, then another forty-five RPM record dropped onto the turntable pile and Acker Bilk's "Stranger On the Shore," the current number one on KNUZ radio, began its seductive work. The couple collapsed into each other's arms and began to slow dance.

Face turned to her hair, Sand inhaled the scent of her shampoo and Chanel #5, as intoxicating a combination as he'd ever encountered. He asked her ear, "Are you sure you'll make it back for our anniversary, m'love?"

Pulling away a little, looking right at him in mild accusation, she said, "Didn't I say I would?"

"I don't doubt you," he said. "But this will be the longest we've been apart since we met."

The laugh bubbled up out of her. "My he-man British spy is in reality a shamelessly sappy romantic. Who would have guessed it?"

"*Ex*-he-man British spy, and if you'd been paying attention, I've been a sentimental fool where you're concerned since...well, since our *stable* relationship began."

She groaned at his pun – not the first time. "A worldly type like John Sand, after two years of marriage... still a lovesick fool."

"Guilty as charged."

Acker Bilk's clarinet soothed and soared. They kissed as they danced. Then they just kissed.

Soon they were on the sofa, undressing each other like children tearing into Christmas packages, and what transpired began slow and tender, turned – after the two slid off onto the floor and the Indian carpet – quick and lusty. Then they lay clinging to each other, naked, panting, thoroughbred animals who'd finished the race together.

A photo finish.

"One month isn't forever," she said, as they sat naked on the sofa.

The living room had become one of their favorite spots in the big house in which to enjoy each other, leading his wife to move the portrait of Dutch Boldt that had long been over the fireplace to a new place of honor in her late father's study. Its replacement here – a painting of the couple they'd commissioned from Norman Rockwell – looked Hollywood glamourous, if more proper than the activities that frequently went on in this space.

He slipped an arm around her. "Why don't I come down to Brownsville next weekend, once you get settled?"

She cuddled closer. "Let's plan on that. No. Better make it two weeks from now. I should have things well set up by then."

"We'll put it on our calendars."

Gathering her clothes, she asked, "Keep me company while I finish packing?"

"Happily," he said, collecting his things. "You know, one of these days Cuchillo's going to get back early from his night off and wander into a scene that may offend his tender sensibilities."

"I would imagine," she said, as he followed her naked-ness up the stairs to the second floor, "that there is little our ex-*federale* friend hasn't already seen in this life. Anyway, he won't be back till late – he had things to do to get us ready to leave tomorrow, first thing. By the way, did you talk to your friend Tom Something?"

She was teasing him – "Tom Something" was the way he referred to the company pilot, who had one of those eastern European names that seemed to Sand to be random consonants in search of a vowel.

"I did," Sand said. "He'll be on hand bright and early, plane ready, flight plan filed."

"You make a wonderful secretary, darling."

They were in their bedroom now, which had once been the guest room where Sand had stayed that first night. They both tossed their clothes on a dresser.

"And I'm pleased to serve as one," he said, following her into their spacious private bathroom, "as long as you continue to pay me like the vice president I am."

"As CEO of Boldt Oil," she said, "I do have some leeway in that area."

"So do I," he said, and squeezed into the shower with her.

She turned on the water, checked the temperature.

"When are you announcing the name change to Boldt

Energy?" he asked, soaping her back.

"Not until the uranium mine is turning out sufficient ore. And we still haven't settled on a location for the nuclear plant. Maybe we'll wait for the re-naming till then."

The warm water sluiced over them and Sand said, "I get excited when you talk business."

"Is that what does it?" she said, washing her hair.

More soaping each other followed, and some playful kissing, but nothing more. They'd had their fun earlier, after all, and his wife did need to finish packing.

Once they'd were dried off, they got into matching white terry robes and Stacey dried her hair while he watched, feeling more fondness for her than he had for anyone outside of his mother, father and brothers. It was love, he supposed. Soon he was lounging on his side of the bed while on her side she carefully folded her clothes into her Louis Vuitton Monogram Canvas Alzer 60 Suitcase.

Yes, he thought, *such a simple Texas girl I married....*

"While I'm away," she said, "you'll need to close the deal with Richmond Oil, remember."

He gave her a blank stare until she stopped folding clothes and looked over at him. "Am I over-managing again?"

"Well," he said, raising himself up on one elbow, "before I entered the dangerous world of oil company management, I did hold the destiny of the world in these hands from time to time, and in the process dealt with homicidal despots, megalomaniac uber-villains, and...you may recall, just last year? Even in retirement, managed to foil a nefarious plot to upset the balance of power in the Caribbean."

She gave him a stare that was definitely not blank. "What happened in San Ignacio was *your* doing alone, was it?"

"All right. All right, that last one we did together."

"Thank you," she said, and a smile blossomed as she closed the Louis Vuitton, "but your point is well-taken. You can certainly handle Joe Musgrave and the Richmond Oil deal without me looking over your shoulder."

"The show of confidence is appreciated. You really do want to avoid emasculating me."

"Definitely."

She came around and sat next to him as he lay stretched out. "I'm done packing."

"Notice I didn't over-manage the process."

"I noticed. It's just...the Richmond Oil deal is key to the growth of the company, John. I really want, *need* it to work out. So forgive me for...hovering."

"It's key, is it?"

"It is."

"Well, that must be why you put your best man on it."

"Why, yes it is."

"Then tell me about the uranium mine."

She crawled up beside him and he scooched over. "It's merely the beginning of the next generation for Boldt Energy."

"Sounds big."

She nodded. "Very. I'll put it in context."

"Please."

"The first nuclear power plant in Shippingport, Pennsylvania, opened three years ago. The Atomic Energy Commission thinks that by the year 2000 there'll be a thousand nuclear power plants in the United States. Someone has to supply uranium for them, and own them, and run them... and why shouldn't it be us?"

"This must be that future you hear so much about."

"It is, if I'm right. In which case we'll be in on the ground floor and can become the energy giant that my father *thought* he was building with Jake Lonestarr."

Sand said, "You have your mother's smile, my dear, but Dutch Boldt's ambition."

"Do you object to that?"

"No." He shrugged. "I told you I was used to dealing with megalomaniacs."

She grinned, a chin-wrinkling thing that was simply adorable, particularly in a CEO, and she began to lightly pound his chest with small fists. He took her in his arms and stopped the assault.

The kiss that followed was long and slow, and when they broke it, Stacey scurried back around to the suitcase, fixed the latches, and Sand followed her and hefted the bag off the bed and hauled it over by the door.

Turning to her, he said, "Anything else that needs doing?"

She smiled, and dropped her robe to puddle at her bare feet.

"Nothing I can think of," she said.

******

The next morning, they said quick goodbyes at the front door, punctuated by one lingering kiss.

"See you in two weeks," she said.

"Two weeks," he said.

Cuchillo, in his chauffeur's livery, had already loaded the Vuitton bag in the trunk. He held the rider's door for Stacey to get in and she gave her husband a little kid's wave and blew him a kiss, and then the Cadillac took them away.

The chauffeur would accompany her on this business trip as her general assistant, a responsibility that included serving as her bodyguard. That latter aspect was a great relief to Sand, who'd had a crash course in the realities of the potential dangers his rich wife could face on that first wild night right here at the Boldt spread just over two years ago.

Last year he had promised Stacey he would never again keep anything from her; but since the aftermath of San Ignacio, he'd been harboring an explosive secret. He had learned, from the lips of a dying woman, that Jake Lonestarr – the man he'd shot twice in the chest, and sent tumbling into the Gulf – was somehow still alive.

The woman who'd taunted him with this news was a lying bitch, but even so, a dying declaration was not to be shrugged off. And ever since he and his wife had returned to the States, to their normal lives as married oil company executives, Sand had taken on a new and very much covert hobby.

Tracking Lonestarr.

If the man was dead, Sand needed to confirm that as best as possible – Lonestarr seemed to have been shark food that night, so corroboration might well be unattainable. But if the bastard was alive, *really was alive*, Sand simply had to know. The man needed killing, and not just because his existence was a threat to Stacey's.

With his bride off to Brownsville for most of next month, Sand would soon be able to turn his full attention to his search for the man who had killed her father. The organization that was Boldt Oil did not need John Sand to function ably, even with Stacey away. Once he had secured the deal with Richmond Oil, Sand's time would be his own until the CEO returned.

The Cadillac was barely out of sight before Sand was

in the house and in the study that had been Dutch Boldt's, back to work on his investigation. He had put feelers out to contacts around the world – former colleagues, ex-snitches, confidential informants, even a few of the more discreet information brokers around the globe; they had all been recruited to help track down Lonestarr. So far, however, all they had come up with was a pound of air.

No one seemed to know anything, or if they did, weren't talking.

When he had tried to contact Double M, even MI6 had stonewalled him; when he reached Kitty Cash's desk, she told him Sir Malcolm Marbury was no longer there – he had retired. He did not doubt the woman, whose voice for the first time in his experience betrayed a touch of emotion.

A fellow officer in the Seven-Seven Section, speaking to Sand from a secure number, confirmed Double M's retirement. The agent also pointed out that Sand himself had reported killing Lonestarr. And in the interim, no intel had emerged to contradict "*your*" report, as his fellow agent had underscored.

Sand had been searching for Lonestarr for most of the last year, and he had nothing. Admittedly, in his current situation – as his wife put it, an ex-spy – he was badly hampered. That dying siren's words – "You'll never stop Jake Lonestarr" – had begun to seem like nothing more than an enemy's final empty taunt, designed to do nothing more than to send him down a rabbit hole of doubt.

If that had been the dead woman's plan, she was succeeding splendidly – Sand was running out of options. He had reports coming in from two more sources, one tonight, one tomorrow. He would continue to exhaust every possibility for the month Stacey was away, and then he promised himself he'd drop it. He would stop driving himself mad.

That evening, he threw on a sportcoat, Ban-Lon and jeans and drove into Houston for dinner at Gaido's Seafood Restaurant; it was probably his favorite dining establishment in the city, but he mostly poked at his food, feeling uncharacteristically anxious. Then he drove to Cobler Books at Richmond Avenue and Main Street, near Rice University, Stacey's alma mater.

At first the store seemed unusually empty, the register inside the door doing no business, the floor-to-ceiling walls of books attracting no browsers. But when he headed to the back, a crowd was seated and waiting patiently, albeit murmuring in anticipation.

Seated before the audience was a striking, dignified woman with high cheekbones and curly light brown hair brushing the collar of her paisley blouse. Rita Copley had been an actress when she was younger, turning down an MGM contract to take over the bookstore that had been her husband's dream until his fatal heart attack at age thirty-nine.

The store had opened while he was still a student at Rice University. Now, it was Rita's and she loved throwing parties for loyal customers and signings for authors she liked. Sand had met her through Stacey, who shopped here extensively, her father having been a close friend of Rita's – Dutch had been one of the financiers of her pet project, the Alley Theatre.

The author appearing here tonight was touting his latest spy novel in a phenomenally successful series that had made him a fortune; it had also led to the demise of John Sand's career in espionage. Seated beside Rita, who was introducing him to the attendees, the author had a deceptively lazy, hooded-eye manner, his wavy, sandy hair parted to one side, his ever-present cigarette holder in his right hand. He wore a tweed jacket over a white shirt with tan slacks and a darker tan bow tie. The dark blue eyes in the oval, grooved face found Sand lurking on the periphery, and a smile flickered.

Sand's former colleague said, "Ladies and gentlemen, thank you for attending, and for your interest in my humble work. But if you'll permit me one last indulgence before we begin signing, I would like you to meet the man you've read about in both *Look* and *Life*, a London expatriate here in Houston but a patriot wherever he might go – the inspiration behind my creation, and himself a former real-life British agent...John Sand."

The fifty people in the audience, every one of whom held copies of the author's new book, oohed and aahed and turned to gawk at Sand, who plastered a smile on his face and nodded, even as he wished that he might strangle his friend by his famous neck.

"Join us, John," his friend said with an open-handed gesture.

"Yes, John," Rita said, "please."

There was no arguing.

As Sand approached the table, the audience applauded (and a few attendees whistled), a pair of Rita's employees rushing to bring out another folding chair and a glass of iced tea for their unanticipated guest.

Rita smiled at Sand, then held up a hand. As the crowd quieted, she said, "Mr. Sand, John...what a wonderful surprise. Thank you for coming. To what do we owe this pleasure?"

"I wanted to chat with the author," he heard himself say. "We haven't seen each other recently. Besides, he owes me a drink for all the money I've made him."

The crowd loved that, giving it a bigger laugh than it likely deserved.

What followed was a question-and-answer session, about a third of the queries coming directly to Sand. He had never spent a more uncomfortable evening, save for the time he'd been penned up in the alligator pit, although he doubted his friend had ever enjoyed himself more.

When the signing began, Sand eased away. Rita joined him. "John, I'd have invited you myself tonight if I thought there was the remotest chance you'd say yes."

He put on a smile. "I wouldn't have. I'll have you know I'm quite miserable."

"Well, it doesn't show. And thank you for coming just the same."

Rita returned to her guest author to oversee the signing of books. Sand browsed and purchased a vintage Raymond Chandler and a new John le Carré. When the appearance finally wrapped up, Sand offered his former colleague a ride back to his hotel.

"Will you ever forgive me, John?" his friend said through a smile as crooked as it was wide.

"No. But you may be able to make it up to me."

"Doesn't *that* sound mysterious!"

They climbed into Sand's British racing green MG, its top down on this starry night.

The author patted the dashboard. "You can take the boy out of England, but you cannot take the Mother Country out of the man."

"I called the Warwick, figuring that's where you'd stay, knowing your tastes. But you weren't registered. Then I asked again using your old alias."

The cigarette holder in his friend's teeth bobbed. "You still have a few deductive abilities left, despite your retired status. Yes, 'Colin Vincent' allows me *some* privacy." He sighed grandly. "You wouldn't know the inconvenience of fame."

"Wouldn't I?"

"Ha! You're familiar with the Warwick?"

"Stacey and I were married there."

"How is the lovely Stacey?" asked "Colin Vincent," having almost to yell to be heard over the wind and engine roar as Sand hurried toward downtown.

"Out of town on business."

"Well," his friend mused, "a kept man like yourself does need the occasional break."

"Save your wit for the books, why don't you?"

The author nodded. "Probably wise. They don't get any easier, writing these things. I meant it to be a lark, not a profession! I quite prefer journalism."

"Any luck with the question I asked you to look into?"

He sighed smoke, which the wind plumed behind him like a gray scarf. "Yes and no."

"You may not be a spy anymore," Sand said, "but you still sound like one."

With a little chuckle, his friend said, "Old habits die hard indeed. The thing of it is, for all my vaunted sources, I can't find a single one who places your Lonestarr still among the living."

Sand felt a pang – Good Lord, he didn't *want* Lonestarr to be alive, did he?

"That," Sand said, "doesn't sound like yes and no to me."

"Well, that was the 'no.' The 'yes' is that – though I couldn't *find* Lonestarr – I was able to locate one of his former associates...a Mexican national named Jesus Guerra."

Braking for a stop light, Sand said, "Lonestarr had plenty of 'associates.' What makes this one significant?"

"Because this Jesus – as opposed to the one interested in saving men's souls – is in the market for buying uranium 235. He pursues this goal in the Kazakh Soviet Socialist Republic, then smuggles it out...but I'm not sure how he's accomplishing that, or where his eventual market might be."

"He's a criminal," Sand said, getting his green light. "You *expect* a criminal to commit crimes. These days the crimes are just more grandiose."

But the word "uranium," after his talk with Stacey last night, did have a glow to it.

"True enough," the author said. "My sources tell me Jesus purchased it for a company called Earl Stron Investments."

Sand frowned. "Who or what is Earl Stron?"

"There you have the proverbial fly in the ointment, John. He doesn't appear to exist. I've searched exhaustively, and there appears to be no such person. Not a single soul on the face of the earth with that appellation."

Sand glanced over at the author, then returned his attention to his driving. "But there *is* an Earl Stron Investments."

He nodded. "Dating back less than a year, well after you thought you'd killed the man. Now here's the 'yes' part – Earl Stron is an anagram for Lonestarr."

Sand let that sink in for a moment, then asked, "So you think I'm right? Lonestarr *is* alive, somehow?"

"Or perhaps his interests are. But if Guerra is alone in this, shipping stolen or black-market uranium to himself...he certainly picked a curious name for his company, don't you think?"

"Curious and curiouser. And it seems an unlikely coincidence. But why uranium?"

But Sand already knew – the future.

The author shrugged, as if contemplating which nightclub to frequent. "What was your mad Texan's original intention?"

"To corner the world's energy markets and take control of the planet."

"I might have to use that one," the author admitted. "Uranium is considered to be a major new power source, after all. Perhaps his plan remains intact, but he's moved from one energy source to another."

"Off oil and onto uranium."

"Possibly," his ex-colleague said. "Or perhaps he's interested in building a bomb."

Sand frowned. "He would need fifteen kilograms for an atomic bomb."

The author's eyes were cold, his face a bland mask. "Would you like to venture a guess as to how much uranium Jesus smuggled from the KSSR?"

Sand said nothing.

"Ten times that, John. Perhaps it's not a bomb he plans to develop, but an atomic arsenal."

Sand shook his head. "Jesus."

"Jesus *Guerra.*"

Another stop light.

"Where is Guerra now?" Sand asked.

"Mexico, presumably, though I wasn't able to get any further than that. I had to break off my intrigues on your behalf when I traveled to America for matters of commerce. I simply don't have the resources to pick up the search from here."

Sand gave him a look.

"Sorry, old boy, but I am not on the Boldt Oil payroll,

and it has been many years since I was in the employ of Her Majesty. I am but a poor scribe who must scribble to make ends meet."

Sand laughed at that.

"On a more personal note," the author said, the Warwick in sight now.

"Yes?"

"There are those who say you are vexed with me for using your experiences as grist for my less-than-literary mill. Is that truly the case?"

Glancing over, Sand said, "Perhaps at first, but by the time I came to Texas and met my future bride, it became clear I was on my last mission. Now I am wealthy with a beautiful wife and the kind of life any man would dream of. I may even be a father one day. And I thank you for that."

"Not fatherhood, you don't! You'll have to shoulder that blame yourself."

Sand smiled. "I might have missed out on this new life altogether if not for your books."

His friend gave a tiny nod. "Worked out well for us both, eventually."

"So," Sand said, pulling up in front of the hotel, "you've put in some real work for me. And, as you point out, you are not on the Boldt payroll. What can I do to settle up?"

A doorman came over to open the passenger door for the author, who climbed out, then swung around to grin at Sand.

"John, when this is all over, you're going to tell me all about it, in excruciating detail...and in the end, I'll have the makings of a cracking good novel."

Laughing as he turned, lighting a cigarette in its holder, the author strolled toward the door.

CHAPTER SIX

RUNAWAY

He would have to tell her.

Sand knew damn well he couldn't just show up in Brownsville with some lame excuse – claiming one day away from her was simply too much to bear...that just would not do. The time had come to inform the former Stacey Boldt that for many months now he'd been doing his best to track Jake Lonestarr down. And that he finally had a lead, however nebulous.

In the study, with Dutch Boldt's picture looking on in seeming approval, Sand set aside his vodka martini and reached for the phone. Coming clean this way might be the coward's way out, but he didn't feel particularly brave at the moment. Let her express her anger over his withholding that terrible woman's dying words with a telephone line between them. Might cushion the blow, for him at least.

He glanced down at the contact information she'd left him, eyes landing on the number of the Hotel El Jardín in Brownsville, Texas. He dialed it.

"Hotel El Jardín – how may I help you this evening?"

"Stacey Sand's room please."

"I'll put you through, sir."

Sand let it ring ten times before he hung up. She'd likely had a long day and might already be asleep. His wife was an extremely sound sleeper, after all; still, a ringing phone at her bedside would surely stir her. Of course, she might be out to a late dinner. He called back, asked for Cuchillo's room this time, and was greeted with another ten unanswered rings.

He sipped his martini. An hour and another martini passed before he reached for the telephone again. He was dialing when a whirring above and outside began to build.

The churning overhead quickly grew closer and closer, until a twister seemed to be hovering over the roof. He hung up and dug one of Dutch's six-shooter .45s out of a desk drawer, his Walther tucked away upstairs.

He strode into the foyer with the weapon at his side, then raised the gun to shoulder level as he cracked open the massive wooden slab of a front door and peered out.

A helicopter was settling down on the lawn just beyond where the driveway circled around, making the short grass bristle. The whirring soon settled into nothing at all, the blades coming to rest, and a familiar figure in a gray Brooks Brothers suit stepped down from his ride and trotted over, black tie flapping, to where an astonished Sand was watching.

"Sorry to just drop by," Phillip Lyman said, brushing back his blond hair. The Havana tan of last year had long since faded.

Sand opened the door for his friend. "Just happen to be in the neighborhood?"

"In Dallas conducting a training exercise. I have some information to share that is better delivered in person."

"Don't they have telephones in Big D?" Sand asked, as

Lyman moved across the foyer.

"Not secure ones."

The CIA agent, who had been here before, strode into the living room, Sand following as if he were the intruding guest.

Lyman plopped down on the sofa and Sand took one of the burgundy leather chairs nearby. The agent smiled as Sand sat with the six-shooter in his lap.

"You appear ready," Lyman said, "to go hunting outlaws."

"Always," Sand said, setting the pistol on the end table nearby. "Care for a drink, Phillip?"

"I'd kill for a bourbon."

"Unnecessary in this instance," Sand assured him.

After pouring two glasses at the wet bar, Sand handed one to Lyman, then returned to his chair with the other.

"I tried to call," Lyman said, "to let you know I was coming, but got no answer."

"I was at a book signing."

"Ah. Your former colleague turned writer. I'm going to guess you've had *him* beating the bushes for Jake Lonestarr, too. He has his own sources, quite separate from the Company's."

Sand sipped bourbon. "He conveyed some information, yes, and now I'm more convinced than ever that Lonestarr is still breathing."

"Mind sharing that information?"

"Not at all. It's just one name – Jesus Guerra. Ring any bells?"

Lyman shrugged. "No. Not a jingle. Should it?"

"I think so. That is, if you're concerned about uranium being sold on the black market, enough to build an atomic bomb or two."

Sand filled the CIA man in on everything his author friend had told him.

Then Lyman let out a long, low whistle. "Some very nasty ramifications in store there."

"Jesus really should have been on your radar, Phillip. And I'm not talking about the Sermon on the Mount."

"He will be as soon as I'm back in D.C."

Sand sat forward. "Why are you here, Phillip? I've shown you mine. Time for you to show me yours."

Lyman raised his free hand, the other busy with his bourbon glass. "Let's start with some context, shall we?"

"All right. Contextualize."

"My sources, while they may not compare to those of a thriller writer, tell me you once had a run-in with an American Indian, a certain Crow Nocona. Brother of Raven Nocona, who worked for your 'friend' Lonestarr."

"Your sources are not wrong."

"Anything you'd care to share?"

Sand shrugged. "That was the last mission I worked for MI6, the same investigation that led me to Stacey's father, who I mistakenly considered the villain of the piece."

"When in fact that was Jake Lonestarr."

Sand nodded. "Crow tried to have me killed in Berlin, but, desirous of an alibi, left the job to amateurs."

"Who apparently failed."

"Apparently. What's pertinent here is that *both* Nocona brothers worked for Jake Lonestarr – they were his favored strongarm specialists."

A mild frown. "You might have mentioned this when you recruited me to help you locate Lonestarr."

Sand shrugged again. "Crow disappeared after Berlin. MI6 hasn't had so much as a whiff of him since, according to my sources. Word has it he's dead."

"Like his brother. Like his boss."

"This assumes the dead are paying us the courtesy of staying that way."

Lyman grinned and saluted with his glass. "What was it Mark Twain said about his death?"

"'The reports of my demise are greatly exaggerated.'"

"The same may be true of Crow Nocona." Lyman sipped, shifted on the sofa, putting an ankle on a knee. "John, we have been keeping track of a German operative named Kyla Fluss. Does that name mean anything to you? In the course of our surveillance, we observed frequent recent interactions between Fluss and Nocona – *Crow* Nocona, that is."

The hair on the back of Sand's neck was standing up. "This was in Germany?"

"No. Matamoros. Mexico."

"...Damn."

"What is it, John?"

"Stacey is in Brownsville, Texas."

Lyman tensed, sitting forward in alarm. "That's, what? Fifteen minutes from Matamoros?...Could be a coincidence."

"Is that what you think it is, Phillip?"

"About much as you do, John."

Sand rose, a bourbon glass in one hand, filling the other with the six-shooter. "Well, I hate to be rude. It was a treat having you drop by. But I have things to do, so you need to fly...literally."

Lyman rose and went over to the wet bar to deposit his glass, frowning in thought as he went. Then he turned to his friend and said, "Keep me posted. I may be able to help out – the Company's taken an interest in Crow Nocona. But it would seem you'll be moving back and forth between borders, so do be careful whose toes you step on."

"If Crow endangers my wife, Phillip, I won't step on his toes, I'll clip his goddamned wings."

"I don't doubt that. Just be discreet about it. Don't sign your name to too many corpses."

Sand watched from the door as Lyman trotted back out to his waiting helicopter, but didn't wait for it to lift off into the night. Instead Sand went back to the study and, when the copter noise had faded, dialed the Hotel El Jardín again. Still no answer in either room. And the check-in clerk had not seen either of the guests since coming on at nine p.m.

Worry was starting to take hold of Sand, but he shook it off. His wife and her bodyguard were checked in, which meant they'd arrived safely – didn't it? He wouldn't bother trying the Boldt office in Brownsville, as it obviously wouldn't be open at this hour, and anyway he didn't have the names handy of those working there.

But he *could* call the pilot who'd flown Stacey and Cuchillo to Brownsville.

Thumbing through Stacey's address notebook to find Tom Something's listing took a while. There it was! What the hell kind of name was Rzepczynski, anyway? It was like that character in *Li'l Abner* who walked around under a black rain cloud – Joe Btfsplk. *That* he could remember!

In any case, he memorized the pilot's number, then reached for the receiver and began dialing. The wall clock said it was after midnight, but anyone on Tom's kind of salary was on call twenty-four hours.

On the fifth ring, a thick voice mumbled, "Hello?"

"Tom, John Sand. Shake the cobwebs – I need to talk to you."

"I'm listening, sir."

"I haven't heard from Stacey, and can't reach her or

Cuchillo, either. Can you confirm their safe arrival in Brownsville?"

"I can, sir. It was a quick, easy flight. A company car was waiting. I watched them drive away before I took off. Everything seemed fine."

"Well, it may not be fine now. How soon can we take off for Brownsville?"

"I'll have to find someone to fuel the plane, file the flight plan. And I'll need some coffee, sir. What time is it?"

"Ten past midnight."

"We should wait until daybreak, sir."

"Not an option. How soon, Tom?"

"Four hours?"

"Three," Sand said, then hung up.

******

After sleeping for two hours, Sand rose to the alarm he'd set, showered and shaved. The windows were still black with night. He tossed some clothes and his shaving kit in a suitcase (Samsonite – Vuitton not his style), then got dressed – a tan suit by Dunhill (very much his style) with a dark brown tie and yellow short-sleeved shirt, his Walther P38 in the shoulder sling and his Beretta 950 in an ankle holster. He might be overdoing it, but preparing for the worst was never a bad idea.

In the kitchen he took the time to pour a glass of orange juice and eat an English muffin, then went out to his MG and headed to the small private airport.

From the hangar he watched the maintenance crew finish fueling the plane. They'd been grumbling when he arrived, until informed they'd be getting time-and-a-half for their trouble and suddenly the boss lady's British hubby didn't seem like such a pain in the ass.

Tom Rzepczynski walked up, his blond crewcut giving him a military look in keeping with his straight, professional bearing. His blue eyes were red-rimmed, but his mug of black coffee would go a long way toward remedying that.

Sand said, "Thank you for this, Tom. I wouldn't impose if I didn't consider it necessary."

"You think something may have happened to Mrs. Sand and Cuchillo, sir?"

Sand shrugged. "With any luck, no. But there's reason enough to be wary, and I need to make sure for myself."

"Understood," Tom said with a nod. Then, careful not to be overheard, the pilot asked, "Could this have anything to do with the work you did for the government last year?"

"Possibly."

"Sir, just so you know – you can count on my discretion. I was a Navy pilot. I understand the sort of work you do. I would just like to help as best I can."

"I appreciate that, Tom. But I don't do that sort of work anymore."

With the barest wisp of a smile, the pilot said, "The gun under your coat notwithstanding, sir."

Sand gave him a rueful shrug. "I stopped having them tailored not to show. Perhaps I was premature."

"Mrs. Sand is good people, sir. Cuchillo, too. You're right to take such steps when it's your family. Just know that I'll do anything I can to help."

"Thank you, Tom."

With a nod, the pilot went off to hurry the maintenance crew and make them earn that time-and-a-half. Within twenty minutes, they were in the air headed for Brownsville, Texas.

The sun was rising when the company's Cessna 310 set down in Brownsville, where a faded yellow 1957 Chevy

Apache pickup waited on the tarmac, a driver next to it.

As Sand went out the open door of the plane, the pilot called, "Happy hunting, sir."

"Thanks, Tom. Stay available – I'll let you know when we're ready to come home."

"I'll be on call till I hear from you, Mr. Sand."

Suitcase in hand, Sand approached the waiting truck, whose somewhat bowlegged driver stood next to it with his arms folded like a harem guard. The man sported the same style chauffeur's livery as Cuchillo, though in this case the unofficial uniform was topped by a white Stetson. At perhaps five ten, with a little Buddha belly and a walrus mustache as white as his cowboy hat, he looked more like a pensioner than the employee of a major energy company.

"Mr. Sand?" the driver asked.

Sand nodded.

The driver stuck out a hand and Sand took it. The grip was firm but didn't show off.

"Charlie Woolford. I'm the driver, not the bellman, so if you want that suitcase in the box, go back around back and put 'er in there."

"Pleased to meet you, Charlie," Sand said, and did as he'd been told, then returned and added, "I'm John."

"Don't mean to be unwelcomin'," his driver said, "but I got a bad back, so I don't lift any more than a fork and spoon and knife these days."

Woolford climbed in behind the wheel. Sand went around to the rider's side and got aboard. In addition to eschewing bag service, this chauffeur didn't open the door for his passengers, which was fine with Sand.

"Where we headed, John?"

The motor purred like a happy cougar and Sand noticed a gun rack in the back window, a lever-action

Winchester rifle riding there. The ex-agent had seen his share of firearms, but one like this? Only in western movies, before today.

"First stop," Sand said, "the Boldt Oil office."

"Can do," Woolford said, dropping the truck into gear and pulling away.

Studying his new companion, Sand asked, "Did you drive Mrs. Sand and Cuchillo yesterday?"

"Nope."

"Do you know who did?"

"Yep."

Half-amused, half-irritated, Sand said, "If we've got the Gary Cooper impression out of the way, perhaps you'd share that information."

Woolford hinted at a smile. "Had another feller from the office follow me out here with a brand-new Lincoln, shiny and black. Mrs. Sand's the company president, you know, so best foot forward. You related?"

"By marriage."

"Ah, you mus' be the husband."

"I have that honor."

"Anyway, that Lincoln was for this feller Cooch-ee-ya to drive her around in. I rode back with the other feller."

"The Lincoln followed you?"

"No. I dropped it off 'fore they landed. I was long gone by the time they come in."

"So you wouldn't know where they went from here?"

"Not a clue. Sorry. They might know at the office."

Brownsville-South Padre Island International Airport sat five miles east of downtown. Traffic was light and the sun loomed behind them as Woolford drove west.

Sand asked, "Did you talk to Mrs. Sand or her driver yesterday?"

Woolford shrugged. "Never had no reason to. Something goin' on here?"

"Possibly," Sand said. "I've not been able to make contact with either."

Woolford glanced over at him. "Meaning no offense, Mrs. Sand has only been in town since a morning ago. Not even twenty-fours since she pulled in. She likely had a busy yesterday. You got reason to think something's gone to hell?"

"It isn't like my wife or Cuchillo not to check in with me. Something may be wrong. I'll have a better idea when I've spoken to the people at the Boldt office."

Woolford didn't say anything, eyes on the road, but his squint was about thinking, not glare. The sun was to their backs, after all.

Sand asked, "Did you serve in the war, Charlie?"

"Seventh Army under General Patton, yes sir. You?"

"I was too young for World War II. I was in the Home Guard, which was sort of like your Civil Defense. I served in the Royal Navy after the war. I would guess you saw your share of action?"

Woolford nodded. "More than my share. Let's just say Casablanca wasn't like the movies."

Sand twitched a smile. "Charlie, do you recall how, just before combat, you got that...feeling? The one where the air becomes very still, as if a storm may hit momentarily, without warning?"

The squint flicked toward him, then back to the road. "I know that feeling, John. Too damn well."

"Well, I've had that sensation since last night, when I couldn't reach my wife."

They rode in silence for a while, then Sand asked, "What is your job with Boldt, exactly?"

"Mostly what you see right now. That and any fetch and carry they need at the office. It's short on glory but it pays the bills. Pays them handsomer than I deserve, if truth be told."

"How'd you rate such a job?"

"Saved Dutch Boldt's ass once. Feller with a knife that Dutch didn't see comin'. Of course the feller didn't see me with that chair, either, did he? After that, Dutch figured it might make sense havin' a friend down this way. Gimme this job, and I had it for goin' on twenty-five years now. You married into *your* job, huh? This that nep-a-tism I heard about?"

"The very thing," Sand said, smiling at having his chain yanked. "I highly recommend marrying money, Charlie."

"I'll keep that in mind."

"But it does have its drawbacks."

"Which is why you're all tore up wonderin' what's become of your missus. Don't you worry, son. We'll find her."

"We?"

This time the grizzled driver twitched a smile. "What do you know about Brownsville, John?"

"That it's in Texas, across the border from Matamoros."

"Guess that's a start. You know where anything is? Who to talk to?"

"You're coming in loud and clear, Charlie. *We*'re going to find her."

"That we are, John."

Charlie pulled up and parked in front of a low-slung stucco building with a sign bearing the Boldt Oil logo.

Woolford said, "Check in with Adam Cameron – he runs things. I'll be right here when you get done. Time for my cigarette break, anyway."

Sand walked into the office. A couple of oscillating fans were stirring the air. Of the two desks, only one was occupied. File cabinets lined one wall and a pair of doors were at the back, private offices apparently. A small, bare bones facility. Not exactly the Houston Boldt Oil HQ.

The only person out here, a young blonde woman in a pink short-sleeve dress, sat behind a metal desk, shuffling papers. Her desktop was orderly, dominated by an intercom phone, a typewriter on a stand nearby. She looked up and smiled as Sand entered.

"Help you?" she asked, chipper.

"Mr. Cameron in?"

"Do you have an appointment?"

"I don't. Is he in?"

The woman seemed to be considering being less chipper. "Uhhh....Sir, you really should call ahead and – "

"If he's here, would you tell him it's John Sand? Executive vice president of the company? Husband of Stacey Boldt Sand?"

He was in no mood to fool around.

The young woman's cheeks turned crimson and the papers in her hands fell onto her desk like a card hand she was throwing in. She gathered and tidied the sheets, then fumbled with the intercom before finally pushing the correct button, and a voice that didn't like being bothered said, "*Yes,* Peggy?"

"Mr. Cameron, John Sand is here to see you, sir."

"John Sand?" Cameron's voice suddenly was fine with being bothered. "I'll be right out."

A few seconds later a sturdy man emerged from one of the offices at the back. Bespectacled with black hair parted on the side, he wore a short-sleeve white shirt and a gray striped tie with darker gray slacks and black wingtips.

"Mr. Sand?" he asked, coming forward, smiling bigger than necessary, and more nervous than need be. He extended a hand, which Sand shook – it was sweaty thing, but then it was a hot day in Texas.

"I'm Adam Cameron, chief engineer down here. I was expecting *Mrs.* Sand. Actually, I was expecting her yesterday."

Sand frowned. "She didn't show up at all?"

Cameron shook his head. "She did not. Does that mean *you* expected her to be here yesterday, too?"

"That was my understanding. Did she call and say she'd be delayed, or...?"

The chief engineer gestured to the empty desk, which he settled behind. Sand took the visitor's chair, sitting forward, elbows on the desk, hands folded.

Cameron said, "She did not get in touch. I talked to Charlie Woolford, but he said he dropped her Lincoln off at the airport."

"That's a company car, not a rental?"

The engineer nodded. "We have enough executives from Houston and other offices come through to call for that."

"Any reason I should doubt Charlie's version of events?"

"You rode into town with him?"

"Yes."

Cameron grunted. "Then you know Charlie Woolford is honest to the point of being a pain about it. He doesn't care what *anybody* thinks."

"That was my reading of the man," Sand said. "Never hurts to get a second opinion."

Cameron's expression was half-thoughtful, half-apologetic. "My assumption was your wife had spent the day sightseeing – plenty to do in this part of the world – or maybe just got herself settled in at the hotel. I was just starting to get concerned, actually..."

"I've been concerned," Sand said pointedly, "since last night when I hadn't heard a thing from her, and couldn't reach her at her hotel."

"Do you think we should involve the police?"

"Not just yet. Do you have the Lincoln's license plate number?"

Cameron nodded and turned toward the blonde at her desk. "Peggy, do you know where..."

Before he could finish his sentence, Peggy – who hadn't had to work at eavesdropping, close at hand as she was – held up an envelope. "I was getting ready to get the new plates this week, Mr. Cameron. I have the form and the old plate number is on that."

She took out the sheet, showed it to their caller. "Should I write that down for you, Mr. Sand?"

"Thank you, Peggy, no. I've got it."

Cameron asked, "What about the police?"

"I'm going to do some checking myself before calling in any authorities, and I'll get back to you when I know what's going on...or if I don't. In either case, just go on about your work. If my wife wanders in, tell her I'm here and looking for her."

"You can count on it, Mr. Sand," Cameron said.

Outside, Sand rejoined Woolford in the truck.

As they pulled into traffic, the driver asked, "Where to?"

"Hotel El Jardín," Sand said. "By the way, we have company."

Woolford didn't even have to check the rearview mirror. "You mean that Caddy, three cars back? Two out-of-towners. Who do you know in Nevada?"

"Nobody worth mentioning." He smiled at his driver. "You're an observant 'feller,' Charlie."

"I like to feel I stay on top of things, John. Otherwise you don't see what's comin' till it's too late. Like me to lose 'em?"

"No, let's just go on to the hotel."

"How long we gonna let them chaperone us?"

"Like to find out what they know before, oh, I hit them with a chair or something. What do you think?"

Woolford was chuckling. "I think you British 'blokes' figure soundin' polite takes the sting out of being a smart-ass."

"Well, we do hope that's the case."

"You ever hear the one about curiosity killin' the cat?"

"The cat wasn't armed," Sand reminded him.

CHAPTER SEVEN
VEGAS IDEA

The Cadillac with the Nevada plates accompanied Sand and his driver all the way to the Hotel El Jardín at the corner of Eleventh and Levee Streets – not too close, always unobtrusive, but never really out of sight. When Woolford pulled up in front of the eight-story, Spanish-style hotel on Levee, their escorts brazenly pulled into a parking place not far behind them, putting only two taxis between Charlie Woolford's pickup and the out-of-state Caddy.

Woolford asked, "How do you want to play this?"

Sand spotted a phone booth on the street corner opposite.

"Sit tight and keep watch," Sand said, eyes on the rearview mirror. "They'll likely size things up before heading in after me, if that's what they're here for. In which case, get over to that phone booth and call the hotel – ask for Mrs. Sand's room. The switchboard will ring the room. That'll alert me I have company coming."

"What if they follow you straight in, right on your heels?"

Sand gave Woolford a cool, hard look. "How are you with that Winchester?"

"I hold my own."

"Well then, as long as we don't find ourselves in a crossfire, we should be fine."

Ignoring the Cadillac, Sand got out and plucked his suitcase out of the truck bed. A doorman came over to help and Sand waved him politely away, then strolled to the double glass doors, using their windows as mirrors. The two men in the Caddy front seat were staying put, but their eyes followed him.

Could their presence be strictly surveillance?

Sand was so accustomed to the heat by now, the air-conditioning that greeted him upon entering slapped him pleasantly. Leather chairs and couches were spotted around the spacious, open-beamed lobby of the 1920s-era hotel, chandeliers hovering, ceiling fans encouraging the cooled air. Several support columns wore tiles halfway up, then gave way to stucco, adding to the half-western, half-Mexican decor.

At the front desk, Sand was greeted by a thin, thinly mustached clerk with (maintaining the theme) thinning slicked-back hair; his gray suit was trimmed darker gray and his name tag said, *Arnold Brewster, Assistant Manager.*

"May I help you, sir?" came a smooth second tenor.

"John Sand. My wife checked in yesterday. Mrs. Sand booked two rooms, the extra one for her driver, Ernesto Cuchillo. It's our anniversary and I'd like to surprise Stacey." He got out his wallet and produced a twenty-dollar bill. "You have a spare key to her room, I assume?"

The assistant manager studied the twenty as if it were a specimen of rarely seen wildlife – perhaps it was.

"I have identification," Sand said, and flipped the wallet open to the card holder.

The assistant manager raised a palm and said, "That

won't be necessary. Do you need help with your bags?"

"No, I just have the one. If you'll check the guest register..."

"No need. It's room 415, our best suite. I checked Mrs. Sand in myself. A very gracious, lovely lady."

"Yes she is," Sand said.

As the assistant manager fetched a key from a half-wall of cubby holes, Sand glanced toward the entry. No sign of his Cadillac chaperones.

"Tell me, Mr. Brewster," Sand said, taking the key, "what time did my wife check in?"

"Around ten a.m."

"Do you know if she left the hotel?"

"She did," the assistant manager said with a nod. "Mrs. Sand came down about an hour later and stopped at the desk. Asked for a restaurant recommendation for lunch."

"And did you make one?"

"I said the hotel restaurant was excellent but also gave her a brochure listing a dozen local spots. She didn't eat here, because I saw her leave out the front."

Damn.

"Was Mr. Cuchillo with her?"

"No. He went out, some time later."

Sand pressed. "Did she come back, do you know? How long were you on duty?"

"Until five p.m. And I did not see her return, or Mr. Cuchillo. But I may have missed it, between guests checking in and out."

Sand nodded. "Thank you, Mr. Brewster."

"Let me know if I might be of any further help," the assistant manager said, with the hopeful look of a man who thought another engraving of Andrew Jackson might be in his future.

Sand got in the old-fashioned lift, where the operator was an elderly Mexican with silver hair and a baggy uniform suggesting the old fellow had either once been more strapping or was wearing a hand-me-down from a previous operator.

"*Hablas inglés?*" Sand asked him.

"*Poquito,*" the operator said. "What floor, sir?"

"*Cuatro, por favor.*"

The operator closed the doors. In Spanish, Sand asked him about Stacey.

Answering in Spanish, apparently pleased with an Anglo proficient in the language, the old man said, "Sí, *la recuerdo bien. Muy bonita.*"

Still in Spanish, Sand asked, "What she was wearing? Do you recall?"

The old man nodded, continuing in Spanish. "Black jumpsuit, very pretty."

Sand knew the outfit well – a sleeveless black number he loved her in. "Were you still on duty when she returned?"

"No, *señor.* If she left, it was by the stairs, or after my shift."

"*La señora,* did she speak to you?"

"*Sí.* She asked where the nearest good *restaurante Mejicano* was."

"What did you tell her?"

"El Paraiso."

"*Donde esta?*"

"Levee and Charles Street."

Sand slipped the man a ten-dollar bill. "*Muchas gracias, viejo.*"

The lift lurched to a stop, the operator opened the scissor-gate door, and Sand stepped out into an un-air-conditioned hall. The nearest door to his right said 421, putting 415 to his left. When he got to the suite, he looked each way down the hall before working the key in the lock and easing the door open.

Cool air rolled out, but also the scent of Stacey's Chanel, its familiarity at once comforting and frustrating, confirming she'd spent time here, giving him the sense that he'd just missed her. Shutting himself in, Sand called her name, not expecting – and not getting – a response.

He quickly checked the two-room suite, a modern sitting area with TV and a comfy bedroom decorated in the Spanish-Mediterranean style. Her absence was no surprise but still a disappointment. Of course, it could have been much worse – she could have been there but not breathing.

Sand scoured the suite for listening devices and clues, checking wastebaskets, dresser drawers, closet shelf, under the bed, behind furniture. Nothing.

And nothing, either, indicating a struggle. Stacey did not seem to have been grabbed. A paperback she was reading was tossed on a nightstand – *Exodus*, providing a cheap irony. The Vuitton bag had been unloaded into the dresser and some clothes hung in the closet, and everything – including her train case of toiletries in the bathroom, not yet unloaded – was here, with only her purse and the black jumpsuit as exceptions.

He used the phone, telling the switchboard to charge the room for the long distance call. The Houston office had not heard from her. He called the local Boldt Oil office on the off-chance she'd phoned in since he'd been there less than an hour ago. She hadn't.

He knocked at the door to an adjoining room that would be Cuchillo's and got no answer; but hadn't expected one. The door was unlocked. He searched the former *federale*'s much smaller quarters just as thoroughly and with the same unhelpful results.

With both Stacey and her bodyguard among the missing, and no clues as to the whereabouts of either, his mind traveled to the Cadillac with the Nevada plates parked down on the street.

Last year in Las Vegas, Sand and Stacey had met with Anthony "Fat Tony" Morello, *capo* of the Cesare crime family, who had tried to intimidate them into an oil company deal. Stacey had turned Fat Tony down in bluntly insulting terms, after which Sand promised to kill the livid Morello, should any harm come to Mrs. Sand.

Could the two men down on the street be Fat Tony's?

Maybe it was time to ask them.

The Cadillac was still in its parking place with the pair in the front seat when Sand exited the hotel. He paused to put on his Ray-Bans; the sun was bright enough to justify that, but it also gave him a chance to take a closer look at the Caddy without seeming to.

The two men were burly, wearing sport shirts that were drab in color – wouldn't want to stick out while tailing someone in their Cadillac, after all. The driver had a nose that had been broken more than once and the rider at least one cauliflower ear. Morello's name might as well have been tattooed on their foreheads.

Sand took his time getting in on his side of the pickup truck. He slipped out of his suitcoat, as a concession to the heat, but also for easier access to the Walther in the shoulder sling.

"Any sign of Mrs. Sand?" Woolford asked.

"No," Sand said, and shared what little he'd learned from the assistant manager at the desk. "Know a place called El Paraiso?"

"Hop, skip and a jump from here. Why, you ready for

lunch? They got some good Tex-Mex on offer."

"What about our friends in the Caddy?"

"You want me to ask 'em to join us?"

Sand smiled a little. "Not just yet. They just sit there the whole time I was inside?"

Woolford nodded. "You know that phone booth I didn't use? One of *them* did."

"Reporting in, perhaps. They seem to be on a rolling stake-out."

"Or calling in reinforcements."

"You're not a glass half-full type, are you, Charlie?"

"Let's just say I prefer drinkin' from a hip flask. You care to tell me who these fellers are?"

"I would imagine they work for Fat Tony Morello."

"The gangster in the papers? The Chicago one who moved to Vegas?"

"That's the Fat Tony in question, yes. He tried to muscle in on an oil deal last year. My wife told him where to go and what to do to himself along the way."

Woolford's grin was lopsided. "I think I already like this girl. Let's find her."

"Capital idea. We can start by seeing what our chaperones have to say on the subject. I suggest we lead them somewhere secluded where we can have a quiet talk. Down an alley, perhaps."

But their escorts had a different idea, picking that moment to pull out into the light traffic and head past the pickup, going northwest on Levee.

"Maybe they lost interest," Woolford said.

"I haven't," Sand said.

"Me neither," the driver said, and dropped the truck in gear and fell in two cars behind the Cadillac, which at the next light swept left and raced southwest down Tenth Street.

The pickup fell behind, but the Cadillac remained visible perhaps two blocks ahead.

"Where the hell are they going?" Woolford asked. "There ain't nothing much down this way!"

"You tell me. I'm a stranger here myself."

The old boy floored it and the truck was closing the distance when the Cadillac swung suddenly right, just past a building labeled in faded lettering, *Furniture Warehouse* – a defunct business, apparently.

"That's a damn parking lot!" Woolford said.

"It's a trap!" Sand said. "Stop!"

But Woolford was already making the turn when the first bullet clanged off their hood. Sand only had moments to take it in, but he counted two more waiting sedans that the Caddy had joined, and five men posted outside their cars, blasting away. In the meantime the Caddy was making a U-turn in the gravel lot, presumably to come right at the pickup as the mobile firing squad fired off rounds.

Woolford hit the brake pedal, jammed the truck into reverse, and backed out onto Tenth as more bullets punctured the truck in a flurry of metallic kisses, then a slug slammed into the windshield, spider-webbing it.

"Get us the hell away!" Sand commanded, the Walther in hand now.

Still in reverse, the driver floored it, backing up till the warehouse was between them and the shooters in the lot.

"How many duck hunters in that blind?" Woolford asked, eyes big, uncharacteristically frantic.

Sand's free hand was pulling the handle so he could jump from the pickup. "I made seven! Now *stop*, and stay put!"

The rider scrambled out and soon Sand was hugging the warehouse wall. He moved quick to the corner and peeked around to see five gunmen heading back to the two waiting sedans, more big men in drab sport shirts. He'd see if he couldn't make those shirts a little more colorful....

Liking them on the move, Sand charged around the corner, Walther barking, and two thugs dropped immediately, squirting red from exit wounds; a third groaned and fell to a knee, and Sand ducked back around the wall, grinning. He still had five rounds and one spare clip, plus the Beretta in the ankle holster; but the element of surprise was gone now.

Can't have everything.

The Cadillac came roaring out. He was happy to see it. The rider had crawled over the front seat into the back and was rolling down the rear window. A machine gun came up, but Sand remained planted, back to the building, ignoring the Tommy, aiming carefully, and squeezed the trigger.

The driver's side window exploded like a shooting-range bottle, and the man behind the wheel suddenly had a head enveloped in crimson mist as the car jumped the curb and hurtled out into Tenth Street, the machine gunner firing wildly from that rear window as the car careened and Sand hit the deck. When the Cadillac crashed into a building across the street, Woolford strode over with his trusty Winchester. As the machine gunner tried to gather himself, the old boy came up and shot him in the head, clean at first, but then the skull came apart in red ragged petals.

Sand, four rounds left in the Walther, headed back to the building's corner and peered around. Two gunmen remained in the graveled lot, hunkered at the far side of a sedan, the wounded man not far away, getting no help from his comrades.

From behind the other sedan, a gunman jack-in-the-boxed up, shotgun in his grasp, and the weapon boomed and boomed again, Sand ducking back around against the wall. Brick dust flew, but he hadn't been hit, though he was annoyed at himself for not taking the shooter down before the man could fire.

Then the pickup came coasting slowly down Tenth Street, driverless – *what the hell was that about?* - past the parking lot, loping by the sedan behind which the remaining two gunmen and their wounded crony now hid. The bullet-puckered vehicle drew their fire, a shotgun blasting into the pickup's passenger door, a .357 mag blowing out the window above.

Sand stepped out and shot both distracted gunmen in their respective heads. They each did a little disappointed dance and collapsed into one awkward pile, like the Queen's playing-card guards in Wonderland.

Moving toward where the wounded man lay on the parking lot's gravel floor, Sand reacted a little as Woolford's Winchester spoke.

Who or what had he been shooting at?

The old boy had set the pickup coasting to walk along beside it on the other side, crouching despite his bad back! Now Woolford peeked up over the truck bed at Sand and pointed upward, indicating what his target had been.

Sand stepped out into the street, looking up at DISCOUNT FURNITURE's roof as a final gunman, with a sniper rifle fumbling from his grasp, tumbled off and made an ungainly dive, landing with a noisy sickening crunch in a sprawl of lifeless limbs.

Sand glanced back toward the pickup where Woolford was somehow behind the wheel again, motioning to him.

"Your ride's here, son!"

Sirens were calling, too, in the distance but calling, building. This was no time to get caught up with the local police and try to explain the trifling matter of seven dead thugs. Woolford was right, it was time to go; but Sand needed to deal with the remaining live thug.

Sand went to the wounded man, who'd taken the bullet in his shoulder, his drab shirt indeed colorful now. The would-be assassin's pistol was in his opposite hand, but that hand was slack, and Sand's Walther was trained on him.

"Two things if you want to live," Sand said.

The face was contorted with pain, but its owner was listening.

"Toss the gun," Sand said, "and confirm this was Morello."

The wounded man dropped the gun and rasped, "Who the fuck else would it be?"

Sand nodded and lowered the Walther. Stuffed it in the shoulder sling.

The wounded man snatched his weapon back up and was grinning like a skeleton when Sand drew the Walther and put a bullet in this one last head.

Sand sighed. "We'll do it your way, then."

"Quit dickin' around!" Woolford bellowed.

Sprinting to the rider's side of the pickup, Sand swept glass off the seat and climbed in. Woolford was on the move again before the door was closed. For all the bullets it had swallowed, the old vehicle was chugging right along.

The driver said, "Take it we're not waitin' for the law."

"No. Go by the office."

"Mr. Cameron's probably gone home for the day."

"Do you have a key?"

Woolford shook his head.

"That's all right," Sand said. "I do."

Taking a roundabout route, Woolford managed to avoid the police bearing down on what was going to make an interesting crime scene.

"Pretty fast draw there you got there, son," Woolford said. "Sure you aren't from Texas?"

"I am now. You know, for a man with a bad back, you're an agile old devil. And nice tactics, there, widening the field of fire like that."

"Well, you smelled that trap before I did. I guess there ain't no flies on neither of us."

"We'll leave those for the dead."

They rode a while in silence. Even two tough men like this could feel the regret-tinged aftermath of a bloody fire fight, exhilaration and relief flowing in conflicting streams.

Sand said, "You're going to have to get rid of this pickup, and anyway it's shot to hell, even if it does still run. Can you manage that without the local constabulary tumbling?"

"You bet."

"When we get to the office, I'll write you a check. Next time you pick me up at the airport, you'll be in a brand-new truck."

"I'll take you up on that. But I'd rather find another one just like this, minus the pockmarks."

"Any ride you want, Charlie."

Woolford frowned in thought as he drove. "This little shooting match just about has to figure in with your wife going missing, doesn't it?"

"Well, it's Morello work. How it figures in, I'll find out."

"You find *her*."

The Boldt Oil office was dark when they got there. After parking in back, the two men threw a tarp over the truck and its telltale bullet holes.

Woolford said, "I'll give this old girl a proper burial Sunday night. I know a nice lake. And Sunday nights are slow in Brownsville."

From his wallet Sand withdrew his little pouch of lock picks and used two on the back door and the men went inside.

Woolford said, "That's your idea of a key, huh?"

"It's not breaking and entering when you own the company."

"You mean, when your *wife* owns the company."

At the absent Peggy's desk, Sand got out his check fold and wrote the man a sizable compensation.

"This is too much," Woolford said, frowning, taking in the glistening ink. "I could buy *two* damn trucks."

"Buy whatever you want," Sand said with a shrug. "Consider it a performance bonus."

They tracked down the keys to another of the Boldt company cars, then – ignoring the fuss of whirling red and blue lights as they crossed Tenth Street – Woolford drove his charge back to the Brownsville South Padre International Airport, where Sand bought a ticket on a late flight out to Houston.

There, Sand phoned Tom Something and told him to gas up the Cessna and file a flight plan for a trip tomorrow morning.

"Where are headed, sir?"

"Vegas."

Tom's voice brightened. "Oh! Did you locate Mrs. Sand? Taking a fun little getaway?"

"A getaway will be involved," Sand said.

CHAPTER EIGHT
WHAT YOU CAN DO

Sand had left a few lights on in the Boldt mansion when he'd set out on this endlessly long day; but when he got back, the place was otherwise dark. The Sands employed no automatic system of lights coming on and off, and no local security company rolled by checking the place from time to time. Cuchillo was their security system, and of course Sand himself.

But when Sand stepped inside, into the dark foyer, he knew immediately he was not alone. He did not hear anything or smell anything, not a foreign aftershave or the scent of cigarette smoke. Nothing solid, rather something abstract – the *feel* of the place. The air had been violated. Was he just paranoid after hours of travel and that fire fight? For too many years he had made his living trusting his senses to start doubting them now.

Someone was inside the house.

Easing the Walther from its holster, he gently closed the front door, then locked it, grimacing at the small but inevitable click. Worth doing, though – no point in inviting anyone else in.

His rubber-soled shoes cooperated silently on the ceramic tile, as he moved with a dancer's grace to the mouth of the unilluminated living room; moonlight through windows revealed nothing but furniture, and the only sounds were his own breathing and the relaxed pumping of his heart. After the day he'd had, and a lifetime of espionage, it would take more than an intruder to raise his pulse rate.

Morello, sending that small army of gunmen after Sand in Brownsville, might have dispatched a backup team here on the off-chance that attack squad had muffed it. The darkened corridor leading to his study at the back of the house gave away nothing, but a thin stripe of light edged the bottom of the study door.

Sand didn't recall leaving that light on. In fact, he was positive he hadn't.

He made his way quietly down the hall and when he neared the study door a light switch went on, revealing two men in suits standing at attention on either side of the door. After a half-second of deciding which one to shoot first, Sand changed his mind, recognizing them.

He knew at once these intruders had not been sent by Fat Tony. That they accompanied not an intruder but a guest – an uninvited guest, admittedly, but someone with an open invitation to just about anywhere.

Snugging away his weapon, Sand said to the pair, "Sorry I wasn't here to welcome you, gentlemen."

The two Secret Service agents, one blond, one redheaded – their gray suits tailored to conceal the jut of their shoulder-slung weapons – gave him smiles so slight it took a trained investigator like Sand to detect them. He'd met these same two in Kanab, Utah last year. They were part of an elite detail protecting a special charge.

The redhead said, "We apologize for the intrusion."

"As well you should," Sand said pleasantly. "If I'd killed one or both of you, or worse if you had killed me, that would have been a terrible inconvenience on everyone's part."

The blond said, "Not to mention embarrassing."

Sand nodded toward the study door. "He's making himself at home, I take it."

"Yes, sir," the blond said. "He's been waiting an hour. I don't have to tell you how unusual that is."

"Helicopter?"

"Nothing so extreme. We're parked in back."

Well, Sand thought, *at least I didn't come home to Air Force One in the front yard.*

"Shall we?" Sand held up his arms. "Walther under my arm, Beretta in an ankle holster."

The redhead raised a palm as if swearing in on the witness stand. "We were given strict instructions not to frisk you in your own home."

"Damned decent of you," Sand said, lowering his hands as the blond agent cracked the door, stuck his head in and spoke.

"Mr. Sand, sir."

Now that he'd been announced in his own bloody domicile, Sand ambled into the study, where President John F. Kennedy sat behind what had been Dutch Boldt's desk, the green-shaded banker's lamp on, a folder of papers open on the blotter. The strikingly handsome president wore a navy blue suit, the collar of his white shirt unbuttoned, his red striped tie loosened.

Looking up without rising, greenish-gray eyes flashing, he extended his hand, that wide campaign smile blossoming. "Do come in, John."

Standing across from the seated leader of the free world,

Sand shook hands with him and said, "Thank you for making me feel at home, Mr. President."

Jack Kennedy flickered that famous smile that was somehow both confident and shy. "Have a seat, John."

How odd it felt, sitting on the opposite side of what was now his own desk. A wing chair had been pulled over, waiting for him. Other than the desk lamp, the room was unlit, though abetted by moonlight filtering in through the flimsy curtains covering the big window on the wall behind the President. Dutch Boldt's portrait, moved here from the living room, looked on approvingly from a side wall nestled between built-in shelves of volumes.

"A fine library you have here," Kennedy said. "Not the usual leather-bound unread tomes of the wealthy. Well-organized – fiction at left, non-fiction at right. Some impressive first editions."

"I can't take credit, Mr. President. This was Dutch Boldt's study long before it was mine, most of the books his. Not meaning to be impertinent, sir, I would imagine your visit is not literary in intent."

This smile was anything but shy now. "Our last meeting made it clear, John, you are, uh, a man who likes to get right to the point. Of course, you've had a busy day, and I'm sure would like to get a good night's sleep in before your trip tomorrow."

Sand said nothing.

Kennedy's eyebrows went up, as if he found something mildly interesting. "A perhaps significant development in my brother's efforts against organized crime occurred today in Brownsville, uh, where you were visiting. Some eight known *cosa nostra* figures – minor but notorious – were found killed after an apparent run-in with an, uh, apparent rival underworld faction."

Sand shrugged. "I didn't keep with the news while I was there. I was busy."

"Obviously. Looking for Mrs. Sand. Yes, I'm aware. And I wish I had something to report to you on that score, but I don't, though I have feelers out."

And this was a man whose feelers could feel a hell of a lot.

"What I'm here for, John, is to offer you a job."

Sand shifted in the chair. "I'm not looking for one, sir. I am quite happy in my current position."

His guest raised a hand casually, but there was nothing casual about the man's expression. "And it won't be necessary for you to give that up. I would, uh, rather you *didn't*, actually, as it rather makes a perfect cover."

"Does it," Sand said.

"What I'm offering is strictly part-time. You'd be on call, but any...assignment you wished to decline would be at your discretion."

"With all due respect, Mr. President, this does not come at a good time. I am concerned *only* with locating my wife. Right now I don't know whether she's been kidnapped or is off on some unscheduled side trip, and there's no room in my mind for anything else."

"She disappeared in Brownsville," Kennedy said, thoughtful, concerned. "My understanding is she *did* show up there."

"Yes. Made it to the hotel, but I haven't confirmed anything else beyond that. No idea whether she's in the states or Mexico."

The President's eyes narrowed. "This mob altercation today – it's the reason you have your pilot readying for a Vegas trip tomorrow?"

"It is. My only lead at the moment is Anthony Morello."

"Those were his men today." Not a question.

"Yes." Not much of an answer. "Frankly, I only came home to regroup and call you. Thanks for saving me the trouble. I was hoping, after the mission I undertook for you last year, you might return the favor and help me find Stacey."

Kennedy sat in silence for what seemed an eternity and was probably ten seconds. Then, from an inside pocket of his suit coat, he withdrew two H. Upmann Petit Coronas and offered one to Sand.

"So you're still able to get these?" Sand asked, examining the cigar.

"I ordered a shipment in January," Kennedy said, using a cigar cutter to clip the tip. "These may be the last for some time."

Sand accepted the cutter from the President. "That would be because you declared a Cuban embargo including these lovely items and much more." He cut off the Corona tip.

"That's true, John," Kennedy said, lighting his cigar with a kitchen match, then extended the flame to his host.

Sand lit his cigar, tossed the spent match into a big glass ashtray with a BOC logo.

The President asked, "I need to pry. With your permission?"

Sand nodded, drew on the strong, distinctive cigar.

Kennedy said, "How have things been with you and Mrs. Sand? Any problems?"

"Minor problems among major happiness. She did not run off, if that's what you're asking. Not from me, she didn't. If Morello has her, I'll find out. If she's dead...well, I'll deal with that, too."

The President's smoke drifted between them. "What

if my job offer served to aid in your endeavor? What if I made it your first mission and gave you whatever support you needed? I can place an FBI man here in case a ransom call comes in, for example."

"I would like that."

"I can also make any questions go away that today's fracas in Brownsville might eventually raise."

"That *would* be an inducement."

"Good. I think it would be best we begin, uh, our negotiations with the embargo you mentioned."

Sand gestured with the cigar-in-hand. "How could your embargo have anything to do with my wife disappearing?"

Flicking an ash into the tray on the desk, Kennedy said, "Maybe nothing, possibly everything. But this much I know – if not for what led to the embargo, I wouldn't have dropped by tonight."

"I'm listening."

The President leaned an elbow on the desk. "I put the embargo in place because Nikita Khrushchev intends to position ballistic missiles in Cuba."

"The hell. Castro won't stand for that."

Kennedy shrugged. "Why, because Fidel wants to be his own man? Yes, I know that theory. But we have solid intelligence that Cuba and Russia are taking secret meetings as well as indulging in back-channel communications. John, things have changed since you and your wife intervened in the San Ignacio problem."

"In what way?"

"For one, Castro is convinced we're trying to kill him, so he's hoping to use Khrushchev as his insurance policy. And with Russia and Cuba newly aligned, our relations with both will inevitably become more tense. In response, I've had my own meetings with other world leaders. The consensus is the best way to protect ourselves in the face of a Russia/Cuba alliance is to pool our resources. We've done so."

"In what fashion, if I might ask?"

"In a *sub rosa* fashion – with our new Global Unit for International Law Enforcement...the acronym, which was quite accidental, is straight out of your ex-colleague's book."

"Out of his *books*, you mean – GUILE. Accidental or not, sir, that suggests a certain...craftiness."

"*Spy*-craft, more like." Kennedy gestured with the cigar. "The intelligence-gathering organizations of Great Britain, France, Germany, Japan, Israel, the Arab nations, Italy, virtually every non-communist country in the world, are working together, albeit not openly."

"Then what exactly *is* 'GUILE?'"

"Call it a clearing house of information, funded by its member nations, enlisting agents, diplomats, scientists, and utilizing agents in an effort to forestall any efforts from any quarters from dominating its member states. Which is to say...the world."

"Are we talking the Communist countries?"

"Yes, but also individuals thirsting for the kind of power and control a petty dictator might only dream of. You've encountered a few of those already."

"And the United States," Sand said, "will be the pre-eminent player in this Global Unit."

"Yes."

"Won't Mr. Khrushchev and Mr. Castro *love* that."

Kennedy's smile was almost a smirk now. "I would imagine, when they learn of our efforts – and obviously they will – my popularity in those camps will, uh, be even less than it is today. Which is why I would like you to be a part of GUILE, John...and I can offer you the princely sum of a dollar a year to do so."

Sand found a smile somewhere. "Well, tempting as that may be, I would have to decline."

"...I'm disappointed."

"To begin with – and, again, meaning no disrespect – the entire concept sounds naively optimistic. Start with who would be in charge of such an organization – what individual on the world stage could command respect from all the other countries without seeming a puppet of the United States? You would need an Allen Dulles, for the skill and substance required, but you would not *dare* make so self-aggrandizing a suggestion."

Kennedy nodded. "Exactly the problem we ran into in creating the organization. Each member nation had a different idea of how it would be constructed, managed, and who would be in charge. Clearly, the latter needs to be someone who, as you say, does not seem our pawn – someone who commands the respect of the member countries, and is experienced in a manner suitable to run a large autonomous agency."

"Good luck finding that person."

"But we did." The President leaned forward on an arm. "John, every country was allowed to nominate its own choice, and then there was to be an election, with the need for unanimous approval, which could have meant the Global Unit would have died at birth. But every country nominated the same person – Lord Malcolm Marbury."

That opened Sand's eyes. "Double M..."

"Double M," Kennedy said. "And I would like you to meet with him as soon as possible."

Sand shifted in the chair again. "I've explained that my personal mission begins tomorrow, in Las Vegas."

"Which, as it happens, is where Lord Marbury is currently working with his support team, setting up the GUILE control center."

Sand frowned. "Why there?"

Now Kennedy sat back, gestured with an open hand. "America is putting up the lion's share of the funding, after all, which is why the other members deferred. Using a vacation location makes travel there explainable for any person from anywhere, which makes its own kind of sense, particularly when at the same time it is essentially out of the way...and yet a quick plane ride to our nation's third largest population center. For us, having Nellis Air Force Base close at hand was a major inducement, as well as Area 51."

"What would Area 51 be?"

Kennedy paused for a moment, apparently having let something slip, then said, "An installation within our test and training range designed to handle anything and all things off the books." He tamped his cigar in the glass tray. "While you're in Vegas, meet with Lord Marbury and see if that's enough to convince you to get onboard. In the meantime, I'll tell him to make all of GUILE's assets available to you in helping find Mrs. Sand."

"That's appreciated, but I'm ready to accept your generous job offer right now....Who can't use an extra dollar a year? My acceptance, however, has to be provisional."

"Why is that?"

"What I have to do in Vegas...what I *will* do in that unique desert community...could attract undue attention. I appreciate your willingness to make it my first mission for the Global Unit, but this is best kept a personal matter."

A slow nod. "When your wife is back safely within these walls, we'll talk again."

"Of course, with Stacey back on the scene, you may have to make your sales pitch all over again. You have veto power over Congress, Mr. President, but my wife has veto power over me."

Kennedy chuckled. "When I get to a secure phone, I'll alert Lord Marbury to expect you some time tomorrow. In the meantime, I'll give you directions to the GUILE control center, and the code protocol. It's better if you don't take notes, of course."

"I won't need to."

"Ah, yes. Your vaunted photographic memory." The famous smile returned. "Does that include issues of *Playboy* magazine?"

"That's a pornographic memory you're thinking of, Mr. President."

Kennedy relayed the information, utilizing a map in a folder he'd brought with him, and shared the code phrases, leading Sand to say, "That all sounds a bit over-melodramatic, sir. I'm afraid my friend's novels have been a bad influence."

"Do you intend to take care of your personal matter first?"

"I do. Lord Marbury needs to know that until my wife is safely home, my sole mission will be making that so."

"Understood."

"And if I don't show up at Double M's new HQ by tomorrow or the next day, I will likely not be showing up at all...except possibly in the Las Vegas papers."

Kennedy's expression grew grave. "I wish you well. In the meantime, I'll call Marbury when I'm back in D.C. and let him know when to expect you."

Sand's guest closed up the folder with the map, gathered his things, and rose. "Find that woman of yours fast,

John. We have things to do, you and I."

The prospective GUILE agent smiled. "Because the country, and the world, are depending on us?"

"Exactly. But, uh...you understand as regards this personal matter, in Vegas? It may be a Global Unit mission, but like many a mission that you will, I hope, be handling for us in the future? You are off-the-books."

"Like Area 51?"

"Like Area 51. If you have trouble with the local authorities, I can't bail you out literally or figuratively. I'm already doing some clean up for you where, uh, your Brownsville shenanigans are concerned. After that, you'll largely be on your own."

"I appreciate your honesty, Mr. President. But after years of bureaucratic MI6 rigamarole, I'm quite comfortable being on my own."

"Plus you'll have your guile to guide you," Kennedy said. "And that's *not* an acronym."

******

Once the President and the Secret Service entourage had gone, Sand went about preparing for the Las Vegas trip. Just last year, he and Stacey had been there, meeting Frank Sinatra and the other notable entertainers in the so-called Rat Pack. It had been a memorable weekend.

So would this one.

He called Phillip Lyman at his D.C. residence. Though it was almost midnight, Lyman only said, "What do you need?" when he heard Sand's voice.

Sand said, "Some information and fast."

After Sand conveyed his needs, Lyman asked, "How fast?"

"Before eleven a.m. tomorrow. Central time."

"All right," Lyman said, and hung up.

First he called Tom Something. He had memorized the spelling "Rzepczynski," but its pronunciation continued to elude him.

"Everything's ready," the pilot said. "Of course, I can't file a flight plan till I know when we're leaving."

"Make it one p.m. I need to catch up on sleep. Now, I'll want you to stay in Vegas and wait for me. I'll book you a room downtown. You'll stay put, use room service, wait for my call. We might return tomorrow evening, but more likely the next morning. Not much longer than that."

"All right," Tom said, not quite hiding the disappointment in his voice. A Vegas trip like the one Sand outlined would have been a letdown to just about anybody.

"When we get back," Sand said, "there'll be a five-hundred dollar bonus for you. Perhaps you'd have won more gambling, but I doubt it."

That perked Tom. "Sounds like a fair trade-off, sir."

Sand oiled and cleaned both the Walther and the Beretta, put them in his duffel bag, as well as a switchblade he'd taken off an assassin. Then he gave the same attention to the Mossberg 500 pump shotgun Stacey bought him for Christmas. That had been for hunting, and tomorrow he finally would be.

Once the guns were ready, he packed several boxes of ammunition into the bag with the shotgun, a pair of binoculars, and a few other supplies, as well as several changes of clothes and a toiletries kit. Then he stretched out on the bed, getting out of his suit coat but not bothering with pajamas or stripping down.

He was still trying to piece together what he might have missed that could reveal what had happened to Stacey when he finally dropped off to sleep, as if stepping off a cliff. His sleep went deep, reflecting his exhaustion, and hours went by as his body replenished itself.

Then the nightmares took over. They were grim – horrific scenarios of finding Stacey over and over but always a moment too late, the woman he loved shot to pieces or beaten to a pulp, or....

He woke up in a sweat. Usually his dreams faded on waking. Today they stayed vividly with him, each and every terrible one.

The bedside clock read 9:48 A.M.

Finally getting out of yesterday's much-abused clothes, he showered and shaved, then dressed for his mission, doing everything he could in the silent house to keep his lingering nightmares from interfering with what needed accomplishing today.

He had just gone into the kitchen to make himself eat something when the phone on the wall rang. He checked his Rolex – 10:27. He figured that was likely Lyman, early with that Morello intel he'd requested.

It was.

"Three shifts," Lyman said. "Four to a shift. Not live-in. There's an adult nephew who lives there, though. No women except working girls on the weekend. He's estranged from his wife, and his daughter is in boarding school in Switzerland. His son, with whom he's also estranged, is in college in the east."

"This is FBI intel?"

"Matthews himself."

"He doesn't know who it's for?"

"No. But everybody in law enforcement and intelligence has heard about Brownsville by now." A pause, then: "I can put a crew together if this can wait twenty-four hours."

"Don't be silly, Phillip. You know the CIA doesn't

operate in the United States."

Both men laughed.

"Thanks," Sand said, "but this is better handled quickly, faster than expected."

"Understood. I hope to see you again."

"I hope to be seen."

They rang off.

In the refrigerator he found a half-eaten pan of lasagna that Stacey had cooked a few days ago. He heated it up and made himself some coffee and stood at the counter and ate food his wife had prepared for him. Right from the pan. He had tears in his eyes but willed them not to fall.

He didn't want to eat. He hadn't eaten since yesterday and the gnawing in his stomach was at least partly hunger. But he needed fuel for what lay ahead, and anyway it made him feel closer to her.

****

By the time the Cessna touched down in Las Vegas, Sand's anxiety had evolved into a cold-blooded rage. If revenge was a dish best served cold, he was prepared to serve up a frozen dinner. Dressed in a lightweight black T-shirt, black slacks, and his rubber-soled black shoes, he carried the duffel bag of weapons and ammo through the airport, rarely rating a glance.

He rented a Ford Fairlane convertible from Avis and drove east on Hacienda Avenue, the same route a chauffeur followed escorting the Sands on their trip last year – dark then, daylight now. The sunny morning provided a view of the new construction in the growing city. Then, as he drove farther east, gaudy civilization gave way to the tan desert and its rocky foothills.

Sand passed the private lane they had driven up last year

to Cesare crime boss Anthony Morello's lavish hideaway. He stayed on the road, drove farther along until he found another turnoff that took him off the paved road and onto a dirt path that led him up into the hills behind Morello's modernistic residence.

The Ford he left a mile or so from the house, just off the path and behind some scrubby brush, not quite invisible but would be when night fell. Anyway, Sand figured he was outside the boundaries of Morello's security. He couldn't imagine the pampered crime boss picturing anybody walking through the desert to settle a score. No doubt in his day Morello had been a tough Roman soldier. Now he was a flabby Nero.

Sand hiked toward the estate, getting close enough to be able to see Morello's place with binoculars. Hugged by stubborn palm and mesquite trees, the unusual house had a rounded look, two gray saucer shapes stacked over a fieldstone base like one UFO had landed atop another.

Prone on the hot dirt there, a low-lying rock shelf giving him cover, Sand used his binoculars to discern that two guards were at the rear of the property, so probably two more were on the front. Or one on the front and the other on the drive.

No sign that security had been amplified past what FBI intel indicated as the usual fare.

He trotted back the way he came, staying low at first, then sat where the camouflaged car gave him cover, leaning against the door. He had a canteen, a couple apples, and patience. Night was coming and when it did, he would make his move.

Fat Tony Morello had started this war, but John Sand would end it tonight.

And not with an olive branch.

CHAPTER NINE

HOUSE CALL

Sand's eyes came open.

His sleep had been dreamless this time, a shallow thing from which the slightest sound would have wakened him. That he was relaxed enough to catch a nap pleased him. A moment ago it had been dusk but that dusk had deepened into a blue cast upon the desert, as if a talented cinematographer had slipped a colored filter over a lens.

Now, he needed to prepare for the fight. He applied black grease on his face for both camouflage purposes and to disguise his features. As night settled over the desert, the ex-spy took his time. He checked his weapons, stuffing the Walther in his waistband, the Beretta nestled in the ankle holster. Then he removed from his duffel a black windbreaker and slipped it on, giving him pockets to hold magazines for both pistols as well as loose shotgun shells for the Mossberg 500. He zipped the jacket up, glad that coolness was conspiring with the night to help him out. Then, carrying his duffel, Walther in hand, he loped back to the low-lying rock shelf overlooking the rear of the estate. He dropped to his stomach and raised the binoculars to try to pick out any guards in the moonlight. One was between the patio and the pool, near the house. On Sand's previous visit a canvas-and-pole cabana had been off to the right, but the temporary structure was gone. Another sentry slowly walked the perimeter where backyard grass ended and desert took over.

Two more presumably out front. If security had been beefed up post-Brownsville, the number inside could be greater – possibly another of the four-man shifts, maybe all three on duty. In that case, he could be facing a dozen soldiers in their uniforms of sport shirts and baggy trousers. A veritable walk in the park – if that park were Dunkirk.

He pulled the Mossberg out of the bag, then from his pants pocket shifted the switchblade into one of the windbreaker's to join the extra clips for the handguns. The Walther went back in his waistband, the Beretta a comforting presence at his right ankle.

He was ready.

Taking his time, moving as soundlessly as possible, Sand made his way down from the ridge to the edge of the property where, about midway behind the house, the perimeter guard had paused to gaze past the backyard to the blue shimmer of pool. He wore an oversize, untucked black bowling shirt with red panels in front, a cigarette dangling from his lips, his expression seeming to reflect the utter boredom of his life's work.

Sand remained enveloped by the pitch black of the desert after dark, not yet close enough to where Morello had planted an emerald carpet likely requiring enough water in one month to put out a forest fire. Music turned up a bit too loud came from a portable stereo on a table near the pool, not Frank Sinatra like last year, but the Dave Brubeck Quartet's "Take Five."

Crouching in the desert, well beyond the spill of light onto the patio, and five or six yards from the perimeter guard, Sand rested the Mossberg on the ground, then got out the switchblade and opened it with an inevitable snick that fortunately got swallowed up by cool jazz. His eyes shifted again and again between the guard at the lawn's rear edge and the sentry closer to the house, beyond the pool on the patio. The pool guard wore a green-and-brown striped short-sleeve sport shirt, also untucked.

These geezers, Sand thought, *look awfully sporty for gun thugs.* But the pops of color made it easier to keep track of them.

Sand crept up behind the bored perimeter guard, who (likely about to start his patrol again) tossed his cigarette onto the ground, where the grass gave way to sandy earth, grinding it out with a toe as Sand rose up to slap a hand over the startled man's mouth, then yank the man's head back and slit his throat. Red sprayed like a scarlet lawn sprinkler, but only for a few moments, as if shut off.

The dead guard went limp in Sand's arms and the agent stepped back to allow the body to collapse to the ground. Then he knelt over the dead man and removed a nine millimeter Browning from his waistband and transferred it to his own in back. He rifled the corpse's pockets, hoping for keys either to locked rooms or vehicles or perhaps to find a walkie-talkie; but no joy. Sand slipped back into the dark. He stayed there a while, making sure he hadn't attracted attention.

Then, keeping low, he padded onto the patio and crept up behind the next guard, who was at the little table where the stereo was playing, in the process of selecting another LP, *More Peter Gunn* in one hand and Bobby Darin's *That's All* in the other.

Surprisingly good taste, Sand thought, and cut the guard's throat, spraying another section of grass just beyond the patio, the red shooting above the portable stereo, not disturbing the music, though when the fresh corpse fell it jarred the table, making the needle slide to the end and the record to skip.

Sand froze, then edged back into darkness, eyes again on the house, to see if that attracted any attention. When it didn't, he returned to the stereo and lifted the needle and dropped it back at the beginning. "Blue Rondo à la Turk" started in.

He trotted back to the shotgun and retrieved it, then waited for a few moments. He was surprised, relieved, but a little thrown. Only two guards at the rear left the other two out front, unless one was within guarding his boss.

Sand moved around toward the front of the house – the few windows on the side of the house were all dark – where the drive looped around to a carport from a blacktop apron with half a dozen or so parked vehicles. Sand peeked around to where the carport emptied out. Across the carport, over at the mouth of it, a third guard caught some moonlight; he was wearing a shades-of-brown batik-print shirt and dark trousers, that blended him in with the night more than the others. He carried a shotgun in his arms like a precious baby.

Sand withdrew quickly. After a moment, footsteps could be heard around the corner, in the carport, echoing. The batik-print guard had heard or seen something and was coming Sand's way to check it out.

And when the sentry came around the corner, Sand slammed the butt of the Mossberg into the oncoming face, driving the frontal bone up and into the skull cavity, killing the man so fast his features didn't register it as he went down.

After tossing the extra shotgun into the darkness, Sand took the dead guard – number three – by the ankles and dragged him alongside the house. Now, where was guard number four?

Sand – still tucked alongside of the house with just the sprawled late sentry for company – had just decided the final night-shift guard must be inside when he heard footsteps again, somewhat distant but clearly audible.

The footfalls grew louder and then, coming around the curve of Morello's private lane, emerged sentry number four. This was a small, unprepossessing individual in a black short-sleeve sport shirt with white buttons, a collegiate-looking chap though no fraternity would likely rush him with that chinless countenance. Nothing about him was impressive at all, in fact, except the UZI in his two-handed grasp.

A weapon of fairly recent design, these open-bolt, blowback-operated submachine guns had become quite popular of late. The Quartermaster had never issued Sand one, but he'd familiarized himself with the weapon in the field, confiscating examples from late opponents.

He could step out and shoot the UZI bearer, of course, but one gunshot would obviously alert anyone inside the house that something untoward was afoot. The switchblade was not a throwing knife. What option was there?

He had just enough time to remove the batik-print shirt from his latest victim and slip it on over the windbreaker. Sand's build and even his hair were enough like the dead man's to pass in the near dark, as long as he didn't step out into the moonlight, positioning himself under the carport. His blackened face would just merge with the night.

"Denny!" the chinless man called. "Got a ciggie you

could spare?"

Sand, his shotgun in his arms in the baby-cradling fashion he'd seen the late guard number three employ, grunted affirmatively.

When guard number four approached near enough to frown in lack of recognition at what should have been a comrade, Sand swung the shotgun butt into the side of the sentry's head, so hard the sound of his skull cracking almost rivaled a gunshot, sending him down in an awkward pile.

Guard four was as dead as if that had been a bullet crashing through his skull, and Sand knelt over him, searching pockets and coming back with four extra thirty-two-round magazines for the machine gun. Not wanting to toss the Mossberg – it had been a Christmas present from Stacey, after all – Sand held it in his left hand and the UZI in his right.

He glanced out and counted eight vehicles parked on the blacktop apron. They ranged from sedans to sporty foreign jobs, with a black Lincoln Continental the odd car out, seeming to rule over this automotive harem – fittingly, as the Lincoln was surely Morello's.

Of the seven other vehicles, one would belong to Morello's nephew, Marco, one of the sports cars probably. That left six. If it was one man per auto, with the four outside guards out of commission, that left two thugs waiting within, plus Marco. Odds he could easily handle.

But perhaps each vehicle had delivered *four* soldiers here – was he looking at a welcoming party of four, or twenty-four? Most likely, something in between....

After tossing the batik-print shirt aside, making the pockets of his black windbreaker accessible again, he paused midway under the carport's shelter. The glass panels in the front door revealed only the sunken entryway, where half a flight of stairs led to a big open living room... which was almost entirely out of sight.

That yawning space could be empty, with the inhabitants off in bedrooms and other areas of the place.

Or not.

He went back around the house, moving past the table with the portable stereo, Dave Brubeck playing "Strange Meadow Lark," and stepping over the corpse of guard number two. Like a party guest, he wandered across the patio by the pool's sparkling dark blue water with its ivory highlights courtesy of the moon, and stood contemplating the double glass doors that opened onto the living room, a view blocked by drapes that looked sheer enough to bleed light, which at the moment they weren't.

If those doors were unlocked, he could walk right in and – if the occupants were indeed in this room and that one around the place, with maybe a few in the living room sitting in the dark watching television or having a friendly chat (perhaps in Italian or maybe Sicilian) – he could go room-to-room dealing with what he encountered, until he had Morello alone and forced him give to up Stacey, if he had her.

Could she be inside?

If the patio doors were locked – no, that was the wrong term: sliding glass doors used latches, not locks, meaning he could simply lift the door off its track and ease it out of the way.

In any case, they weren't secured, whether latched *or* locked, and he slid one half-open and stepped through the drapes like an impresario about to have a word with the audience. The room was very dark, but only for a moment, because the house lights came up and a tableau appeared before him that Sand would not soon forget.

Wearing his trademark Hawaiian shirt, Morello sat in a big comfy-looking off-white armchair, a throne of a thing, and his court was assembled at either side of him, where gently curved couches were on the mobster's right and left. But his courtiers were not seated there, rather standing in front of those couches with weapons in hand with eyes wide and smiles in many cases wider still.

The array of thugs, mostly in sport shirts, a few in the Hawaiian-style to honor their boss, and a couple wearing rumpled suits, should have fired immediately. Sand's storied career would have been over had they done so, his death just another footnote in the life that his writer friend had chronicled so loosely and imaginatively.

But they didn't, because Fat Tony – not really as corpulent as his hated nickname implied, more like heavy-set, his hair dark and slicked-back, his features thick, nose a lumpy potato, smile wolfish and white – had apparently ordered them not to.

He wanted to have his moment with Sand.

"Did you think, you limey son of a bitch," Morello said sneeringly, "that you could wipe out eight of my best men and not pay for it?"

Sand answered by sweeping the UZI across the six men at Morello's left, the weapon chattering, sounding like a grotesque shuffling of cards, then skipping the mob boss before the nine-millimeter slugs continued to arc across the other six. Shells flew, spirals of blood twirled and splattered, and limbs and torsos were chewed up and spit out, heads exploding into chunks of bone and bursts of blood and gobs of brain, and like the worst chorus line in history, the twelve men danced in an ungainly, awkward, entirely undignified manner.

Puffs of gray smoke gathered into a drifting cloud. Immediately a putrid, but all-too-familiar bouquet of evacuated bowels and coppery blood filled Sand's nostrils. Morello, who sat in his over-stuffed throne like the over-stuffed mobster he was, smelled it, too, his nostrils flaring like a rearing horse, his eyes wide enough to fall out of his head if he wasn't careful.

"A surprise party?" Sand said to the gangster, slamming a new magazine into the feather-light machine gun. "For me? You shouldn't have."

From a hallway charged the nephew, Marco, spiffy in a sharkskin suit, trying to be worthy of his uncle as he ran in screaming with a .45 way too big for the fist brandishing it. Sand cut him down with a short burst and the younger Morello was lifted up and slammed back down, as if he'd slipped on a banana peel.

His uncle, still in his throne, glanced back in disgust, pronouncing a fitting epitaph: "Useless."

Sand moved closer. Not much, though – too many dead to trip over, too much blood to slip and fall in, soaking the carpet like bloody Rorschach blots.

"Well," the mobster demanded, his hands on the arms of the big chair. "What the fuck are you waiting for?"

"Class till the end, Tony. Class till the bitter end."

The big man was trembling, whether in rage or fear or a combination, Sand couldn't guess. Nor did he care.

The agent said, "This can go two ways."

"Don't tell me," Morello said with a contemptuous laugh. "The *hard* way or the *easy* way. I don't give a shit! You *won*, you prick. Or are you going to stand there gloating like an asshole?"

Patiently, Sand said, "You can tell me or I can start shooting you in various tender places. Feet. Knees. Arms.

Testicles, if that's what is necessary."

"Tell you *what* the hell?"

"Where is she?"

"Where is who?"

Sand's turn to sneer. "Don't play cute. It doesn't become you. *Where is Stacey Sand?* Where is my wife?"

"No idea. You can shoot my dick off and I still won't know."

"She disappeared in Brownsville the day before your kill squad ambushed me. *Tried* to ambush me."

The dark, soulless eyes narrowed. "Why deny *that*? They were my boys. *Of course*, I tried to kill you. I learned you were flying to Brownsville, and I sent my guys. I have no idea where your wife is. But if I *did* know, asshole, I would thank the one who took her."

Sand punched Morello in the face, smashing the man's potato-like schnoz, blood shooting from his nostrils like celebratory ribbons.

"You broke my goddamn nose! You *bastard*! You English prick!" Morello tried to stop the bleeding with the front tail of his shirt, the red adding to the festive Hawaiian design.

"I'm not in a good mood, Tony. I was here when you threatened her. *You* did this."

Still wiping away blood with his shirt, Morello said, "I did not! It was *you* who threatened *me*. I don't take a black eye like that from *any* man! Your wife, she ran off at the mouth, but she's a broad. Who gives a shit what a broad does? But I can't have *you* disrespecting me! That gets around, I'm dead."

Despite Morello's babbling, Sand found himself starting to believe the gangster. "If you didn't take her, who did?"

His bleeding under control, Morello said, "No idea. Ask somebody who gives a shit. Killing your limey ass was what *I* was after."

"You knew I would be in Brownsville how?"

"*You* used to be a spook – you know how easy it is to buy people, particularly underpaid little shits. How many nobodies knew you were going to Brownsville?"

"Very few."

"Yeah?" Morello counted on his fingers. "Pilot. He have a co-pilot? Either way, there's a flight plan filed. How many people at the airport knew about that? How about the mechanics that made sure the plane was fit to fly? The guy who fueled the plane? The ape that pulled the plane out of the hangar? I only needed one of those guys to be a gambler, a junkie, a pussy hound, or just a good old-fashioned greedy bastard. Sand, I've been watching you since you came back from San Ignacio. Sooner or later I knew I would get my chance. Nothing to do with snatching your wife."

"Why should I believe you?"

"Because I waited for a trip where that bitch wasn't with you. I didn't want *her* dead, you dumb-ass. I wanted her to know I killed her fucking husband and that I could take everything away from her that she ever wanted, whenever *I* wanted. I wanted her ass to suffer."

Sand's gut clenched. The sadistic bastard was telling the truth. This gangster had surely *not* kidnapped Stacey, which meant that Sand was wasting his time here.

"I believe you, Tony."

"You get rid of me, whoever next sits in this chair will hunt you down and kill you like the dog you are."

Sand laughed at that. "Whoever takes your chair will likely write me a note of thanks. And if not, he'll realize I killed all of your people, here and in Brownsville, taking out twenty-some of your 'best.' He won't want a war with *that* man. I promised if you messed with my family you'd regret it. The next one in this chair'll know that too. Will know that the only reason he's sitting there is because of me. That *I* put him in the chair, and I can take him out. Just like I did you. But if he *does* come, Tony, I'll just empty that bloody chair again, and for as many times as it takes."

"I hope you find her, Sand – *dead.*"

Sand stitched a row of nine millimeter slugs across Tony Morello's chest. The gangster looked down at the small black holes weeping scarlet tears, then frowned as his eyes went to Sand's.

"Hell," he said, and then his chin came down with a final jerk.

In the distance sirens were nice enough to warn Sand. He returned to the patio and collected the shotgun his wife had gifted him and headed back out into the desert. At the rental Ford he put the duffel in the trunk, from which he took a rag to wipe most of the black grease off his face, then got behind the wheel.

Going back the way he came, just under the speed limit, he passed the first police cars headed for Morello's house. Sand continued on back toward the smear of colorful lights that were Las Vegas. With Stacey's whereabouts unknown, and Morello a literal dead-end, the only person who might be able to help Sand now was Lord Malcolm Marbury.

CHAPTER TEN
AGENT OF GUILE

Sand made a stop just outside Vegas at a gas station where he washed up and got into a quick change of clothes from the duffel – fresh Ban-Lon, jeans, and sneakers, all in black, which didn't look that different from his combat garb but at least didn't smell of blood, sweat and excrement. Smiling at himself in the bathroom mirror, for having just nearly quoted Churchill, he looked presentable enough to risk going straight to his old boss at the new headquarters.

Soon he was on Interstate-15, the new superhighway connecting Las Vegas to Salt Lake City. He drove northeast out of town, putting the city's glitter in his rearview mirror. By the time the desert surrounded him, Vegas was a dim if insistent glow behind him.

About eleven miles out Sand took an exit, the ramp leading down to a narrow two-lane. He turned right, kicked on the high beams, then followed a blacktop for nearly a mile. His headlights revealed only negatives – no buildings, no plants, not a stray road sign, not even a jackrabbit.

Had he memorized the directions wrong?

Then, through the blackness to his left, he glimpsed

a chain link fence, extending down the opposite side of the road past his high beams. He slowed and eventually the fence was interrupted by a gate, yawning open onto a gravel drive.

If this was indeed his destination, Sand was either expected, thanks to the President's doing, or whoever was in charge of security here figured the installation was so far out in the boondocks that no one would ever find it.

He drove until high-mounted security beams came on – indicating he'd either been seen or had triggered them - illuminating a graveled parking area with just a beat-up pickup truck - in only slightly better shape than Charlie Woolford's after it got shot up - fronting a sizeable Quonset hut behind which a massive-looking barn loomed, time having stripped most of its red paint off and leaving only gray behind, a structure that looked like it wouldn't take much of a wolf to huff and puff it down.

The security lighting was bright enough to make silhouettes out of a sea of towering shapes surrounding the Quonset hut. But as Sand climbed from the parked Fairlane, he realized what he was looking at – a sort of junkyard with one theme: aisles of dead, oversized signs, the neon refuse of hotels, casinos, restaurants, and bars in Vegas that had either gone out of business or redesigned their logos. These electric, but unlighted, tombstones constituted a sort of neon graveyard.

Three creaky steps led to a small porch up to the Quonset hut's door where a sign in the window said, "BY APPOINTMENT ONLY," with no phone number posted to make that possible. But when Sand tried the door, it was unlocked. He shrugged and went on in.

The interior was an antique shop of sorts, its theme consistent with the neon cemetery outside – Vegas memorabilia, chiefly ancient slot machines but also standees of entertainers (faded and familiar), framed posters of acts for both showroom and main stage (long forgotten and legendary), display cases of gaming chips and dice, hotel room keys, ashtrays and matchbooks with the stamp of casinos (defunct and still going). The lighting was low, the air musty, the offerings dusty. A pair of ceiling fans churned the staleness as if an old plane had crash-dived nose first into and through the ceiling.

Sand approached the counter at the rear of the shop, where a wall of neon beer signs buzzed and shorted in and out. On a barstool, with a hand underneath the counter – accessing a weapon? – sat a gray-haired old boy with a prospector's beard, a cigarette dangling from his lips, and alert light blue eyes that didn't fit the otherwise sunken-cheeked profile. His faded, fraying yellow shirt was home to a name-tag badge that said ED.

"Got an appointment?" he asked, blowing smoke out his nostrils like a grumpy ancient dragon.

The old boy couldn't be begrudged for having an attitude, sitting behind the counter of a dingy tribute to yesterday at nearly two o'clock in the morning. Recalling the words on the card Kennedy gave him, Sand suppressed a chuckle, then said, "'When bad men combine...'"

"'...the good must associate.'"

"Who was it said that?"

"Edmund Burke."

The code phrase seemed a little on the nose to Sand. Back in MI6 days they were mostly non-sequiturs.

"You're Sand," Ed said, unenthusiastically.

"John Sand, yes."

"Hands on the glass, please. Fingertips only."

Sand pressed his fingertips to the glass top of the counter's display case, which held matchbooks and ash trays and such from dead casinos like Club Bingo, the Royal Nevada, and the Pair-O-Dice.

The glass top glowed light blue.

"Lift 'em," Ed said.

Sand's fingerprints glowed white, then the glass turned green.

"Don't tell me," Sand said. "If the glass went red, I'd be..."

"Unwelcome," Ed said, glancing down.

Hand still under the counter, Ed hit switch and a section of the back wall, beer signs and all, slid away to reveal a metallic tunnel with recessed lighting.

"Come on around the counter," Ed said. "He's waiting. You were expected sooner, you know."

"I had things to do, Ed. Sorry to keep you."

Ed shrugged. "You didn't. This is night shift for me."

The corridor was no more than eight feet, leading to a steel panel above which was mounted a rounded camera eye under a protective glass hood. Bullet-proof glass, one would think.

Sand took the steel panel to be a door, though neither knob nor hinges confirmed that. He stood before it and looked up pleasantly at the red, unlighted camera eye; it glowed redder momentarily, the steel slab glided away, and what Sand entered was certainly not the warehouse of a dusty collectibles shop, rather a high-ceilinged, expansive control room right out of NASA.

Huge Univacs bore whirling tapes, punch cards flipped into waiting beds, row upon row of orange lights on control panels winked on and off in sequence, while technicians in white lab coats attended the massive machines like doctors with patients; the techs carried piles of continuous paper, and men in suit coats sat around tables studying materials delivered to them like fat menus, which they handed back after examination to the next passing white coat.

To one side of Sand, a man and a woman conversed seriously, their backs to him, both presumably field agents judging by their understated business dress. When the pair parted in opposite directions, they revealed – as if human curtains (near a wall but not encased in an office), a man at a desk. This was like saying Henry the Eighth was a man in a chair.

Lord Malcolm Marbury, behind his snooker-table-size mahogany desk – which (like him) was an anachronism in this ultra-modern facility - was going over computer print-outs. He was seated in the same high-backed button-tufted burgundy leather chair as back at MI6.

Double M seemed little changed in the two years or so since Sand had seen him last. His hair had receded slightly, and the navy blue Savile Row suit with its three buttons and vest had been replaced by an otherwise identical gray one. He wore his typical starched white shirt, of course, cufflinks identifying him as an Eton alum, and when he turned to look at Sand, his eyes were the same ice-blue as the Tower of London skating rink.

"John, I'm pleased to see you," Double M said, the corners of his lips nearly threatening a smile. This was more warmth than the man had expressed in Sand's entire tenure. "Do sit."

His host gestured toward a waiting chair, a modern-looking teak-and-black-vinyl number. Sand sat. It was as comfortable as falling down.

"Do I detect fatigue, Triple Seven? If I might be allowed the liberty of still calling you that."

Sand couldn't quite get used to this deference. "I've

had a busy evening." He gestured to himself. "I actually stopped to clean up a little."

Marbury nodded slowly. "I understand you've already... gone calling."

Sand was not surprised that Double M was aware of his activities. Knowing things was the man's business.

"Anthony Morello will not be missed," Marbury said, "although the local constabulary are already beside themselves. Apparently it's the worst underworld slaughter since a certain St. Valentine's Day in Chicago, some years ago."

"Well, these mob squabbles do get out of hand, sir."

Double M shrugged. His mood was unusually upbeat and familiar. "Not any of our concern, is it? We have matters of our own to discuss."

"Do we?"

"As you know, the President has selected you as his personal representative with our budding organization."

Sand glanced around the bustling computer center. "Looks well past 'budding' to me, sir. And, yes, he did invite me to be part of your group."

Marbury folded his hands and sat forward. "If I may be frank?"

"Of course."

"John, I told Mr. Kennedy I had certain misgivings, despite your stellar record of service at MI6. Now, when he asked me to help you find your missing wife, I of course said I would do what I could for an old comrade in arms."

"May I ask...what misgivings?"

Sitting back but with his hands still folded, Marbury said, "Well, there are a number. Our mutual former colleague turned author has outed you as a secret agent – dramatically, thoroughly...and widely. This obviously limits your usefulness."

"I don't disagree."

"Beyond that, there are your methods of operation. Even among Double-Sevens, you were a loose cannon, a rule breaker, and...if I may at least obliquely refer to the earlier events of this evening...rather prone to deal with situations in a violent and showy fashion."

"There's an American saying about omelets, sir. That you can't make them without breaking a few eggs."

"This evening, that would be *yeggs*."

Sand smiled. "Usually *I* do the jokes, sir."

"Perhaps you've been a bad influence on me. And of course you would be an *American* agent, in this instance, though you remain a subject of Her Majesty."

"I now hold dual citizenship, sir."

"Given. But we are a new organization, rivaling the United Nations in number of members. And, as I say, you're a loose cannon, Triple Seven – even in retirement that's the case. Take that business in Jamaica with Raven Nocona. And that Dominican affair, and of course San Ignacio. I was still at MI6, at the time, John, and there you were – back on our radar! And we were never able to determine in whose interests, beyond Boldt Oil, you might have been acting."

Sand said nothing. If Kennedy hadn't seen fit to share that information with Double M, Sand certainly wasn't about to.

"Because of these actions," Marbury continued, "and knowing Mr. Kennedy's inclination to recruit you, we've been keeping a collective eye on you post-San Ignacio, after you and Mrs. Sand returned to the States."

Sand chuckled mirthlessly. "And here I thought I was merely a paranoid case. I *felt* from time to time I was being followed."

"Only when you traveled away from Houston." Marbury shifted in his chair. "John, do not assume that I advised the President against your participation with the Group Unit. In fact, I rather sang your praises...albeit in a context of your, uh..."

"Failings?"

Marbury again nearly smiled. "I had a responsibility to give Mr. Kennedy a frank and accurate assessment. But, having spoken to your sponsor, I understand you have your *own* misgivings."

Sand folded his arms. "If I may be frank?"

"Please."

"Until my wife is safely back at home, I can't give the 'part-time job' the President proposes due consideration."

Double M nodded. "You are understandably distracted. And as I indicated, we are prepared to help you. This organization is in early days, but we *will* help...whether you pledge to come aboard, or not."

"Is that an invitation?"

"Yes."

"Without equivocation on your part?"

"Oh no. I have plenty of that."

Both men laughed.

Marbury said, "At any rate, I understand your position, Triple Seven, given the circumstances. Your missing wife is understandably your priority...but if I may say, it's also a concern of ours, another reason why, frankly, I was not enthusiastic when your name came up."

"How so?"

"Mrs. Boldt is a strong woman, the CEO of an important company, and a potential target for authoritarians, malcontents, and the criminally ambitious. She represents an Achilles' heel in your make-up."

Sand couldn't argue with that, either.

Double M said, "Before Anthony Morello's premature passing this evening, may I assume you questioned him thoroughly about Mrs. Sand's disappearance?"

"I did. He claimed to have had nothing to do with it."

"And was this claim credible?"

"Actually, it was."

"What was his motive for the attack in, where was it? Brownsville, Texas?"

"Yes, sir," Sand said, and explained the history between the Sands and Morello, and the mobster's desire to kill the husband and leave the wife to grieve.

"Do you understand," Marbury said, "that as an agent of GUILE, your tendency toward administering justice personally is less than desirable?"

"It's never desirable, sir. But sometimes it's necessary. If I were to sign on with this new organization, I would expect my old license to liquidate without prejudice to be restored."

"That was MI6. This is a different animal."

"I won't promise that *I* would be a different animal."

Double M mulled that, then said, "Would it be asking too much to request that you employ...discretion?"

"No. That's reasonable."

"More discretion than this *evening*, perhaps?"

Sand raised an outward palm. "Let's leave the discussion there. I am not inclined to decide on the invitation to join your ranks until my wife is home, or..."

"Or if she isn't – properly avenged?"

Sand looked at his longtime employer with as hard an expression as he could muster. "If I was not so inclined, would I be of use to you or anyone in our business?"

Marbury's expression was stony yet not disapproving. Then he said, "There is a piece of news that bears upon how this situation may develop."

"News?"

"We have been looking into Mrs. Sand's disappearance. I can tell you, and this is *without* equivocation...that she was not kidnapped."

"Not..."

"She left of her own volition, John."

It was if Marbury had struck him a blow.

Sand said, "That can't be."

"I'm afraid it is, John. As I said, you've been on our radar for some time. That includes Mrs. Sand. When she went to Brownsville, she traveled with a ghost."

Meaning someone from GUILE had been following her.

"The night she disappeared," Double M said, referring to notes, "she went to a restaurant."

Sand frowned. "*El Paraiso*?"

"Yes. On..." Back to his notes. "...the corner of Levee and Charles. When she emerged, something caught her attention...as if..." He read from the report. "'She had seen something or someone she recognized.'"

Sand held out his hand and Marbury passed him the handwritten field notes.

Double M said, "After this apparent sighting of some sort, Mrs. Sand did not return to her hotel. Rather, she crossed the bridge into Mexico. Our ghost followed her into Matamoros, but, unfortunately, lost her. When your wife's chauffeur, Ernesto Cuchillo, came along, Mrs. Sand's ghost shifted to him, but lost the man shortly after he crossed the bridge on foot. Apparently this Cuchillo person has skills of his own. At any rate, they would both appear to still be in Mexico, John."

"So you've narrowed it down for me – to a country. You GUILE people are good."

Marbury ignored the sarcasm. "I promised the President we would help you. And we are. We're still tracking down some leads, Triple Seven. I'll have something for you, but it's going to take some time."

"Situations like this don't lend themselves to taking time."

Marbury's sigh seemed to come from the bottom of his being. "John, you're exhausted. You have put yourself, as they say, through the mill. Check into your hotel. Vegas is a twenty-four-hour town, you'll be able to get something to eat. Do so. Above all, get some sleep. Come back in the afternoon and I'll have more information which, with any luck, should narrow your search parameters. Agreed?"

"Do I have a choice, sir?"

"No."

"Then...agreed."

Double M looked past Sand and waved someone over.

The two agents who'd been talking earlier responded and Sand, getting a better look, realized he knew them both. The male agent – blond, brown-eyed, tall, athletic – came over with a big smile. He had met Lucas Claes, formerly of the Belgian intelligence service, when the two men were assigned to intercept a NATO traitor in Luxembourg. They'd stopped him from fleeing into Germany.

Sand should have recognized Charlotte DuBois, even from behind – perhaps especially from behind. The leggy brunette, slender in a curvy Bardot way, had been a top field agent in the French Service de Documentation Extérieure et Contre-Espionage, a decade ago. The SDECE had more than its share of good agents, but Charlotte, who had assisted Sand on more than one occasion, was as lethal as she was beautiful. Those high, sharp cheekbones could almost cut a man, the bright blue eyes, unusual in a brunette, cut even deeper.

She'd lost none of her appeal, her lithe figure encased in a tight black skirt and a white blouse beneath a black blazer. No woman ever looked better in six-inch heels than Charlotte. But here, at work, she wore sensible black shoes with rubber soles.

"I don't believe introductions are necessary," Double M said.

They weren't: Charlotte presented herself for kisses to either cheek, after which the two men clasped hands firmly.

"It's been a while," Sand said, looking from one to the other, a statement equally applicable.

Claes said, in his smooth, appealing accent, "We've been working on this unfortunate situation with your wife. We hope to be getting somewhere soon."

Charlotte took one of Sand's hands in both of hers and said, "I am the agent who followed Stacey to Brownsville, John. I have let you down. It won't happen again."

Her grasp was warm with a meaningful squeeze that somehow conveyed the affection of their once-upon-a-time, very steamy affair. She was one of the few women with whom he'd ever considered tying the knot, prior to Stacey. Possibly that he'd once witnessed her tying a knot around an adversary's throat had been a factor in deciding not to marry another spy.

Workplace romances, after all, so often didn't work out.

In that subtle, enticing French accent of hers, she said, "We will find her, John."

Double M said, "Triple Seven, don't let me see you back here any sooner than ten hours from now. Refuel.

Get some rest."

"Yes, sir."

He knew enough not to argue. Giving Marbury and his people a chance to pull together more intel was his best tactical move at the moment. And recharging was a necessity.

Sand made his way back out the metallic tunnel and, after a nod to Ed, headed through the musty shop and out into the parking lot where the Fairlane awaited. Less than half an hour later he was checking into the bland-for-Vegas Elwell Hotel on South First, not far from the Pioneer Club and its iconic looming neon sign known as Vegas Vic – unlikely to join Ed's neon graveyard any time soon.

Sand deposited his suit bag, shaving kit and himself in the clean, spare room. He shaved and showered before going to bed, just to feel better about himself. He had a towel around him when a knock came to the door.

Frowning, he went out and got his Walther from the nightstand and, positioned to one side of the door, said, "Yes?"

"John," a familiar female voice said, a fetchingly accented one, "May I come in? May I see you?"

He lowered the weapon and opened the door. Charlotte, her brunette hair a lovely tangle, no make-up on the perfect features but for some lipstick on the puffy lips, wore a raincoat, though it not only wasn't raining, it didn't look like rain.

She stepped inside and opened the coat. A diaphanous pink negligee was beneath, covering no surprises but her presence. Noting his towel, she flipped it off.

"You are glad to see *me*, too," she said.

Their reunion was immediate. She took charge, as she so often had, and led him to the double bed, and turned off the bedside lamp that was the only light in the room. She pointed as if instructing a dog to sit, and he lay down on his back, and she began to kiss him, not starting with his mouth.

With only the gaudy endless day of Vegas night filtering through the windows, the slim, muscular woman with the pert handfuls, nipples almost too large – almost – had her way with him. When he recalled it later, the lovemaking would be a dream with fast motion and cuts and slow motion, like something in a film, a French film of course, her smooth creamy flesh all over him, his hands filled with her plump bottom, his face nuzzling her breasts, her blue eyes rolling back, as man and woman climaxed.

She went off to the bathroom to tend to things and came back to find him standing naked at the window, looking out at the neon night, smoking a *Gauloises*. She stood at his side and looked up. Her fingers touched the tears on his face, gently.

"It is not betrayal," she said. "We are such old friends."

"That's not the question."

"What is the question?"

"Has she betrayed *me*? I thought she was taken, but she went off of her own free will."

Charlotte took him by one arm and that was enough for her to turn him to her. "I am the ghost who haunts her, remember? I saw her with no other man. She sees *something* – something that put a look of...of terror on her face."

Sand frowned sharply at her. "What are you saying?"

"You still need to save her. Forget your guilt and come to bed. We will sleep, *mon amour*, and you will add one more memory to our story, then go out and continue yours and your Stacey's. She is out there, waiting for you, I promise."

They went back to bed and slept. Only slept.

CHAPTER ELEVEN
NEON GRAVEYARD

When Sand awoke naked and alone in the double bed, the light coming in the window was the work of the sun and not Las Vegas neon. The nightstand clock said 11:17 A.M. next to a note on a Hotel Elwell pad, reading (in handwriting that after all these years was still familiar to him), "We will find her, *mon amour*," signed, "C."

He felt well-rested and loose and himself. If there had been nightmares, he didn't recall them nor did their mood linger. He brushed his teeth, shat, shaved, showered, threw the Ban-lon and jeans on, went down for breakfast in the hotel restaurant – eggs, bacon, toast, coffee – and read the story about Morello's death on the front page of the *Las Vegas Sun*. The "apparent war between underworld factions" had happened so close to deadline that there were scant details, no photos other than a file shot of Morello.

Returning to his room, Sand got into a gray Botany 500 suit he'd brought along – it had hung out nicely in the closet – with the Walther in its holster under his left arm and the Beretta 950 in its ankle holster. He gathered the suit bag (the duffel remained in the rental Ford) and went down to the desk where he checked out.

The return trip to the antique-shop front and the GUILE control center was an easier, quicker one by daylight, easier also to feel sure he wasn't being followed. The remoteness through which the two-lane blacktop cut was less atmospheric, of course, though he was surprised to find the gate in the chain-link fence still yawning open.

Pulling into the gravel apron, Sand noted the same beat-up pickup truck but also, next to it, a sleek black Chrysler parked diagonally near the Quonset hut's entry. A customer for the cover business? Or perhaps another first time visit from a prospective operative like Sand? The staff here clearly parked elsewhere, perhaps in back and at any rate not in the open.

Atop the little porch with its few steps, the door to the shop was agape.

Sand swung the Ford around so that it blocked entry through the gate, shoved the gear shift into park, climbed out, went around to the trunk and, from the duffel, extracted the Mossberg shotgun. He jogged to the rear of the Chrysler and determined no one was waiting in the front or back.

The keys were in the ignition.

The driver had obviously not anticipated dealing with anyone who wasn't already inside. Quietly opening the door, Sand pulled the keys from the ignition, pocketed them.

He almost rushed up those three wooden stairs to the front door when the sun glinted off the tripwire across the second step. His immediate assumption – that GUILE was under attack – was revised: whatever happened here was almost certainly already over.

But then why was this Chrysler unmanned with its keys in the dash?

As if in answer, a machine gun burst ripped behind him, aimed at the other side of the small parking lot and his rental Ford, its metal pinging and sparking and pock-marking, the windscreen an array of spider webs around each punched hole in its glass.

The shots had come from beyond the Chrysler's passenger side, which meant the vehicle - presumably getaway car – was between him and the shooter. The burst seemed intended to both cripple his car and force him inside, presumably to trip the wire and get blown to bloody pieces.

Kneeling by the Chrysler's driver side rear tire, between it and the parked pickup, Sand explored his limited options. Avoiding that tripwire wouldn't be hard, going slow and easy; but rushing up those stairs...? Of course, Sand could always stay out here while the machine gunner repositioned himself for a better bead on him....

And there could be more than one gunman – the safest place among the various dangerous possibilities would be inside. Shotgun in both hands, he duckwalked along the Chrysler until he was even with the driver's side front tire. Perhaps five feet separated the big black car and the bottom step.

He rose from his crouch and, leaning forward, ran those few feet before launching himself, the unseen machine-gunner firing and splinters flying, diving over the three stairs, tripwire included, gunfire chewing wood right behind him. He landed on the porch on his belly, then scrambled like a crab through the open doorway as a fusillade ripped into the landing.

Within the musty shop, staying low, shotgun in his hands, Sand scurried down the central aisle with ancient slot machines and other vintage Vegas memorabilia on either side. The only danger now would be through the windows, where machine-gun fire could reach him; but the likelihood that whoever this was had left an accomplice behind in the shop was nil, not with the place wired to blow. He was lucky to be inside and not hit; lucky, too, that those machine-gun rounds – which had let up – did not trigger the tripwire or otherwise set off the explosives positioned God-knew-where, which even now could blow him to kingdom come.

Midway down that aisle he was far enough away from the windows to get upright. Bearded, bored Ed was not at the counter, though a splash of blood on the wall was still dripping off a Hamm's beer above an empty stool.

Behind the counter, he was not surprised to find the old boy sprawled on the floor, a .45 automatic in his limp fingers, an entry wound in his forehead, his dead eyes staring and somehow accusative, as if he'd died thinking Sand had brought all of this on.

Perhaps he had.

The tunnel was open not just at this end but on the other.

GUILE headquarters was a bloodbath. Everywhere technicians were scattered like so many bowling pins, their white lab coats dotted and spotted red, the wounds in rows suggesting machine-gun fire. The massive computers no longer spun tapes, bullet holes puncturing and rupturing them and leaving them standing as upright mechanical corpses. Agents in business suits sprawled over tables, occasionally draped over each other, men and women alike, flung to the floor, riddled with bullets. Only occasionally did any of them have a gun in hand. The carnage at Morello's was no competition to this, though the stench of death was similar.

When he didn't spot Charlotte DuBois among the dead, Sand allowed himself a tentative feeling of relief. Perhaps she'd left his hotel room only moments before he woke, and had stumbled off to wherever she lived in Vegas and crawled back into bed, and not yet made it into work.

What, satiated and exhausted from a lovemaking sensation with the great cocksman? he asked himself ironically. *Not bloody likely.*

As for Lucas Claes, he lay on his stomach, shot behind the ear, face down atop a grotesque pile of several agents. Sand knelt for a moment and squeezed his dead comrade's shoulder, then moved on, quickly sweeping the room, but it was clear. No one here but the dead.

And no sign of Marbury at the big mahogany desk – *where the hell was he?* At least he wasn't another machine-gun-mangled corpse. He searched the desktop for any clue Double M might have found, and left for him, about Stacey's disappearance.

Nothing.

Why wasn't Marbury's body among the dead? This had obviously been a surprise attack with everyone gunned down in seconds.

A noise behind him swung Sand and his shotgun around.

Lucas Claes's body, flung on top of several other corpses, started to move. Could he still be alive? Shot behind the goddamn ear like that?

Then Charlotte DuBois crawled out from under Claes and the sprawl of bodies. On her hands and knees, her suit jacket soaked with blood, she looked up at Sand as if he might be a mirage.

A trace of a smile appeared on the puffy lips. "You are a quiet one, John. I did not know you were here. I...I thought I was alone." Her hand covered her face. "I...I *hoped* I was...."

He went to her and knelt there, putting an arm around

her shoulder, the shotgun held in one hand. "My God. How bad are you hit? Where...?"

"Not hit at all," she said with a sigh. "The blood, it is not mine....Are they gone?"

"There's one outside. What the hell happened here?"

"When the attack come, half a dozen of them, they rush in with *la mitrailleus.*"

Machine guns.

"And Claes, he joins in," she went on. "He *let* them in, John. *C'était une taupe!*"

"He was a mole? Whose?"

She shrugged. "No idea. So rude of him not to say, before he shoot me."

"You said you weren't hit."

"I was and I was not." She pointed to a bullet hole in her coat over her left breast.

From her jacket she withdrew the silver cigarette case Sand had given her years ago. He'd had the case engraved with a dove, one of the meanings of *chérie*, his term of affection for her – a woman who did undercover work dare not risk initials. Now, the case was dented where a bullet smashed into its center, distorting the dove. Saving her.

"To think," she said, managing a small smile in the midst of all this carnage, "I almost throw this in the Seine, John, when you leave me."

"What did they look like?"

"They come in shooting – men in business suits but also Balaclavas. Lucas with them, their...their escort. *He* shoot me, I go down, hit my head on the table edge. They think I am dead. When they kill Lucas...because who wants to do business with a traitor, *Oui?*...he fall on top of me and... some others." She shivered. "I've been through much in my time, John, but this? *C'est trop!*"

"Are you all right? Do you have a concussion?"

"I don't know. I don't think so."

"Whoever they are," he said, "the one outside with a machine gun will come in looking for me, soon."

"Not just one," Charlotte said and held up two fingers. "I hear the leader say, Kelso, you and Cook stay behind in case Sand, he come back."

"What became of Double M?"

"I see them drag him out. He was shooting when they overtake him."

Sand looked around the terrible tableau. "I don't see any of *their* dead."

"None to see. They must be wearing the bullet-proof vest and what little resistance we give them, it is overwhelmed by those machine guns. John, those technicians, they are not armed. And only a few of the agents. *C'est un massacre.*"

"Marbury was the target. He's an incredibly valuable hostage – think of the information he carries around in that head of his....I trust there's another way out of here."

"There is, but surely they would know this, from Lucas. If they have it covered, we won't last long."

"How long will we last going out the front way? Where we *know* there's at least one of them? And by the way, that shop in front is rigged to blow sky high."

An eyebrow raised. "Then shall we depart through the back, *mon cher?*"

She led him through the slaughterhouse the control room had become, moving in and around the dead, careful not to slip in the still wet redness, and escorted him into what proved to be a parking garage for the help, accommodating dozens of cars.

One mystery answered, Sand thought.

A double roller-door was how vehicles accessed the garage. A regular-sized door was beside it.

"What's out there?" he asked her.

"A gravel drive through the neon junkyard. For several hundred yards it extend to the fence."

"More chain-link?"

"No. That fence is steel beam, and the gate the cars of GUILE personnel enter, it is also steel and open only with the remote control."

"You have one of those?"

"I do."

"Is your car here?" He nodded to the rows of vehicles.

"It is."

He locked eyes with her. "You'll drive your car out of here, slow just enough for me to jump out half-way down the lane, then you take off like a bat out of hell, while I position myself to return any fire you get, and draw theirs, while you make it out through the gate."

"And wait for you where?"

"Nowhere near. Take your pretty backside away from here. I'll get one of these cars running – plenty to choose from – and we'll meet in town somewhere."

"This plan I do not like." She clutched his sleeve. "Come with me. Like the bat out of hell, you say? We will go that fast without me slowing or you jumping."

He took her by the small of her arms, gentle but insistent. "No, *chérie*, I need to stay behind. I *want* these two. And I need at least *one* of them alive long enough to talk. I have to know if the attack on GUILE relates to my wife's disappearance. The leader knew my name, remember."

Her eyes narrowed. "Lucas may have told whoever pay him that you are here yesterday. I have the other idea."

"I like my idea."

"Listen to mine. I will stay with you. We will position ourselves along the lane in the graveyard. They will know about it from Lucas. You can be sure they will check it out."

She was right.

"You kill one," she said, "and we will question the other. *Très bien?*"

"All right," he said. "Do you have a gun?"

From under her jacket she withdrew her Manurhin PP automatic, a French pistol manufactured under license from Walther.

"Put that away," he said, handing her the shotgun. "This will give you more range."

She nodded.

At the door onto the neon graveyard, Sand – the Walther in his right hand, the knob in his left – said, "They could be waiting. Move left and find cover. I'll do the same at the right. Fast."

"Like the bat from hell?" she said with a smile.

"Like the bat from hell. Can you use your singular skills to clamber up onto those old neons?"

"Of course."

"Then do so. Make it about half-way down the lane – you know how to time that, *chérie*, you're familiar with it and I am not. We'll situate ourselves for ambush."

"We cannot know how they will deploy themselves."

"True. And they may be positioned in the lane already, so we each must react as need be."

She shrugged and her brunette hair bounced. "It is a plan such as circumstance allow....On three, *mon cher.*"

He returned her smile and began the count for her: "Un...deux...*trois!*"

Then they were moving into a world of towering

defunct signs down a single gravel lane, a street cutting through surrealistic skyscrapers. Sand loped along at a moderate pace, staying low, his back to the row of signs, ducking into shadows and moving from one recession between signs to another.

Across the way, Charlotte ran, vaulted, climbed, and ended up atop the row of decrepit signs from old hotels, casinos, restaurants, bars, leaping from one to another with grace and yet staying low, cat-like and quick. He marveled how she moved, utilizing training called *parcours du combattant,* a technique she had tried to teach him with little success.

With Charlotte taking the high ground, she would have a clean line of fire if one of the gunmen popped out near him from hiding. In anticipation of that, he checked every shadowy spot and each dark corner, and listened for any indication of movement. If he heard something, it could be the scurry of a rat, perhaps the human variety.

He glanced up – Charlotte was hunkering down, almost out of sight. She gestured with an upraised palm – this was the half-way point. He nodded. Then she frowned, her head bobbing to his left, her eyes wide – someone was coming up on his side of the aisle, following the same path, edging along.

Sand pivoted and threw himself, belly-down, onto the gravel, and lined up the stocking-masked, business-suited gunman in the Walther sights. The stalker's machine gun swung toward Sand, who fired, hitting him in the knee. The crunch of it was awful, with blood spurting like oversize tears. The gunner howled, dropping onto the other knee, his weapon firing wildly as he toppled to the dirt, and in the same instant Charlotte's shotgun barked. The gunman jerked back as the shotgun round tore half of his head off, and he fell sideways, as if the missing piece of him had made him lose his balance.

Sand got to his feet, irritated with Charlotte for killing the man, ready to give her a calming palm signal when machine gun bullets tore the top off the signs where she perched, Charlotte backing away.

Swinging around, Sand fired at the second gunman, who had materialized from somewhere, missing him, and sending the gunner ducking behind a big casino sign. Hugging the row, Sand moved sideways down to where the second man had slipped behind a dead neon; ears perked for the slightest sound, Sand quickly scanning the dark recessions between massive signs, looking for a stray shadow to spill into the dirt and indicate someone hiding nearby.

At the row's end, near the back of the barn within which the GUILE HQ hid, Sand got down on his haunches and peeked around. He saw the gunman sprinting away, alongside the building, heading toward the parking lot...where that black Chrysler awaited!

Swearing under his breath, Sand took off after him. The gunman was far enough ahead to make the Walther essentially useless. The agent ran hard, knowing something the fleeing gunman did not – the keys from the Chrysler's ignition were in Sand's pocket!

And as he closed the gap, Sand raised the Walther to take the man down, without killing him, he hoped....

The runner looked over his shoulder, saw his pursuer gaining, and abruptly stopped and spun with his machine gun to make it spit again. Sand dove for the dirt as a deadly burst of bullets flew over him. Prone, Sand fired and a round caught the shooter in the thigh. The man shot at the sky as he tumbled to one side and hit the ground and sat there, a small red spot of blood expanding until, from his belt to his knee, a glistening wetness soaked his pants leg.

Sand rose, not bothering to brush dust from his suit as he moved forward, the gun like a divining rod pulling him to blood not water. The gunman struggled to regain control of his machine gun and bring it to bear, but Sand simply fired another round, hitting the man where his shoulder met his chest, and the assassin dropped the machine gun. Holding his arm, the masked gunman managed to get himself into a seated position, his entire left pant leg glistening now, his arm leaking blood through his fingers.

Kicking the machine gun away, Sand pointed the pistol at the man's head. Three eyes – Sand's and the gun barrel's – stared pitilessly at him.

"Where's my wife?"

"*Blya.*"

An all-purposes Russian obscenity.

"Let's keep it in English. Who hired you?"

"*Blya,*" the gunman said again, smiling at Sand, showing him lots of white teeth, then bit down, and, damn! The man's mouth was swimming with foam....

"Bastard," Sand said, and shook him. But what can you do with a dead man?

And he was dead, all right, tongue poking out as if in one final insult. Goddamn cyanide anyway.

Sand almost shot the corpse to work off some rage, but didn't waste a bullet and anyway there was Charlotte to check on. He headed quickly down the aisle to where she had slipped from sight.

He climbed up to where she'd been; the shotgun was there and he retrieved it. Spots of blood atop the sign indicated she'd been hit, then they trailed away. He climbed onto the sign behind this one, following the blood trail, and found her sitting below, in the next aisle over, leaned against the sign on which he stood.

Climbing down, he knelt beside her. She was bleeding from both legs and one arm.

"Charlotte," he said, frowning. "What have you done?"

"I get myself shot, John," she said. Beads of sweat pearled her forehead. She looked very pale. Shock was setting in.

He pulled off his belt, wrapped it around her left leg where the blood loss seemed the worst. "We've got to get you to a medic."

She managed a weak laugh. "I'm not sure it will help, *mon cher*."

"Nobody likes a pessimist, *chérie*."

He picked her up into his arms.

She said, "There is a thing you do not know."

"Don't talk."

"No, it is an important thing," she said, as he began to make his way slowly down the aisle. "Double M, there is something he learn. Your wife's man – Cuchillo. He is seen in Acapulco."

"What? When was this?"

"Just yesterday."

He had a hundred other questions, but said, "Thank you, I can use that. Now shut your pretty mouth."

"No. Double M say the man who see Cuchillo is some-one who *know* him. Who *recognize* him."

"Tell me later," Sand said.

They were at the black Chrysler. He somehow got her into the passenger seat.

"I'll be a moment," he told her.

She nodded, barely awake.

As badly shot-up as the rental Ford was, it still started and rumbled on its two good tires and two shot-up ones out of the way, unblocking the gate. He got his things from the trunk and threw them in back of the Chrysler. Then they were heading back to Vegas, fast.

Charlotte said, "I thought I do not understand him."

"Him? Who?" Was she delirious?

"Lord Marbury. When he tell me who... *who* recognize Cuchillo."

"Who was it?"

"John Wayne. *Le grand* cowboy. Could that be? Do I dream, *mon cher*?"

He glanced over at her. Her blue eyes were still bright and she was definitely not delirious.

"John Wayne is a friend of my wife's family," he told her. "Now rest."

******

Sand parked in the AMBULANCE ONLY spot outside the emergency room of Nevada Memorial. He got out of the Chrysler, then eased Charlotte over behind the wheel. She was breathing and asleep. He kissed her cheek, then leaned her forward to where she pressed against the horn. As it blared, he turned and walked away.

His to-do list now included tracking down Double M. Sand walked to the nearest corner and hailed a passing taxi. Climbing in, he said, "McCarran, please."

"Got the money for that, bud?" the driver asked.

Sand's suit was disheveled, covered in dust and dirt, as well as random splotches of Charlotte's blood. From his pocket, he withdrew his money clip and peeled off a hundred for the driver.

"That kind of change I don't carry," the driver said.

Sand met the man's eyes in the rearview mirror. "I don't remember asking for change. I remember asking to be driven to McCarran."

"And I am thrilled to do it."

After this taxi ride, Sand's next stop would be Acapulco. If he could find Cuchillo, he could find Stacey.

But as they neared the airport, he was mulling whether GUILE headquarters had been stormed by hired Kazakh assassins. Plenty of other Russian speakers in the world, right? But his author friend had told him Jesus Guerra, a Mexican national, was smuggling uranium from the Kazakh SSR. Was that a coincidence?

That probable Kazakh assassin considered suicide preferable to failing his employer. Few men commanded that kind of fear.

One who did had been an associate of Jesus Guerra.

Jake Lonestarr.

CHAPTER TWELVE
FUN IN ACAPULCO

The Acapulco Hilton – less towering though far wider than its neighboring competition – might have been a huge white domino set on its side along the beach of the bay. The previous Hilton to welcome Sand had been in Havana, courtesy of Fidel Castro, who'd taken the hotel over as his occupational headquarters; though less than a five-star stay post-Batista, Sand's unscheduled visit had at least been something he managed to live through. The recently opened Acapulco Hilton promised a warmer welcome.

At McCarran he had immediately gone to a phone and put Tom Something in motion, including having him make a hotel reservation. Then in a men's room Sand managed to diminish his disheveled appearance enough to join other travelers waiting in the General Aviation area. Several hours later he was told he could go to the gang hangar where various private aircraft were housed, his company plane and its pilot awaiting. He slept for much of the flight to General Juan Alvarez International Airport in Acapulco.

Despite the cramped quarters of the Cessna, he'd gotten himself into the last clean change of clothes from his duffel bag. The fresh if rumpled wardrobe allowed him to get off the plane looking at least tolerably presentable, while a men's shop at the airport refreshed his duffel with more than just weapons. Now he would be neither the best nor worst dressed vacationer in Mexico.

Also at the airport he rented a Jeep and drove himself to the Hilton. If John Wayne really was in Acapulco, Sand knew right where to look for him; but nearly nine p.m. was a little late to come calling. Anyway, he hadn't eaten since breakfast, and it made sense to find some dinner and a good night's sleep before first tracking down Wayne...and then, he hoped, Cuchillo.

The Hilton's expansive swimming pool, a particular draw for tourists, was every bit as round as the moon turning its shimmery surface into an ivory mirror. A restaurant, La Isla, was positioned at the pool's center like a flower that had floated there and stayed put. A bridge walkway led to the entrance where awaited a pretty young Mexican woman in a peasant blouse and green-sashed red skirt with multi-color satin ribbons – just what a tourist might expect a Mexican girl to wear every day. Sand knew such finery was really only for weddings, dances, and other special occasions, if the family could afford them at all.

"This way," she said, although "this" sounded like "these." With a lovely smile, she led him (at his request) to a table well away from the bar.

The man tailing him was better than he had any right to be – a pasty-faced twenty-five or so in an ill-fitting suit, too-tight tie, and a short haircut, so nondescript he stood out. Sand was ordering his meal when the guy strolled into and settled at the bar, where he immediately began chatting with the bartender.

Earlier, Sand – in a pink polo, dark gray blazer, gray

chinos, and black lace-up sneakers – had gone into the gift shop and purchased a pack of *Gauloises*. He took a hike around the big pool before returning to the lobby, ostensibly to pick up an Acapulco newspaper, finally heading back for the restaurant. This had taken perhaps ten minutes, enough time to confirm he was being followed.

The only negative about being well away from the bar and his shadow was the difficulty of knowing whether a bribed bartender was mixing a drink that included something other than the usual ingredients. With no desire to toss down a Mickey Finn, Sand ordered a highball with dinner but didn't touch it. A bottle of wine and the water already on the table would have to suffice.

Guerrero, home to Acapulco, was known for *jueves pozolero*, a pork and hominy soup served only one day a week. *Jueves* was Thursday in English, and since this was a Thursday, Sand was in luck. The bowl of soup soon arrived with its accompanying array of avocado, oregano, cilantro, lemon, and chiles – how much to add of each was his choice, a ceremony rivaling a religious ritual.

The soup was as tasty as he remembered from a previous visit to Guerrero. He ate slowly, savoring the dish, keeping a discreet eye on the discreet eyes on him. His shadow seemed particular about what he drank, too – or perhaps was too professional to get tight, much less sloshed, on the job.

After dinner, Sand wandered out onto the beach – just another late diner walking off his meal and enjoying an after-dinner cigarette before bed. Somewhere back there the tail would be accompanying him. An open area like this made the tail's job easy; but at the same time, even after dark – it was a moon-swept night – being made was the issue for his escort. It wasn't as if there were a crowd to get lost in.

Sand stopped and lighted up a *Gauloises*, let the obscenely rich tobacco have at his lungs, then continued to stroll along. His hotel room might provide safer harbor; but out here on the sand, in the Pacific breeze off Acapulco Bay, it was easier to think.

Why on earth had Stacey crossed the border from Brownsville to Matamoros? That Mexican city was in the country's extreme northeast corner, yet somehow, for some reason – just days later! – her man Cuchillo was spotted in Acapulco on the *southwest* coast of the country, some thirteen hundred kilometers away.

It baffled him.

Under what circumstances would she have taken off, to parts unknown, without letting him know? He'd checked in numerous times with the FBI man on the phone at the mansion, and neither she nor any kidnapper had yet phoned. And his efforts to find her had been interrupted at every turn by killers, from Morello's men to foreign assassins probably linked to a man he himself had shot multiple times and apparently killed.

How could he make any sense of this?

But if he could find Cuchillo, perhaps that one piece of the puzzle would make the rest of the fragmented picture discernible, if not clear.

Sand approached a stand of palm trees two hotels down. He paused, stubbed out the cigarette in the sand, then slipped into the shadows of the trees. He dropped to his stomach, and waited.

He didn't have long to wait.

Panicked at losing track of his subject, the tail halted by the handful of palms and frowned at the empty beach ahead. Footprints in the sand stopped here, smooth sands lay ahead. The tail turned suspiciously toward the trees just as Sand's hand snaked out, grabbed an ankle and jerked him down, rudely, onto his buttocks. The shadow's other foot kicked out, but Sand, on his knees now, blocked it with a fist, which he swung down into the man's belly, like a hammer into an anvil, minus only the clang.

Then he dragged the man into darkness and, still on his knees, Sand pummeled him with body blows. Just to soften him up before questioning. Where the knife came from, Sand couldn't tell, but it was a knife all right, and it slashed at him, ripping the front of his Polo, and cutting him, but not bad. Sand retaliated by grabbing the man's wrist, twisting it, and with his other hand taking charge of the knife. That kept Sand too busy to see his opponent slip a hand under the baggy suit coat and pull a revolver. Sand reacted at once, pushing the arm with the gun-in-hand away and stabbing the man three times in the chest. It happened so quickly the man hadn't mustered a scream.

"Damn it," Sand growled under his breath. Was he so out of practice he didn't know how to keep a bloody flunky alive?

He rifled the pockets of this young man who was now as old a man as men ever got. U.S. dollars, Mexican pesos, a 9mm Tokarev TT30, and the knife, a Kizlyar dagger – Sand pocketed the lot of it. Leaving the body within the palms, he peeked out, looking left, looking right, to make sure he was alone on the beach.

Sand strolled back to the hotel a bit unsteadily. The moonlight told him the cut on his stomach was superficial, and he could keep it hidden by buttoning his blazer as he ambled through the lobby. He stopped at the hotel gift shop again, just before closing, and picked up a replacement Polo, pink again, staying touristy.

In his room, he cleaned his wound, bandaged his stomach, took a few aspirin, and got into the new shirt. It wasn't safe at the Hilton now, so he packed his duffel and simply walked out, having the parking attendant bring up the Jeep. He drove off onto Avenida Costera, thinking that he'd have preferred waiting till morning to find Wayne, but now no longer had that luxury.

Somebody unfriendly was interested in his presence in Acapulco. So making contact with the actor soon had become a priority.

Even at night, with lighter traffic, the drive along Avenida Costera took twenty minutes, getting from the Hilton to Los Flamingos in Las Playas. At least there was a nice breeze off the bay. He'd never met his wife's family friend, however much it might feel like you already knew a movie star. What would Sand say to this complete stranger at nearly midnight? How to convince a pestered celebrity to talk to him?

Los Flamingos was the obvious place to start looking for John Wayne – the actor had been one of the owners till not long ago. He had come for a vacation once and liked the hotel so much that he and several of his Hollywood cronies had purchased it, making the place their private clubhouse. They'd sold it back recently, and Los Flamingos was again open to the public.

Sand knew all this because Stacey had suggested Acapulco and the hotel for their honeymoon. She'd told him that Wayne had offered them the Casa de Tarzan (named for the role the actor's fellow investor in the hotel, Johnny Weissmuller, had famously played on screen). Seemed Wayne had a standing reservation for Casa de Tarzan during the season. But when Sand and Stacey set a date for their wedding, the bungalow was unavailable for the honeymoon and they'd gone instead to Port Royal in the Caribbean.

The roundhouse was a bungalow set apart from the rambling forty-six-room hotel that hugged the cliff near La Quebrada, where Acapulco's famous divers showed off their prowess, timing their leap to catch incoming waves in the cove below. Sand had seen the divers when he was here about four years ago, on a mission, and it had been quite a show – not the mission, the diving. Well, the mission, too.

After witnessing those astonishing high dives, he'd wondered how people could ever think *he* was reckless. Compared to those daredevils, he had an office job.

After parking the Jeep in the hotel lot, figuring to head the front desk, he decided instead to go to the Casa de Tarzan bungalow. A few dim lights among the palms provided more mood than illumination as he followed a winding sidewalk through the hotel's lawn, making his way with the moon's help to the roundhouse, which – like the other bungalows with their thatched roofs – was a bright pink that put Sand's pale Polo to shame.

A light shown through the curtains of the small window in front. Sand stepped onto the porch and as he raised a fist to knock, a deep, familiar voice said, "I wouldn't do that, friend."

Sand turned to where a big man sat at a glass table in the shadows, a bottle of tequila before him, the red tip of a burning Camel in his fist.

John Wayne added, with just a hint of menace, "I don't give autographs at this time of night."

"I'm not here for an autograph, Mr. Wayne. Forgive my showing up at this late hour, unannounced."

"Then maybe you better announce yourself."

"Sand. John Sand."

A big smile blossomed in the craggily handsome face.
"You're the spy that got too famous for his own good.
Had to marry Dutch Boldt's little girl to support himself."

"I can only plead guilty, Mr. Wayne."

"Pull up a chair."

Sand did. "I apologize for intruding."

"I should do the apologizing. I promised little Stacey
the use of this hut for your honeymoon, had to back out."

Anyone who had known Mrs. Sand long enough to refer
to her as "little Stacey" really was a longtime family friend.

Wayne looked rangy just sitting there, his thinning
brown hair starting to recede, his brown eyes sharp with
a Leprechaun twinkle. He wore an unbuttoned white shirt
and khaki shorts and was barefoot.

The actor's smile faded. "As it happens, though we
haven't met, I tried to call you yesterday."

"How is that, sir?"

"That's enough of that 'sir' business. Call me 'Duke.' I
need to back up. You've come around because you heard
I saw our mutual friend, Ernesto Cuchillo, right here in
Acapulco. Am I right?"

"You are."

Wayne was stubbing out one Camel and shaking
another out of a pack. "Cigarette?"

Sand got out his *Gauloises*. "Have my own."

"Those are strong medicine. Tried them once."

They fired up their respective smokes.

Hefting the bottle, Wayne asked, "Care for a nip?"

"Thank you, Duke. I would appreciate that."

Wayne poured two fingers of tequila into a glass and
slid it over. Sand picked it up, saluted his host, who clinked
the glass with the bottle, and they each took a drink. The
tequila made a pleasant burn going down.

Sand was doing his best not to show irritation with this big, famous man's slow pace – Duke had apparently been drinking a while.

"Cuchillo?" Sand prompted.

Wayne nodded. "I ran into him at *El Tepito* market-place over in the old part of town. The wife likes to shop over there. Really, I didn't run into him – *he* ran into *me*. Right into me."

"What was he doing in the market?"

"Not shopping. But he was in a hell of a hurry, going where I have no idea. When he saw who it was he bumped into, he made no small talk and he sure wasn't impressed. But he asked me to call you. Gave me the number and I put it to memory. Gotta be a quick study in my business."

"Call me, and tell me what?"

"I'll get to that. First he gave me one specific instruction – talk to no one but you. John Sand himself. Real spy stuff, like out of the books. No one else, he said...but it wasn't you I got. It was a male voice, no British inflections, and when I said I wanted to talk to you, you weren't available."

"What did you say to that?"

"Nothing. I hung up. I know how to take direction."

"That would have been an FBI man on the phone."

Wayne lifted an eyebrow. "So something *is* wrong?"

Sand said, "Stacey has been missing since Monday."

Quickly he filled the actor in, leaving out the carnage, saying only that he'd had obstacles thrown in his path.

"When you called, I was already looking for Stacey and Cuchillo," Sand said. "The FBI is covering the phone in case she calls or a ransom demand comes in. But ransom, a conventional kidnapping, is not what this is about."

He frowned, his concern obviously genuine. "What *is* it about, John? Was I right to call a friend I know in government, who might pass the information along to you? He *must* have, because here you are."

"Who did you contact?"

"Fella I know in the spook trade, a consultant on a picture of mine, *Big Jim McLain*."

Sand frowned. "His name is McLain?"

"No. Phil Lyman. He's retired now."

Sand smiled a little.

"Then you know the man?"

"We've met." Sand didn't bother to tell Wayne that Lyman was anything but retired. "You were to call me, and tell me something, presumably."

"Yes. Cuchillo said you were to go to the El Tepito marketplace, find a woman selling serapes. Tell her you're looking for her son. That was the extent of it. Then he was gone."

Sand finished his drink and put out his cigarette. Got to his feet and stuck out his hand. "Thank you, Mr. Wayne."

"Duke, damn it."

Wayne shook his visitor's hand. "John, you go find my friends, Stacy and Ernesto. Scratch that – I *know* you'll find my friends."

"Thank you, Duke."

"I'd offer to come along and help, but if you're like the guy in those books, you'll do better alone. Anyway, when I pack a gun, it's usually loaded with blanks."

******

Finally Sand had a lead, a genuine lead, he could pursue; but not until the sun was up. Going back to the Hilton was out of the question, and seeing if Wayne could provide a room at Los Flamingos would risk putting the actor in harm's way. Sand got back in the Jeep and drove off *las Playas* peninsula to the mainland. From his prior visit to the area, he knew where the marketplace was; but he couldn't go there in the middle of the night. He could get near it, though.

El Zocalo, the central plaza of Acapulco, was the city's oldest and, like all the others in every town in Mexico, it faced a church. After parking the Jeep two blocks away, Sand walked to the plaza and found himself standing before Acapulco's Catholic cathedral, *Nuestra Señora de la Soledad*. He wasn't a praying man generally, nor did he really think a confessional could settle the score for the men he'd sent to hell...not even just the ones since Monday.

But with his wife among the missing, Sand could use a little good karma wherever he could find it, however inappropriate his terminology.

He entered the darkened church. Worldwide, cathedrals were always open, and early on he'd learned that meant he always had somewhere to go. Call it refuge, call it sanctuary – he had long ago lost count of how many of God's houses he spent nights in over the years. They outdistanced even all-night movie theaters and bordellos.

He took a pew in a dark corner at the rear of the church and did his best to make himself comfortable in the wooden seating. He looked up at Christ on the cross over the altar, and may have bowed his head, and might have whispered a prayer for the safe return of his wife. He certainly asked no forgiveness nor mercy, either. In any case, it wasn't long before he went to sleep, sitting up.

When he woke the Rolex on his wrist was still there – a small miracle in the big church. It told him nine A.M. was nearly here. He'd slept longer than anticipated. With the breakneck pace he'd been maintaining, however, that was not a bad thing. And the market might already be open. If so, that would be good, too.

A few others were in the cathedral now, including a priest down front; no one appeared to be paying any heed to the man in the blue blazer and pink shirt at the back of the nave – just another tourist who wandered in after a rough night.

Sand exited the church, the morning sun waiting with a blinding welcome. He let his eyes adjust, then began walking. *El Tepito*, the local name for *El Mercado de Artesanías Parasal*, the oldest market in Acapulco, was five blocks northeast of *El Zocalo* plaza. He had gone less than a block when he picked up not just one tail, but two. He was not about to guide them to *El Tepito* and risk his only lead.

He needed to shake them, and fast. No specific clock was ticking on Stacey's absence, but as with a homicide investigation (a thought giving him a momentary shudder) he knew that with every passing hour, the road got rougher and the threat more foreboding. At the next corner, he took a quick right, and ran. Both men – in ill-fitting suits and the kind of short haircuts you got on a Russian military base – followed and planted themselves with their weapons raised, zeroing in on him. They might have been brothers of that shadow he killed in the palms last night.

As he ran, Sand filled his hand with the Walther and a bullet zinged past his head and took a bite out of the corner of an adobe building. Stopping, spinning, Sand saw one shooter had him dead to rights, the other farther back. The forward man aimed, but as he fired, the world fell away from him.

From all *of them – Sand included!*

Barely hanging onto the Walther, Sand found himself on his back, like an upended bug, his head aching from where it smacked the street, its bricks suddenly uneven. Somehow he had the wherewithal to roll over onto his stomach. The world was still shaking violently, and he knew at once....

...he, and his pursuers, and everybody else in Acapulco, were in the throes of an earthquake!

Locals and tourists alike were trying to run, often losing their balance and falling to an unfriendly earth, screams cutting through the rumbling roar as if God's stomach were growling. Three Anglo men were sprawled in the road, in loud touristy garb, apparently separated from their wives. Hispanics in far less gaudy garb moved along as best they could as if walking a highwire act. From above Sand, dust and plaster particles fell as the corner of a building wrenched itself free from the structure, poised to fall. It cracked ominously, but held.

Both gunmen had gone down, the eyes of one seeking the gun he'd dropped; the other tried to get to his feet, without success, then gave up and simply crawled toward his own fumbled pistol.

Sand couldn't get up either, but he wasn't about to play helpless target. *He* hadn't lost his weapon. He aimed the Walther carefully and, when the shaking eased at least momentarily, he fired off a round. The standing gunman, seeking his pistol, gurgled and shimmied as the shot meant for his chest went through his neck. Scarlet squirted, fingers went uselessly to the wound, and he sank to the pavement, painting it a brilliant red.

Sand kept track of the cracked corner chunk of the nearby building threatening to break off and fall on him, but also monitored the second gunman, who finally reached his pistol and got hold of it. Sand fired his Walther three times, hoping one of the bullets would hit the man and stop him. To Sand's surprise, all three hit the man – one in either shoulder, the lucky third striking the would-be gunman in the forehead, shutting him down like a machine whose plug got pulled.

Sand crawled around that crumbling corner, away from the teetering chunk, holding onto the Walther, and as the earthquake subsided – later he would learn it had been a magnitude seven – he finally made it to his feet and walked away. He did so as fast as he dared, his equilibrium a mess, people around him staggering in terror, looking at one another trying to comprehend what had just happened.

Buildings were leveled, goods were scattered, but Sand was alive and on the move. He still needed to get to *El Tepito* to see the damage there and if the woman who sold serapes could help him find her son Cuchillo.

He only hoped they were both still alive.

CHAPTER THIRTEEN
HERDING CATTLE

El Mercado de Artesanías Parasal on *Calle Cinco de Mayo* was both the oldest and largest open-air market in Acapulco, but now it was just part of the disaster area that the city had become. Finding "a woman who sold serapes," without even a name to guide Sand would be a feat on a normal day – in the aftermath of an earthquake, it would take a miracle.

He had been to any number of such bazaars in numerous countries. Hundreds of stalls trafficked in everything from onyx chessboards to embroidered dresses, sombreros to bootleg records, spices to chiles. You could walk naked into such a place with nothing but money, and walk out with a new wardrobe and enough furnishings to set up housekeeping.

That was on a normal day.

On this day, everything had been thrown to hell and gone, aisles blocked by end-over-end merchandise, people frantically searching for loved ones, tourists seeking only a path out of this Armageddon of scattered goods, ruptured stalls, and overwhelmed souls.

He passed a booth with its front table upright but the glass figurines - dolphins, roosters, dancing Mexican girls, Mariachi musicians – knocked over, mostly in pieces. The woman running the stall, black hair in a severe bun, her navy blue dress dusty from where she had hit the pavement, was in tears as she sorted through the rubble, looking for stock she might salvage.

Sand walked deeper into the marketplace. Despite the state of disrepair booths had suffered to varying degrees, the vendors were doing their best to clean up the mess and fend off looting and yet somehow continue to hawk their goods.

He approached a stall that was already in a semblance of order, where a heavyset man with exaggerated features – his white shirt and black slacks both relatively free of dirt or dust, his black hair slicked back with oil – was selling sombreros, most of which he had stacked back onto the table.

Sand said, "*Perdóname, señor – donde esta la mujer que vende sarapes?*"

The man pointed farther down the aisle, responding in Spanish, "Down that way, *amigo*. But there are three of them."

That three stalls would specialize in serapes was hardly a surprise. But before Sand could ask if the women worked together or at three separate stalls, the vendor shifted his attention to a passing tourist, who was pale and sweating, just another disoriented survivor.

That didn't stop the vendor. In broken English, he pressed, "Hey, *gringo*! Give that pale skin some shade – you need a nice, big sombrero to keep the sun off! Ten pesos only."

The tourist stumbled on, whether hearing any of that or

not, Sand had no idea.

This did not stop the vendor, who called out, "Did I say ten? I meant *five* pesos!"

Sand was about to ask his follow-up question when the vendor turned his attention to another passerby, this one a tourist in a straw fedora, but that didn't prevent the vendor from trying to peddle a wider-brimmed alternative. Sand, realizing this merchant had already reached his limit of help, trudged on around scattered goods still not recovered from the aisle. It was a slow go.

Gradually every stall was getting itself reassembled and tidied, and those fleeing were already outnumbered by shoppers starting to fill the pathways of commerce again. He had gone another hundred yards or so when he paused where a short, rather stout woman of at least sixty perched behind a table of serapes, working on another at a backstrap loom. Her dark hair going gray, she wore glasses and a white, go-to-church dress protected by a shades of blue apron.

Sand fingered one of the brightly colored serapes, then asked, "*Quanto?*"

"Fifty pesos," she said in a bored but melodic voice, paying him scant attention, immersed in her weaving.

In Spanish he said, "I have one hundred American dollars if you can tell where to find my friend Ernesto Cuchillo."

For a moment the woman paused, then resumed her weaving. "This name I do not know."

After his years in MI6, he trusted his own instincts better than a polygraph. This lie, so casual in its delivery, suggested much to him.

"*Mi nombre es* Sand," he said. "John Sand." Continuing in Spanish, he said, "Dutch Boldt was my father-in-law, and I believe you are the mother of my friend, Ernesto Cuchillo. If you are not, you may know who she is and can direct me. It is important I find him."

She continued her work.

Sand said, dropping the Spanish, "He told you I would be coming, didn't he?"

For a long while the woman kept weaving. She might not have heard him, or perhaps his shift to English had been Greek to her.

But finally she looked his way. Her English was just fine: "If you are who you say you are, tell me something about Ernesto that only you and his mother would know."

Sand considered the question. Then: "My friend Cuchillo is a modest man. He does not display his body, though he is muscular and fit. I have seen him but once without his shirt. On his chest is a tattoo of a beautiful young woman. A woman who is close to his heart. You are that woman, *señora*, older now but still very beautiful."

Her smile was small but spoke volumes. Her eyes shone with tears not cried. "I feared you might never come, *Señor* Sand," she said, her English measured but not halting. "We must make haste – Ernesto, he is badly hurt. I have returned only just now to check on him after *la conmoción. Estaba muy asustada!*"

"That you're frightened," he said, "is understandable."

Turning to the neighboring stall, the woman said, "Juanita, watch *mi barraca* – there is an errand I must run. I will be back soon, I promise."

In the next booth a slender woman, perhaps thirty, frowned a little. "*Pero tia* Maria – you have just returned!"

"Juanita, *es muy importante.* I will be back before long."

She nodded. "*Tia* Maria, I will watch like a hawk."

Maria Cuchillo came around the table, already on the

move. "Come, *Señor*, come quickly." She was nearly a foot shorter than Sand, yet he had walk to fast to keep up, a soldier jogging alongside a tank.

She trundled through the market in the bright sunshine, then up a street, down an alley, dodging dislodged bricks, overturned outdoor furniture, the occasional fallen window air conditioner, and other remnants of the quake. For a moment Sand thought she might be trying to lose him, but soon, on a narrow street, Maria stopped before a faded blue door at a four-story faded-yellow stucco building almost overwhelmed by its protruding, haphazard balconies.

Maria looked all around, seemed satisfied, then led him inside. The hallway was dark after the sun, and on the left a staircase rose to more gloom. The building was almost ancient, but in no way dingy. He followed her up to the second floor, then the third, and down a corridor lit only by a window at the far end. Halfway down the hall, she unlocked and opened a door, led him inside, then closed and locked it again, putting the chain on.

Had you entered this living space a hundred years ago, it would not have seemed significantly different. The room was barely four-and-a-half meters square, a sliding glass door to the minuscule balcony opposite. To the left as Sand came in behind her, a plump worn sofa hugged the wall. A rectangular table and four chairs dominated the center of the room – together, they comprised the living room and dining room. The walls and the surfaces of modest furniture bore religious images and artifacts.

To his right was a sink with a small stove wedged in the corner, a short counter and a tiny icebox – the kitchen. An alcove that was probably considered a hallway led to two closed doors and an open one that gave a glimpse of a bathroom.

Maria led her guest down the alcove and opened a door, saying, "*Hijo*, I am home again already. *Your Señor* Sand has arrived."

Sand followed her into a compact bedroom where Cuchillo lay with covers at his waist, a revolver raised rather feebly in his hand. His black hair was wet and lank, hanging to his shoulders like moss from a tree, his skin pale and sweaty, chest bare with its tattoo of the younger Maria but with three bandages – two stained pink, one showing red. Sand's stomach muscles tightened.

"You look like you have a story to tell," he said to his friend.

Letting his hand with the gun rest on the bed, settling back on his pillow, Cuchillo said, "There is a short version, Mr. Sand, and a long one. The short version is, I got ambushed."

Sand sat at the bedside on a chair Maria provided. "What about Stacey?"

"She is alive as far as I know. But I hadn't caught up to her when..." He nodded to his bandaged torso.

A hundred questions boiled in Sand's brain, but he managed, "*Who* ambushed you?"

Cuchillo didn't answer, his eyes instead going to his mother near the open doorway. "*Estoy bien, mamá.* Go back to the market and tend to things. *Señor* Sand and I need to talk."

"*Estás seguro, Hijo?*"

"*Sí,* Mama, *estaré bien.* Juanita has her own stall to run."

She didn't look convinced, and raised a nearly scolding forefinger. "I will be home for lunch, *Hijo.*"

"I'll be *fine,* Mama."

Under other circumstances, Sand might have smiled at this so typical exchange between a mother and son, the hard-bitten Cuchillo reduced to just another cub.

They waited quietly until they heard the apartment door close, followed by the click of a key. The room was sparsely furnished – a single-drawer nightstand with a small lamp and a pitcher of water with half-full glass, a small dresser with a Virgin Mary picture above, and the straight-back wooden chair Sand had been provided. A window let some sunlight filter through flimsy, filmy curtains.

Sand said, "Start at the beginning. If you're not up to chapter and verse, I'll settle for the highlights."

Cuchillo nodded toward the water glass. "If I pass out, see if you can make me drink. If not, throw it in my face. There are things you need to know."

"Tell them to me."

As he spoke, Cuchillo often did so with his eyes closed, as if summoning pictures.

"All seemed fine until we got to Brownsville. At the airport, Mrs. Sand turned white as a sheet. She saw something or someone I didn't see, and it spooked her. I asked what was wrong, but she just shook her head. I thought we might go directly to the mine, and if not to the office. But as we were leaving the airport, Mrs. Sand told me to take her directly to the hotel."

"To settle in? Freshen up?"

"She didn't say and I didn't ask. She is *la jefa,* is she not? I drove her where she wanted to go."

"So you checked into Hotel El Jardín. Then what?"

"We had adjoining rooms. She knocked on my door, said she was going out shopping. She didn't need the car and I should stay at the hotel."

"Did you?"

"Yes. Understand, going shopping by herself was not unusual on such trips. Doing so before attending to business matters, perhaps. But not enough so to be overly concerning."

"Mildly concerning, though."

Cuchillo nodded.

"And then she, what? Just disappeared?"

"No. She came back, late afternoon. We discussed going to the office the next morning, visiting the mine, everything as planned. And then she said she wanted to go out for dinner by herself. That was *not* as usual."

"In what way?"

"When we are on business trips, Mr. Sand, I accompany Mrs. Sand at meals. This is partly to serve as protection. But we are longtime friends, despite our roles. By this I mean, despite her wealth and standing, she does not put on airs. We always dine together. Converse. It pleases me that she will inquire of my opinions about business, about the people she has met."

"I know she considers you a good judge of character."

"Which is why I was surprised when I asked at what time she would like me to bring the car around, to take her to dinner, that she said she was going out alone. That she needed to think. To...how did she put it? 'I need to reflect on what's ahead tomorrow.'"

Meeting with that two-person crew at the local Boldt Oil office wouldn't have required much reflection on her part.

Sand said, "Something must have been troubling her."

"I offered to drive her, drop her off and pick her up, but she said she hadn't decided where she was going. She wanted to walk to the area with restaurants nearby, and see what drew her in. She was acting very strange, Mr. Sand. Something was obviously bothering her, but I didn't pry. If she wanted to tell me, she would have told me."

"She went out to dinner, and you stayed in your room."

"No. I followed her."

Sand sat up. "To El Paraiso."

"You have not lost your skills, Mr. Sand. You questioned that assistant manager at the desk?"

"Yes, but I got that from the elevator operator."

Cuchillo smiled. "Smart old *viejo* like that sees everything."

"You followed her to the restaurant."

"Yes, but not into it. If she dined with someone, I did not see it. I waited across the way. When she came out, a car came down the street between us. Not going fast, almost...as if it were slowing for her. Again, as at the airport? She *saw* something, Mr. Sand. It was like she saw a ghost."

"A ghost called Lonestarr," Sand muttered.

Cuchillo lurched forward, despite his condition. "*Madre de díos*, but you killed that *cabrón!*"

"Maybe not. I *shot* him. He went over the side. We all assumed he was dead. But a dying woman in San Ignacio told me, 'You will never stop Jake Lonestarr.' And, Cuchillo, I believed her. Ever since, without my wife's knowledge, I've used every resource, pulled every available string, to track him down."

"And you think he got to Mrs. Sand first?"

Sand ignored that. "She was still there after the car went by?"

"Yes, and do I have to tell you how impulsive this woman is? She took off on *foot*, chasing that car!"

Sand leaned forward. "Didn't you yell at her? Let her know you were there?"

"No. I was on foot, too, remember, and just ran after her. I tried to keep up, but she is younger and she is faster, and in this? She was *relentless*. Finally, I shouted at her, calling her name...but if she heard me, she took no notice. She was headed for the bridge."

"The bridge to Mexico."

"Yes. Because of who I am, and Texas being Texas, I always carry my passport...but a block before the bridge, a car cut me off. Different car, and on purpose or not, I cannot say. But by the time I made it around the auto, and over the bridge, Mrs. Sand had already been swallowed up into Metamoros."

"What did you do?"

"I followed her. This old *federale* is good at finding people, whether they want to be found or not – especially in Mexico."

"*Did* you find her?"

"I found her trail. She had a head start, so it took tracking. I talked to cab drivers and rental companies and contacts going way back. You know how it's done. I followed her to San Luis Potosi, Guadalajara, Mexico City, and finally Acapulco."

Hope spiked through him. "Did you make contact?"

Cuchillo shook his head. "I never got close enough. But I established she had gone to the airport here. And that from here she went to Curacao."

Sand's hands were fists now. "Who or what is in Curacao?"

"I never got the chance to find out. At the airport, I bought a ticket on the flight after hers, which had just gone out. I had a two-hour wait. I had a meal. I went into the men's room to freshen up. Someone followed me in, shot me three times. I should have died."

"But you wound up here?"

"*Sí.* One of the ambulance workers knew my mama – convinced his *compadres* to take me to her, not the hospital.

And no police. She got the local doctor, a priest from the cathedral. The doctor patched me up, the priest prayed over me – no Last Rites, not yet."

"Let's put that off for a while."

"Heaven is okay, but I like it here."

Sand was up and pacing. "Someone didn't want you to follow her to Curacao. How many people knew that was where you were going?"

"From a distance, I saw Mrs. Sand go through the boarding gate to the plane for Curacao, before I booked the next flight. No one but the woman who sold me the ticket knew where I was going."

"Did you get her name?"

"Daphne, her name tag said."

"Local, do you think?"

"No. Blonde, blue-eyed. Pretty girl with the airline, like a stewardess but working the ticket counter. The only locals who work at the airport are baggage handlers and a few mechanics."

Sand had stopped pacing, standing at the foot of the bed. "All right, I always wanted to visit Curacao again. I need one more thing, if you can help me."

"What's that?"

"You wouldn't happen to have a pistol with a noise suppressor?"

Cuchillo managed a weak grin. "In the bag next to the nightstand."

Sand went over and fished it out – a Tokarev TT30 with a noise suppressor. "Where did you happen onto this?"

"I took it off the man who shot me three times. One of the men herding us."

"'Herding' us?"

"Make no mistake, Mr. Sand – Jake Lonestarr, or

whoever did this, wasn't trying to kidnap Mrs. Sand.
He wanted to lure her somewhere, maybe Curacao, but
somewhere. I followed her across Mexico. They could
have grabbed her, but they didn't. They also didn't let her
get discouraged and turn back. She was led into a trap. A
trap set for her, maybe. Or a trap for both of you. I can't
tell you that. But this was a cattle drive, pure and simple.
You and she are the beef."

"And you know," Sand said, "how a cattle drive works
out for the beef."

Somewhere a dog was barking.

"I was an annoyance they wanted out of the way,"
Cuchillo said, indicating his wounds. "If they have her
now, they must know you'll come for her."

"It's her they were after," Sand said. "They've tried to
kill me, too. More than once....Mind if I take this?"

He held up the pistol.

Cuchillo nodded, and said, "Not really mine, after all.
I'm embarrassed to say that the *bastardo* I took it from
slipped away before I could even the score."

"Perhaps I can do that for you."

Sand put the pistol in the back of his waistband; it rode
rather bulkily, but sufficed.

"You get well, *mi amigo*," Sand said. "I'm going to get
Stacey and bring her home. When we get there, and the
world is normal again, we'll need you."

Cuchillo said, "*Gracias*, my friend. But what is 'normal'
in this world in which we live?"

******

At the airport, after returning the rental Jeep, Sand had one
last thing to do before boarding the company plane for the
Curacao flight. Tom Something would have the Cessna

fueled up and ready to go, so they could leave as soon as Sand finished that task.

At the ticket counter he was pleased to find blonde, blue-eyed Daphne ready with a smile as wide as it was practiced.

"May I help you, sir?" she asked, chipper.

"The next flight to Curacao – when does it leave, and is there a seat available?"

"Well, let's just see, shall we?"

For some reason doing this took a phone call, one that Daphne made quietly, standing well away from the counter, occasionally flashing Sand a smile that somehow got even wider.

He paid cash, didn't check a bag, and when she handed him the ticket, he noticed she dipped her head slightly toward him, then, "Thank you, sir. Enjoy your flight."

"I'm sure I will," he said, smiling back at her, curious as to who behind him had been alerted by her signal. Shouldn't take long to find out.

Sand headed for the nearest men's room, entered, but instead of walking to the line of urinals to the left, he positioned himself with his back to the wall by the door at right. Sinks lined the wall near him, stalls at the rear. Several men made use of the facilities, then no one. Sand withdrew the Tokarev with the sound suppressor from his waistband.

Two men came in with pistols drawn. They had a professional look, unlike the rumpled bargain-basement East European rabble he'd been getting lately. This pair were clearly in good physical shape, one blond, one dark-haired, both in black suits with white shirts and black ties, like pallbearers. Their eyes went to the urinals.

Sand shot the gunman nearest him in the back of the head, glad to be far enough away that neither blood mist or, worse, blood and brains got on him. Instead, gore splashed the other gunman from behind, startling him, slowing his spinning around. The result was a bullet in the man's head that he had the chance to see coming, a rather neat between-the-eyes job.

Sand hoped one of these two had been the shooter who put the three bullets into Cuchillo. But this would have to do.

He used a damp paper towel to wipe his fingerprints off the silenced Tokarev, then dropped it into the waste bin with a clunk. When he exited, he noticed a DO NOT ENTER – CLOSED FOR CLEANING sign on the door, and of course left it there. They'd been professionals, all right. Just not professional enough.

At the ticket counter, he approached Daphne, whose smile turned into an O mimicked by her big blue eyes.

"I've changed my mind about going," Sand told her. "Refund, please?"

"Of...of course, sir."

She counted out the total, laid it on the counter with unsteady fingers. He traded her the ticket, gave her wink, and made his way to the terminal where the company plane awaited.

His send-off from Acapulco had certainly been memorable. Sand could only wonder what kind of warm welcome awaited him in Curacao.

THREE

A MOST DANGEROUS GAME

MAY 1962

CHAPTER FOURTEEN
DUTCH TREAT

Having left scenic Acapulco behind in the aftermath of an earthquake and a trail of bloody bodies, Sand gazed out at vivid blue, crystal-clear Caribbean waters surrounding an island that looked like he could put it in his pocket.

His destination was Willemstad, capital of Curacao, and the only city of any size there. After Tom set the Cessna down at the International Airport, Sand told the pilot, "Grab what you need. I hope to have Mrs. Sand in tow when we leave."

"Any idea when that will be, Mr. Sand?"

"None. In the meantime, I'll get you a room at the Avila Beach Hotel. Nicest hotel on the island."

"You've been here before, sir?"

"A few years ago, yes."

A taxi took them to the hotel, whose main building – the Belle Alliance – was an old Dutch colonial mansion from the late 18th century. Now it was a spruced-up peach-colored two-story with white shutters and the only hotel in Willemstad on the water.

At the front desk in the modern lobby, Sand booked a

room for a week for Tom and sent him off with his key, then lingered for a talk with the front desk clerk. Tall, thin, his crisp jacket the same peach shade as the hotel's exterior, Claude – as his ID badge labeled him – had close-clipped blond hair, a sharp chin that lent him a triangular look, and a bored professionalism.

"Was there something else, sir?"

"My wife isn't expecting me," Sand said, "but I believe she's registered here. Mrs. John Sand. Stacey Sand."

The man nodded. "Mrs. Sand *was* a guest here for two nights, sir. She checked out yesterday afternoon."

"Leave any forwarding address?"

"I'm sorry, sir, she did not."

"May I be frank with you?"

"Sir?"

"We had a spat a few days ago. Then I went off on a short business trip, and discovered when I returned she'd gone off without me. My travel agent says she came to Curacao and had a reservation here. I am hoping for a reconciliation."

Understandably, this was not a conversation the clerk seemed comfortable having. Somehow he managed, "Well, sir, I wish you luck. But I don't see how I can help."

"I wondered if you knew if she had received any visitors. Perhaps dined here at the hotel and met with friends of ours on the island. Anything at all you might remember."

"Not really, sir."

Sand dug out his money clip and peeled off a twenty American, dropped it on the counter. "Anything?"

"I was the one who checked her in, Mr. Sand, Wednesday. And as it happened, I checked her out yesterday afternoon."

"No one was accompanying her? Meeting her?"

"No, sir."

Sand pushed the twenty forward.

The clerk shook his head. "That's not necessary, sir."

"Keep it. Now...I'd like to book a room for myself."

Sand checked in and took his duffel up to a room with a lot of charm – rattan furnishings, more peach coloration, and a view of the beach and cottages lining it. He put on a pale blue Polo, got into his shoulder sling with Walther, and slipped on a dark blue blazer. He was ready to go.

But where?

He was a day behind Stacey, unsure of where to look next. Now that she'd checked out, she could easily have yet another stop on her peripatetic itinerary. Should he return to the airport and ask at every ticket counter if she'd booked herself somewhere? Of course, she might have gone by boat, which meant checking at steamship offices.

No, he thought, *you're getting ahead of yourself.* He hadn't even determined she'd left the island.

As he'd told his pilot, Sand had been here before. In 1958 he joined CIA agent Lyman and several Dutch agents to protect Curacaoan oil refineries from Russian interference. Those refineries – which provided seventy percent of the oil used by the Allies in World War II – were no less important during the Cold War. And MI6, the CIA, and the General Intelligence and Security Service of the Dutch government had successfully prevented saboteurs from setting the refineries ablaze.

With those memories stirring a thought, Sand went down to the lobby and out of the hotel to take one of the waiting taxis. His driver was Afro-Curacaoan in loose-fitting white shirt and slacks, with an easy smile under a pencil mustache and short black hair visible beneath a straw Panama hat.

"Where to, boss?"

"Netto Bar."

"Good choice, boss." He put the taxi in gear. "No danger in Curacao. Very safe place."

That would make a nice change.

A pleasant breeze riffled Sand's hair and the brim of the cabbie's Panama, as they traveled with the windows down. Even though it nestled in the sunny Caribbean, Willemstad reminded Sand of The Hague or Delft, cities in the Netherlands where buildings huddled close together. The difference was the exterior walls here were painted brighter colors – blues, greens, yellows. Within fifteen minutes, the cab pulled up in front of the Netto Bar.

Sand asked the cabbie, "Would one-hundred dollars American buy me a driver for the rest of the day?"

Big smile under the little mustache. "It would buy *this* one, boss."

Sand gave the friendly driver a fifty and told him to stay put, adding that the other fifty would come at day's end.

The words *Netto Bar* were splashed in blue script on a red facade with jailhouse-like red doors slid aside to reveal customers on stools at the edge of the beckoning darkness, away from insistent sunlight. About the size of a carriage on the London Underground, with one end open onto the street, the dive boasted small round tables and a few mismatched chairs scattered along at left, a bar running down the wall opposite. Rounded off at the end near the entry, the counter itself had a leaping swordfish painted on it. Unframed watercolors of Willemstad scenes were stuck on the yellow walls here and there, as were snapshots of happy customers. A laundry line of Christmas bulbs hung across the room for a year-round festive flavor.

Four patrons were dispersed two to a table, with

another standing at the bar (it bore no stools). The latter customer slipped into the men's room as Sand approached the counter.

None of the patrons seemed threats; no Russian military base haircuts among them. Those at the tables were obvious regulars, and the gent who went into the GENTS was an aging, stooped career drinker. The bartender was female and stood perhaps a meter and three quarters, her body lithe under an orange football jersey (of the national team of the Netherlands) and tight jeans. A messy pile of brown hair, barely held in check by a wide red headband, rose above her ivory forehead, her features splitting the difference between pretty and cute. She had the look of a woman who could teach you things.

Her big brown eyes seemed happy to see him, but she was already shaking her head when he leaned on the bar and said, "I'll have a Red Stripe."

"Why, you think this is Jamaica, cowboy?" the bartender asked with a faux Jamaican accent.

"You had it the last time I came in."

She grunted a laugh and went to the cooler, pulled a bottle of Red Stripe, and slid it down the bar to him. "How the hell have you been, John?"

He shrugged. "Good days, bad days, and the inevitable in between. How goes it with you, Lena?"

A tad closer to forty than Sand, Lena De Jong had been a member of the Dutch contingent on the refinery mission. Sand had heard that she walked away from espionage after that episode – it had been a bloody affair...the mission that is, not *their* affair – and had become a bartender and co-owner here at Netto's, where she'd worked undercover.

"Not a dull life," she said. She had a cloth and cleaned the bar in front him, sporadically. "But not a lively one, either."

"Miss it?"

She shrugged. "If I get an itch, there's always a couple of loudmouths getting into a fight I can break up."

"Which makes you feel like a real woman again?"

"Which makes me feel like a woman who can handle *any* man. I heard *you* found the exit, too."

"I did. I'm an executive now. A vice president. Still in oil, like the last time I was on the island. Only this job pays better."

She smirked prettily at him. Or perhaps cutely. "Pays better to have a rich wife. But why is a vice president, an executive, packing heat? Surely you can afford having a tailor make that less obvious. Or are you just glad to see me?"

He patted the Walther under his left arm. "If you think it comes up to here, Lena, your memory's playing tricks. But thanks for the compliment."

She eyed him skeptically. "In a way I'm not all that surprised see you."

"Oh?"

"I heard there was a big-shot Brit on the island. I just didn't know it was you."

He frowned. "News travels fast on Curacao, considering I just got here."

"Not *that* fast," she said, frowning a little. Then she shrugged. "Wasn't you, then. That rumor goes back a day or so."

Could the rumor have referred to Lord Malcolm Marbury?

Sand was half-way through the Red Stripe. It wasn't particularly good, but had a sweetness and heavy carbonation he liked, and reminded him of his time with Lena.

He asked, "Where's this Brit staying, do you know?"

"Not in town. Up north somewhere. Some rich guy has a compound up there." She held his gaze. "It's one of those places you hear about."

"*What* do you hear about it?"

"Weird things."

"Such as?"

Her eyes widened momentarily. "Such as people go there and never come back."

"Lose anyone you know?"

"Not yet." She smirked again. "Don't pay that any heed. This is an island, and all islands are superstitious."

"Certainly. They avoid walking under ladders in Manhattan, for instance. Shun black cats."

"I don't."

Sand filed away Lena's rumor. He would find Double M, of course, but the priority – obviously – was Stacey.

He said, "You seem to know who I'm married to."

"Of course. For a spy, you're famous."

"Thanks so much. My wife came to the island alone, two days ago. Lena, no prying questions, now. Where would you suggest I look for her?"

"Alone, you say."

"I think so."

"You've tried the Avila Beach Hotel?"

"I just checked in. But she checked out, yesterday."

A slow nod from Lena. "And you don't know if she's left the island."

"I do not. But I do know she is almost certainly in danger."

"I thought you were retired, John."

"Tell that to the assassins I've been killing left and right."

That didn't even faze her. She just rubbed the bar down with her cloth and thought. And thought.

Finally she said, "There is a man. Surprisingly young man. He came to the island a year ago. He's an investor here, has pumped a lot of money into Curacao. And he's made it part of his business to always have his finger on the pulse of whatever's going on."

"I assume he has a name?"

"Milan Meier. His company is *Energie-Instituut* – the Energy Institute. Perhaps you've heard of it."

He hadn't. "Where can I find this Meier?"

"At his *landhuis* – how do you say it in English? A manor, near *Boka Labadera,* that cove across the island from here. He calls it *Landhuis Paradijs.*"

"Paradise Manor?"

"Yes."

"This isn't that place up north where people disappear?"

"No." She smiled. "That's a different eccentric rich guy."

"What kind of man is *this* 'eccentric rich guy'? Have you met him?"

She laughed lightly. "Well, he's not a regular at the Netto. But I *did* meet him once, at a charity event at the hotel – a rare public appearance."

"Keeps to himself?"

"That's fair to say. He's unmarried but, as far as I know, isn't seeing anyone, at least not on the island. Younger than either of us, maybe...thirty? For someone not known to be sociable, though, I found him charming. They say everything he touches turns to gold, or perhaps platinum. As I say, he's put plenty of money into the island. I haven't heard a bad word said about him, not even a jealous one. They say he always knows what's going on everywhere – not just on the island, but around the world, in commerce, in politics. I've heard it said he's something of a...a seer."

Sand thought that was a little much, but he said only, "You think this Meier might be able to help find my wife?"

"If anybody can. You could go to the police, the airport, go door to door to every home on Curacao, do all of that yourself – but I would start with Milan Meier. He can get all of that for you and more with a few phone calls."

Sand leaned over the bar. "If I tried to tip you one-hundred American dollars, what would you do?"

She kissed him, short and sweet. "Just pay for the Red Stripe and we don't have to mess up your marriage."

He complied.

Climbing into the waiting cab, Sand said, "The Milan Meier manor – know it?"

"For a hundred dollars," the cabbie said with a grin, "what *don't* I know about Curacao? Seventeen kilometers. Other side of the island."

A tall stone wall surrounded the estate with a high wrought-iron gate; it might have seemed an impenetrable fortress if that gate weren't standing open, unguarded. The big wide two-story house – burnt-yellow with an orange-tiled roof and prominent peaked gables – stood out against the blue water behind it like a huge yellow ship ready to set sail. Its windows and trim were painted white, the double door a rich forest green. The buildings on Curacao were nothing if not colorful. This one might have been a church on the Island of Lost Boys.

The taxi came up the bricked circle drive and stopped behind four cars parked there, a steel blue Jaguar convertible, a silver Aston Martin, a pale green Studebaker Avanti, and a black Lincoln Continental.

"Your wait may be minutes," Sand advised the cabbie, who was already unwrapping a sandwich from somewhere, "or it might be hours."

The cabbie had a bottle of Coke now, too. "I live much of my life in this buggy, boss. Whether it's rolling or not."

Sand accepted that at face value and walked across the brick apron to a surprisingly modest stoop up to the two twin green doors within their white cathedral-like framing. The place said money, but did so cheerfully.

He was just about to knock when he heard voices neither nearby nor distant – from the back of the mansion? The big structure was surrounded by brick walkways and Sand took the one to the left, which widened behind the house into a patio overlooking a swimming pool and, beyond, a drop to a private beach and of course the endless cool Caribbean Sea.

Two men lounged in Adirondack chairs, a small matching table nearby with a pitcher of probable martinis on a tray with cocktail glasses. The man nearer Sand was perhaps sixty, in a loose-fitting lightweight white suit, his Panama hat in his lap. Shirt white, tie muted blue. Hair graying at the temples and clipped short, his face was a narrow oval, his slitted eyes overwhelmed by out of control eyebrows.

"I will put that in motion," he said, matter of fact. "It will be done before the end of the day."

The other appeared no older than Sand and possibly younger, yet with utterly white hair combed back on a high brow, very pale skin, and piercing ice-blue eyes. His off-white shirt was open at the throat, his slacks a slightly darker shade, a light tan jacket slung over the back of the chair.

He had already noticed Sand. His cupid lips were pursed in an almost smile, as if he might laugh at any moment if only someone would say something funny, but no one ever had.

The young man with white hair said, "You look lost."

"I don't believe I am," Sand said, stepping deeper onto the patio, "if you're Milan Meier."

"Then you *aren't* lost."

Sand's eyes went from his sudden host to the man's other guest and back again, then said, "I really don't mean to interrupt."

"Petrus was just about to leave," the white-haired young man said. "Isn't that right, Petrus? Aren't you just about to leave?"

The older man thought about that for a moment, then stood. "Yes, yes I was. I will take care of what we discussed."

Sand and the gentleman exchanged nods as the latter headed around the house.

Just the two of them now. Sand said, "My name is Sand, John Sand."

And finally the white-haired young man had heard something that could make him laugh, clapping his hands as he did so.

"I've been known," Sand admitted, "to make the occasional bon mot. But never before has just my name done the trick."

His host rose from his chair with an apologetic expression. He was almost as tall as Sand and at least as fit.

"Forgive my laughter, Mr. Sand. Certainly I'm not laughing at you, and considering what I *know* about you, I hope I'd never be so foolish. No, I am laughing at the serendipitous nature of this world of ours." Milan Meier extended his hand. "I am delighted to meet you."

"And I you," Sand said, as they shook hands, his host's grip firm and confident, but not showy.

"I have of course heard of you, Mr. Sand, and I really should have recognized you from the newspapers and magazines. Of course, I'd venture to say you were known in some circles well before your former colleague began plundering your past for thriller fodder."

"It didn't feel like 'fodder' at the time," Sand said with a smile. "What is it you find serendipitous about my dropping by?"

The white-haired young man raised a forefinger as if testing the direction of the wind. "As your host, I reserve the right to postpone my explanation for a short while longer."

"I would prefer you didn't."

He held up a palm. "Your abilities are legend at this point, but I am really quite impressed that you found your way to my door. You simply must share how you managed that."

Getting irritated, Sand said, "I'm here because I was advised you might be able to help me find my wife."

Meier huffed a chuckle – at least it wasn't a full-throated laugh or Sand might have throttled him.

"Mr. Sand, this just gets better and better. You mean to say you were not already aware that she's here?"

"*Here?*"

Meier gestured vaguely. "Just inside. Freshening up after a swim, and no doubt trying to call you for the umpteenth time. She'll join us here on the patio any moment now."

Sand started toward the house and Meier stepped between it and him. They almost collided.

Meier's eyes lit up. "Come and sit. Let me pour you a martini – the taste should be familiar, because Mrs. Sand whipped up this batch herself, in your honor...vodka. I understand that 'shaken but not stirred' stuff is nonsense. Come, come and tell me how you found us. Stacey will be along in a moment."

After all he'd been through, Sand felt both gobsmacked and blindsided. He actually could use a martini. He sat near the table and accepted a glass Meier poured for him.

"Stacey is *here*," Sand said, still not quite believing it. "For how long?"

"Since yesterday," Meier said. "A contact at the hotel informed me of her presence. I was pleasantly surprised to find Mrs. Sand on the island. I've been eager to meet her, to make contact. I'm hoping my *Engerie Instituut* might do business with Boldt Energy."

Rather numbly Sand said, "We haven't announced the company name change yet."

Meier smiled, shrugged, beyond casual. "It is my business to know the competition, to learn about my possible partners, Mr. Sand...and keep tabs on the industry in general. It's not enough to know my business. I need to know everyone *else's*."

Stacey's voice: "He's still not there! I keep getting that person who may or may not be an FBI man."

She strode quickly out of a back door onto the patio, typically beautiful in the sleeveless black jumpsuit she'd been wearing when she disappeared. It looked none the worse for wear – freshly washed by her, most likely. Sunlight highlighted her auburn hair as it careened off her shoulders, and a few moments passed before she saw him sitting there large as life, her green eyes going so wide they showed white all around, her expression almost comically stunned.

Perhaps not almost: their host was laughing again.

"Priceless," Meier said. "The look on her face!"

Sand wore no expression. Relief surged through him, and anger, and the two emotions fought within him leaving his reaction outwardly blank.

She rushed to him as he stood. Looked up at him. "What are you doing here? *How* are you here?"

"I was looking for my wife," he said. "And I seem to have found her."

She clutched his sleeve. "John, Lonestarr's alive! Jake Lonestarr is *alive!*"

"Never mind any of that," he said, and took her into his arms and held her. They clutched each other.

Meier was looking on, clearly not knowing what to think, much less to say.

"With apologies, sir," Sand said, without looking at him. "Could you give us a little time?"

Their host nodded graciously and went quickly into the burnt-yellow house through the door Stacey had exited.

They took the two chairs and scooched them together, sitting with knees touching, bending toward the other, grasping each other's hands.

"I knew the bastard was alive," Sand said, "or at least suspected."

He told her what the dying woman had said in San Ignacio, and admitted privately searching for Lonestarr through various contacts.

"So much for no more secrets," she said quietly, not looking at him, withdrawing her hands.

"I didn't *know* he was alive. I suspected, I said."

Now she looked at him. "Well, *I* saw him."

They held hands again.

And she told him her story, of glimpsing Lonestarr at the Brownsville airport, of seeing a car with him smiling at her from the back seat outside El Paraiso, then speeding off. Of following him on foot across the bridge to Matamoros. By cab to the airport where he went to Mexico City, and then on to Acapulco. She lost him there, but then she'd bribed a blonde ticket clerk to give her the Curacao lead.

He began to tell her his story, but she stopped him at the Brownsville fire fight.

"That was *you?*" she asked, wide-eyed again. "I read about it!"

He nodded.

She was thinking "Wait...and Morello? That was *you, too?*"

He shrugged, vaguely embarrassed. "I thought he took you."

Her eyes were wide again. "You've been busy."

Then he told her about Las Vegas, and GUILE, and how Marbury was taken and the wholesale carnage left behind by the raiders, discreetly leaving out Charlotte's role. He told her briefly of the East European hitmen he'd tangled with in Acapulco, the earthquake, and what happened to Cuchillo, who'd been tracking her. It took some reassuring to calm her, after she heard Cuchillo had been shot.

Sand said, "Cuchillo says we were being herded into a trap, but I can't put it together – everyone seems to want *me* dead, but there seem to have been no overt attempts on *your* life."

She confirmed that. "I've been the one hunting," she said. "I should have talked to the FBI on the phone, shouldn't I?"

"Yes, but I understand your hesitation. Just because someone says he's FBI doesn't make him J. Edgar Hoover or his janitor for that matter."

"The only voice I would've believed was you." She came over and sat in his lap. "You came looking for me. You came looking and you killed anyone who got in your path. For *me*."

"Well, for you and my own bloody ass."

She laughed and played with his hair. "What now? Back to Houston finally? Regroup and figure what the next step is where Lonestarr's concerned? Of course, this may all have been about shutting down this new spy group you're embroiled in, this GUILE."

"It might be at that. Which leads us back to Lord Marbury."

"Your precious Double M. But what can we do about that?"

"I have a lead," he said.

CHAPTER FIFTEEN
FIRST LONESTARR I SEE TONIGHT

As they talked, the Sands took a stroll around the pool. Its sparkle of blue was but a prelude to the vast blue of the ocean below and beyond, which glimmered with gold from the dying sun as if thousands of pirate doubloons were scattered just beneath its surface.

"How did you happen to end up here," he asked her, his hand slipped in hers, "as a house guest?"

"Milan called me at the hotel," she said, "and invited me for lunch. I knew of him, of course – and he'd been pointed out to me at an International Atomic Energy Agency seminar. You remember me attending that last year?"

Sand nodded.

"He drove me personally to Jaanchie's in Westpunt. Lovely part of the island, oldest restaurant in Curacao."

"I've been there. I hope you tried the iguana."

"Uh, no...I'm more a Mahi Mahi girl. At any rate, in the midst of a nice relaxing lunch, Milan said he didn't wish to concern me, but a man eating alone over in the corner had followed us. At least Milan thought he had."

Sand stopped, locked eyes with her. "Tell me."

"Well, of course, I hadn't mentioned my real reason for coming to the island. He knew nothing of my hunt for Jake Lonestarr. But the man he pointed out, I'd seen before. He'd been driving when I saw Lonestarr in that car in Brownsville. A Latino, probably Mexican."

"Possibly Jesus Guerra. A crony of Lonestarr's."

"We were almost finished dining. Soon we were back in Milan's Jaguar, and we were followed, all right. But Milan outran him. And despite the high speed, he questioned me, and I told him why I was in Curacao, and why I was trying to find Jake Lonestarr."

"Did he agree to help?"

The lap, lap, lap of the pool water in the sea breeze might have soothed Sand. It didn't.

"Actually he got very quiet," Stacey said. "Milan insisted I leave the hotel and come stay here until he could do some checking – that if Jake is on the island, Milan would find out. He drove me back to the Avila and I got my luggage and checked out, and moved in here."

"What's Meier's interest in all this? Or is it the obvious?"

"The obvious?"

He gave her half a smile. "What any heterosexual male wants from a woman who looks like you."

That prompted the bubbling laugh he knew so well. "He doesn't want my body, John – he wants my uranium."

Sand thought about that. "Well, maybe he isn't heterosexual."

"It hasn't come up," she said.

He gave her a look. "I'll do the jokes, dear. But I do see your point. You're good at your job and make a practice of knowing what your competitors are after."

"That's right," she said. "And what Milan's after is any uranium we don't utilize in the United States. He has power plants planned all over Europe."

"A man who looks at you and thinks only of his profit margin has warped priorities."

The laugh bubbled again. "As a man *Life* magazine described as 'Mr. Kiss Kiss Bang Bang,' you may have warped priorities yourself, John Sand. Actually, Milan's priorities include hoping to improve life on this planet."

"Better here than Mars, I suppose."

They began to stroll again.

She said, "Milan is keenly aware that fossil fuels – oil in particular – will be played out sometime in the next century. Mankind itself is at stake. And he views Jake Lonestarr as an ecological menace."

"He might well have felt the same way about your father."

She shrugged. "That's occurred to me, but it's a moot point. And Milan knows I am looking ahead to atomic energy. He wants to help us find and stop Lonestarr. He's a pacifist, and would *not* be happy to know how we might deal with Jake."

Sand shook his head. "Getting Lonestarr extradited from here to the United States would be virtually impossible."

"I'm aware of that."

As they continued to romantically stroll, Sand said to her, "Darling, I intend to kill the son of a bitch."

"And I intend to help you. But where Milan is concerned...let's stop short of making that point, shall we? Discretion, John. The most famous spy in the world certainly knows how to be discreet."

"If I were discreet," he said, "I wouldn't be the most famous spy in the world....let's go talk to our host."

She led him directly into a spacious living room, its walls white and tastefully popping with paintings by Kandinsky, Pollock and Rothko, abstract works any museum might envy. The furnishings were modernist as well – functional but elegant, colors limited to black-and-white, though chrome gleamed here and there. The oak flooring somehow went well with it all, as if Nature was reminding anything manmade that She was here first.

Windows on the ocean side of the place were tall and cracked open, letting a breeze blow gently through and making wispy ghosts of filmy curtains. In the middle of the room was a circular black carpet with a geometric design in white, about three and a half meters in diameter, where sat a half-circle white couch across from its white mate, which formed the rest of the circle. In between was a chrome-and-glass coffee table, its top empty but for a black onyx ashtray, an under shelf bearing a few Dutch periodicals – *Elsevier, HP/De Tijd, Autoweek.*

They were looking around for their host when, providing a glimpse of a modern kitchen, he emerged from an open doorway with a Deco silver pot and tray, the latter bearing jade-green glassware – three cups, sugar bowl, small pitcher of cream. Wearing the tan jacket over his white shirt and slacks, he placed the tray on the coffee table and asked, "Coffee? Or does my British guest prefer tea? I chose this over more cocktails, as I assume we have things to talk about."

"Coffee is fine," Sand said. He nodded around. "These paintings are original, I take it?"

"Yes. When I began to make money, they were among my first purchases. As was this home."

The white-haired young man gestured for them to take one of the half-circle couches and began to pour for them, leaving any sugar or cream to their discretion; both husband and wife had theirs black.

Meier took cream and sugar. He settled back with his cup and stirred. "This villa was built in 1750 and I've found I take rather a perverse pleasure in melding the old with the new. It is a reminder that we have been here a while but have come a distance."

Sand got out his deck of *Gauloises*. "Do you mind?"

"Not at all," his host said. "You two were able to... catch up, I trust?"

Stacey said, "We were, Milan, thank you."

Sand let the rich smoke have at him, let it out, then said, "I see no sign of security here. And those paintings, and for that matter I would imagine much else, would be well worth stealing."

"I do have a security staff. But they keep out of sight, particularly when I have guests. Obtrusive security can make one a prisoner in one's own home."

"No one stopped me just walking around the house," Sand said. "Perhaps they could stand to be somewhat *more* obtrusive."

Meier smiled, shrugged. "They'd been told you might drop by. I distributed a photo of you."

Sand's eyebrows rose. "You happened to have one on hand, did you?"

"No. I clipped it from a magazine."

"You were expecting me?"

Meier sipped coffee. "Not necessarily. But after talking to your lovely wife, I thought it highly probable you might drop by out of the blue. And, if so, did not want you to feel unwelcome – or, perhaps, encourage you teaching my security team any new tricks."

The hotel had probably informed Meier of Sand's presence, as they had about Stacey when she registered. But Sand said nothing, not wanting to be a bad guest.

After another drag on the cigarette, Sand said, "My wife tells me you've been kind enough to inquire around about Jake Lonestarr. Have you had any luck?"

Meier finished his coffee and set the cup back on the tray. "I have not been entirely frank with either of you."

Sand and his wife traded sharp, troubled looks.

Meier raised a calming palm. "Nothing to be alarmed about. It's just that I started looking into this matter some time before Mrs. Sand asked me to. You see, when the rumors began to circulate about strange things happening at a certain hunting lodge up north, I inquired into who the new owner was. The name on the deed was Joakim De Ster, but people upon whom I rely, who had met him, informed me that he was American, not Dutch. But as far as confirming he was indeed Jake Lonestarr, I was at a dead-end."

Sand asked, "Were you ever able to establish it?"

"I was. I have."

"How?"

"I met him. Face to face. *He* was in magazines and newspapers from time to time, too, you know."

Sand sat forward. So did Stacey.

"We met at that lodge itself," Meier went on. "He rarely leaves there, but apparently my inquiries attracted his attention. He invited me and I went – some of that security I mentioned accompanied me. But nothing sinister or threatening transpired. He wanted to talk business."

"Uranium," Sand said.

"Energy in general, but yes. Uranium. It was a preliminary talk, no follow-up as yet. This was just a little over a week ago."

Sand and Stacey exchanged glances – Jake Lonestarr was not only alive, he was indeed on this island.

"Let me first say," Meier said, holding up both palms now, "that this individual has never been officially suspected of any crime on Curacao much less charged with any. Obviously, he committed crimes in the United States, but that is of no concern here...and, anyway, he's not Lonestarr here, but De Ster."

How long had Lonestarr had been using the De Ster alias, Sand wondered? Could it have been as far back as when that German gunman in Berlin had warned him about "der Hollander"?

Sand asked, "Have you alerted the American government that Lonestarr's on Curacao?"

"I spoke to the counsel, but – as the man who 'killed' Jake Lonestarr, Mr. Sand – you can surely imagine the re-action. Then I got in touch with various American contacts, in and out of government, and got nowhere. Jake Lonestarr is a dead man, as far as officialdom is concerned."

Stacey was frowning. "Milan, if you knew all of this when I first told you I was looking for Lonestarr, why in God's name did you keep it from me?"

His sigh was endless, his eyes downcast. "Forgive me, but...Stacey, you made your intentions clear to me. At least you did before you knew my position on violence – that I would never condone extra-legal retribution."

"Are you sure," Sand said, biting off the words, "this isn't more about protecting your precious position on the island? About not risking your reputation or suffering any legal repercussions?"

Meier gave that a dismissive wave. "Those are consid-erations, yes. And I certainly don't rule out helping you. What would you have me do? Keep in mind I won't be party to murder."

"If I pledge to you," Sand said, "that you would not be

aiding and abetting such an act? That I will limit any show of violence to self-defense? Would that be enough?"

"What will you do with him, this Lonestarr-by-any-other-name?"

"Throw him on my private plane and fly him to American justice."

Their host considered that, then asked, "What do you want from me?"

"Strictly information. No one will know you were who directed us to that hunting lodge. It's information we could get elsewhere, after all. Why not save us a step?"

"True." He shrugged. "It's near Savonet Plantation – hectares of jungle where Lonestarr and his cronies hunt."

"Do you know, or can you at least estimate, how many people he has? Can you give us the layout of this lodge?"

"Before you go I'll put something on paper for you. But there's something you don't yet know – the nature of those rumors that initiated my interest in 'Der Ster.' The reason why they say people go there and don't return – the nature of the game Lonestarr hunts."

Sand knew at once. "People."

Stacey hadn't guessed it. She didn't scare easily but when Sand glanced her way, she'd gone white as the walls around them, her eyes wild as the crazy paintings hanging there.

Preparations were made – a roughed-out floor plan, just the first floor, as Meier hadn't been on the half-floor where the bedrooms were; a map of as much of the grounds as Meier had seen, including private quarters for staff.

They had cleared the glass coffee table and were going over sketches Meier made when Sand asked, "Any idea how many men he has?"

Meier said, "I saw three, no, four locals. And the Latino

who followed Mrs. Sand and I to Jaanchie's. And then there's a right-hand man, a formidable fellow. Those locals called him *Kraai*. That's 'Crow' in Netherlandic."

Stacey gripped Sand's arm.

Meier looked up, his expression regretful, almost sad. "I cannot offer you any of my security team. No men. No guns."

Sand said, "I'm not asking for any."

"Do you have a car?"

"I hired a cab. That won't do. I'll dismiss him."

Meier nodded. "Take one of my vehicles. Can you... what's the American slang for starting a car by connecting wires in its electrical system?"

"Hot-wiring," Stacey said. "I'll do it."

That impressed and amused Sand.

Meier said, "You will take the highway forty kilometers northwest of Willemstad."

Sand asked, "Which car shall I take?"

"The Jaguar. Why not live a little?"

"I hope to."

Stacey said, "Why are you doing this, Milan? Why take *any* risk helping us?"

"If the rumors are true, this man is a monster, and a blight on my little island. And don't forget if you are successful, a ruthless competitor of mine will be eliminated. Then, too, you will be grateful for my assistance when we next sit down to discuss business."

With a half-smile, Sand said, "And here I thought you just wanted to make the world a better place."

Meier's head went back as he shrugged. "We in the Netherlands have been prosperous since the war. We have great freedoms, possibly more even than America. Am I an altruistic dreamer, believing every citizen of the world is deserving of those same freedoms? Anyway, my friend – weren't *you* trying to make the world a better place in your former profession?"

"Mostly," Sand said, "I was just trying to survive."

******

Before they left, Sand escorted Stacey outside onto the patio. The sinking sun had set the sea on fire, a conflagration that would soon go out with a dousing of night. He asked her to please stay here and let him do this alone.

"No," she said.

"I'll spend all of my time worrying about you, and – "

"No," she said.

"We've been through some dangerous times together, but nothing like this. Do this for me. Stay here."

"No," she said.

It went on for a while. She hot-wired the car while Sand went to send the cabbie off, with a final fifty dollar payment. He came back and shook Meier's hand and thanked the man. Then Stacey gave their host a perfunctory hug and they were on their way.

Traffic was almost non-existent on the quiet highway.

"What's our plan?" she asked.

"Kill Lonestarr."

"Not throw him in the Cessna, and – "

"Is that your preference?"

"Hardly. But you promised Milan that – "

"I'm a spy. Spies lie all the damn time."

"You're an *ex*-spy, my darling."

"Yes." He grinned at her, enjoying the feel of the Jag, the power. "But not an ex-liar."

They turned off the highway onto a two-lane dirt road that eventually narrowed into one lane with only the Jag's headlights guiding them through the thickness of jungle, a canopy of branches keeping even the moon from being much help.

"Where's this celebrated compound," Stacey said as they bounced along the rutted road through too much darkness.

"I think we're in it," Sand said.

"No walls? No guards?"

"Possibly the latter. They could be spotted all along here. That there's one lane doesn't exactly make guarding it harder."

They were several kilometers from where the dirt road had left the highway when headlights burst on behind him.

The Range Rover had either been tucked into a jungle path or possibly followed them from the turn. Stacey was staring back at what was like a bright-eyed beast bearing down on them.

Sand picked up speed, braving the rough dirt road. At least nobody was shooting at them from the Range Rover, which meant somebody wanted them alive. With only one direction in which to travel, Sand said softly, "Goddamnit," and let up on the gas.

She said, "Why the hell are you slowing down?"

Stacey was frightened and he hated that.

"We can't outrun them," he said, "and we're trashing Milan's lovely car. We're being herded again, darling, and we might as well go along."

"There must be *something* we can do!"

"There is. Let them take us to Lonestarr. We wanted to find him, and it looks like we have."

"You're awfully relaxed about it!"

"I killed him once." He gave her a jaunty smile showing more confidence than he felt. "I'll just kill him again."

"More thoroughly this time please!"

The Jag, taking its time now, followed a curve in the path, then Sand slammed on the brakes when the headlights of three vehicles came on at once. Three more Range Rovers were spread at rest across a sudden widening of the road, and now there was nowhere to take the Jag at any speed.

They stopped.

Waited.

The passenger door jerked open, and Stacey lurched toward Sand, who slipped his right arm around her shoulder. A pockmarked face leaned in – Jesus Guerra, most likely, black hair slicked back, his smile going up, the tips of his bandito mustache going down. In his unbuttoned-at-the-neck white dress shirt and black slacks, this might have been a waiter who had just knocked off for the night.

Guerra grabbed Stacey's arm and she squealed, punching at him, but the man was stronger and dragged her out of the car and away from Sand, whose hand went under his coat for his Walther, but the driver's side door swung open and Crow was there, big and ugly as life, in a blue-and-black tropical-print camp shirt and jeans, a .45 auto in his fist.

"Go ahead and draw," Crow said, grinning. "I can wait."

Sand removed his hand from under his coat and let Crow pry him out from behind the Jag's wheel. Crow helped himself to the Walther, his .45 still trained on Sand.

"Let's have the Beretta, too," the big Indian said. "Two fingers – be stupid, if you wanna be dead."

Sand did as he was told, then once the guns were gathered by others, Crow motioned toward Sand and a crony frisked him, relieving the prisoner of his switchblade as well. The Indian marched Sand into the still-burning headlights of the Jag, merging with those of the Range Rovers. Crow, .45 on Sand, turned his captive around to face the trio of vehicles and their near-blinding lights. Guerra did the same with Stacey.

From between the middle Range Rover and its neighbor, emerged a tall, thin, gray-haired man sporting a salt-and-pepper mustache that overwhelmed his grin. He was decked out in a khaki safari suit like a big game hunter, if a big game hunter wore a black Stetson.

"Well, the Sands," Jake Lonestarr said. "How long has it been, anyway?"

Stacey hurled a physically impossible suggestion at her father's old partner, but he only chuckled.

"You have spirit, girl. You always have had." The lanky sociopath turned his attention to Sand. Lonestarr was keeping his distance. No need to get spat on or jumped by a heroic husband trying some stunt.

"I'm going to make this short," Lonestarr said. "We have options, you and I." He was speaking to Stacey again. "Your father could have done business with me, if he'd had the sense. I took his life, but it was self-defense."

Now the madman spoke to Sand.

"*You* were there! He came aboard, and so did you, with guns, ready to kill us! You *tried* to kill us! We were too strong for you, Raven and I. He had brawn and I had a bullet-proof vest." His laugh was a cackle. "But you, darling child..." Eyes were back on Stacey. "...you are a better 'man' of business than poor Dutch ever was. Oh, he was strong in his day, but he got soft. And he didn't keep up. You keep up!"

She made the same suggestion as before, but a sob interrupted it.

"If only your father had...kept up, listened to reason,

been as smart as his daughter. Why, we could have all been rich together. We *still* could! You have better sense than him, Stacey. You already figured out that atomic energy is the future – that uranium mines are the new gold and silver."

"If you think I'd do business with you," Stacey said, "you're even crazier than I thought."

"Don't be so hasty, child. That's how your father got himself in trouble. I'll make you a partner. You can run things in America. And we can all be filthy rich."

"I'd sooner do business with Hitler," she said.

Lonestarr shrugged. "You're too tired from what I put you through to think straight. My fault, really. You had such a long road gettin' here. Took time and effort to lure you two in. It's understandable you're beat. I'm gonna haul you folks back to the lodge where you can rest up proper. Make sure you get a good night's sleep before you make your, uh, final decision."

"You can't hold us here," Stacey said, chin up, nostrils flared, eyes narrowed. "Milan Meier knows we came!"

Lonestarr's laugh was a ragged thing. "Oh, Stacey child, don't be naive. You're smarter than that! Who do you think delivered you to my very door if not *der Hollander*?"

Lonestarr nodded and Guerra produced a hypodermic and injected something into Stacey's arm. Sand was struggling when a needle jabbed him the same.

Sprawled on the dirt next to his unconscious wife, Sand thought, *Meier – the Dutchman.*

Of course.

CHAPTER SIXTEEN
QUICK SAND

John Sand's eyes came openly slowly and focused the same way. Groggy, he sat up. He was on a chaise lounge in a vast room with a two-story cathedral ceiling, knotty pine walls, and hand-carved rustic log furniture, though this chaise and a few select pieces were brown-red over-stuffed leather.

Staring from the walls, with a particularly regal example looming over the massive stone fireplace, were mounted deer heads with magnificent antlers and glassy eyes, eight-point, ten-point examples – a virtual museum of taxidermy. Ruling over it all was a grotesque chandelier fashioned from an unfathomable number of antlers.

Overlooking this cavernous area was the balcony of a truncated second floor with a row of doors (to bedrooms presumably) and a walkway along which a trio of well-spaced Latino guards in camouflage gear leaned against a rail with their rifles.

Stacey, on her back on a matching couch, was still out after their hypodermic nightcaps. Neither Sand nor his wife were bound. Crow was seated on a leather chair across from Sand with a shotgun in his lap. He wore a red-and-black plaid shirt, jeans, moccasin boots, and a smirk. A low-slung rustic coffee table with a carafe of orange juice, a platter of cinnamon rolls, and napkins separated Sand and Crow.

"I'm going to check on my wife," Sand told him.

Crow's shrug seemed to allow that.

Crouching beside her, Sand said, "Darling...darling, wake up."

Her eyes fluttered.

"Morning, my love," he said gently, a hand on her sleeve.

Slowly, lifting a hand to a skull that must have been aching as much as his, she groaned and opened her eyes.

"Are we dead?" she asked.

"Not quite."

Footsteps on wooden flooring announced Jake Lonestarr striding in, again wearing that stupid damn safari get-up with the black Stetson, a snap-holstered sidearm on his right hip. He was not alone. One arm around her shoulders, the other around his waist, Lonestarr had at his side – in a catsuit not unlike Stacey's, but black leather, as if to upstage her – was Kyla Fluss.

Kyla Fluss, the bosomy blonde betrayer who had led Sand into Crow's clutches back in Berlin. Kyla Fluss, who had rutted with this monstrous mad Texan in that stable stall in Houston.

Lonestarr arranged himself and his female companion in front of the stone fireplace. Perhaps God would drop the antler head down on them, crushing them, although in Sand's experience the High and Mighty left it to his earthly children to sort out their own affairs.

"Well, you kids both look rested," Lonestarr said, hugging his honey. "I have a full morning planned for you folks. Help yourself to the orange juice and a sticky roll. Normally I set out a full breakfast spread for my guests, but you two will want to be lighter on your feet than that."

Sand said, "What did you give us?"

"Just a little something to help you sleep. You'll soon shake it off....You remember Kyla here, don't you?"

Looking directly at Stacey, Kyla said, "Oh, I'm sure he does. Just like I remember the scars from each and every bullet and knife wound on his lovely body."

Stacey obviously didn't like hearing that. What woman would?

Sand said, "It's true I've had to put up at times with disgusting indignities for Queen and Country."

Kyla pretended to pout. "So ungentlemanly, John. It's not like you. What's become of your fabled *savoir faire*?"

Lonestarr gave her a peck of a kiss and she stroked his face, played with a tip of the elaborate mustache. He told her, "I won't forget how rude he was to you, darlin'."

She smiled. "Whatever is best for business, *liebling*. Your Kyla is nothing if not practical."

They kissed again, longer. Sand grimaced. Stacey frowned.

"Now you run along," Lonestarr told her, "and tell our friend Milan we'll have that Boldt uranium deal in our pocket in two shakes. Scoot!"

She scooted, in a manner that Sand felt would have embarrassed Jayne Mansfield.

Stacey said, "I made my position clear last night, Jake. And a drug-induced 'good night's sleep' has hardly changed things. You will never get your hands on any Boldt Oil holdings."

Lonestarr turned to Sand. "You share that opinion, son?

Or are you content to let the little lady run things?"

Sand nodded. "I'm in charge of the big things in the marriage – like ridding the world of megalomaniacs."

Lonestarr chuckled. "Such bravado. You've started to confuse yourself with the fictional version, Johnny." He sighed, shook his head, returned his attention to Stacey. "I am just sentimental enough a soul to prefer getting that uranium by having you sign it over good and proper, making fair payment and all. But that would be the easy way, so we seem to be headin' into that hard way you hear so much about. Hard for *you*, that is. Easy for me."

Stacey's laugh had a bitter edge. "You really think with me out of the way you can take over my company? Everyone on the board *revered* my father. *Worshiped* him! They wouldn't do business with you even if you somehow could crawl out from behind the murder I saw you commit. Of my father!"

Lonestarr stalked over and, with the coffee table between them, shook a finger at her as if she were a naughty child. "I told you, you stubborn little colt, that was self-defense!"

"You'd kidnapped me! Like you're doing now!"

"That was strictly business. But you're right about one thing – it's better I stay dead. It won't be me who approaches the board and your heirs – it will be my friend Milan Meier."

Silenced draped the room. A dozen dead deer seemed to be listening intently.

"So," Stacey said, "what, then? You're offering us our lives for our cooperation?"

He spread his arms and opened his hands. "I am. Bygones be bygones. Cling to memories of better days. I don't want to steal a thing from you, Stacey child – I will pay."

"Yes you will," Sand said.

Lonestarr turned his gaze on the agent. "You are an arrogant son of a bitch, John Sand. I could kill both of you, here and now. There are guns on you all around. You can *see* that. But I prefer to be sporting about it."

"You're going to hunt us," Sand said.

Stacey hadn't put that together and her look of alarm cut Sand.

But he didn't show it, only shrugging. "Well, we're at a hunting lodge, after all. I'd hate to disappoint."

"Why on earth," Stacey said, and she'd recovered quickly, which made him so proud of her, "do you imagine we'll play your psychotic game?"

Lonestarr unholstered his sidearm, not surprisingly a Colt .45 revolver, then turned to Crow. "Keep the little lady company for a few minutes, would you, *kemosabe*? I have somethin' I want to share with my other guest.... Come along, Johnny."

With the .45, Lonestarr nudged Sand down a corridor past three closed doors, each with a Latino guard with a rifle in his hands just outside. Lonestarr stopped at corridor's end.

"My study," Lonestarr said, and opened the door. "Go on in....Normally I keep this locked up and private, but I thought a man of the world like John Sand might appreciate it."

The room was not large, and definitely cozy – built-in bookcases on either side, a desk tucked in one corner, a liquor cart in the other, and a small stone fireplace on the facing wall beyond a dark-red leather overstuffed chair by a table with a lamp on it, a hardcover book folded open – *Something of Value* by Robert Ruark. Above the fireplace were the mounted heads of four men and two women, all

Afro-Curacaoan, arranged in a gentle half circle with a space reserved right over the hearth.

"That's where you and the missus will reside," Lonestarr said, gesturing with an open hand. "Place of honor. My first Caucasian trophies."

Sand looked at the grim, staring faces, and was glad he hadn't been served that big breakfast. He had seen much in his years on Her Majesty's Secret Service – cruelty, barbarity, madness. And this combined, and outdistanced, it all.

Lonestarr paused to look from one wall of books to the other. "One of these will have to go," he said absently. "Pity, as there are some nice leather-bound volumes here. But I need the expansion space....Shall we rejoin the charming Mrs. Sand?"

She was boiling as they re-entered. "There is no way in hell we are going to play your sick game!"

"Your hubby may want to weigh in on that," Lonestarr said. "Might be time for him to assert himself. Wear the pants in the family, for a change....Uh, *Hay-zoos!* Bring out our other guest!"

Jesus Guerra came out of the corridor where Sand had recently been. The camo-clad thug had a .45 automatic in one hand and with the other dragged by the arm a hand-cuffed, bound-at-the-ankles, square-framed man with a burlap bag over his head. The rumpled gray suit, loosened narrow-striped tie, and Eton cufflinks made his identity clear to Sand even before Lonestarr yanked the bag off the blinking man.

Lord Malcolm Marbury, working to get used to the sunlight streaming in, gave Sand a wan smile. "I'm afraid we were betrayed, John. Not sure by whom."

"The Belgian," Sand said.

"Ah," Double M said. "You're looking well, Mrs. Sand. I don't believe I've seen you since the wedding."

Stacey summoned a brave smile. "Pleased to see you again, sir. Despite the circumstances."

Lonestarr said, "Aren't reunions a joyous thing?...Now, Johnny, the little lady was just saying she doesn't want to play the game. But I prefer that you do, both of you, together. If you choose not to participate, that's your howdy do. I'll just send Lord Marbury in your place...he'll have an hour to make it through the jungle to the beach. He'll get a ten-second *head* start..."

The emphasizing pun would mean nothing to Stacey, but Sand got it, all right.

"It's a good thirty seconds to the trees," Sand said.

"Lord Marbury," Lonestarr said, nodding, "will surely die. I'll shoot him down myself. But seein' as you're my old dear friends, I'm gonna allow you a runnin' start of ten minutes."

"Before you come after us," Stacey said.

"That is how the game is played, darlin'. Of course, I will have an unspecified number of my associates hunting with me – that may seem unfair, but hunting always has been a lopsided affair, a group of humans tracking a single beast. You have it better than most – there's two of you!"

Stacey asked, "And if we reach the beach?"

"You will be free. The hunt will cease. And so will my efforts to pry that uranium away from Boldt Oil. You have my word."

Dryly Sand said, "Who could ask for more?"

"Now," Lonestarr said, "if you're thinking of following the dirt lane to the highway, I'm afraid I have other men posted all along to make sure you don't cheat. Because no one likes a cheater, as we all know!...Shall we head outside?"

Lonestarr gestured to the balcony and his men in camouflage gear made their way down, and soon a small army – including Crow and Guerra - filed behind their slender, elaborately mustached honcho in his black Stetson and ridiculous khaki safari suit as he and his .45 revolver showed their guests outside.

Through an open porch with rustic furnishings, they went down half a dozen steps to a gravel apron with a showroom's worth of parked Range Rovers beyond which stretched a manicured yard complete with such Texas touches as picnic tables and a barbecue pit - a bit like that party the night Sand and Stacey first got to know each other. He doubted this would make Stacey feel at home, particularly since a primordial jungle awaited forty meters beyond.

The sun wasn't high yet but it was already hot. A breeze riffled through the trees, though, with some sea smell to it. At least Lonestarr's promise of a fairly nearby beach was not just another lie.

Someone handed the country-fried bwana a Remington Autoloading Rifle with scope. He held it to him in both hands, as if he'd already won a prize. Sand glanced back at Lonestarr, who was just behind the couple, bringing his wrist around the weapon to check his Cortébert watch, which was too good for the bastard.

"You kids best get to runnin'," their host said pleasantly. "Ten minutes starts *now*!"

They ran hand-in-hand across the open yard, as behind them Lonestarr cackled and his boys guffawed. Stacey was every bit as fast as Sand and they didn't let go of each other as they sprinted into the jungle along a narrow path through a gauntlet of leafy branches.

He squeezed her hand, and they both came to a gradual stop, bending over, hands on knees, catching their breath.

"This path," she said, huffing a little, "goes east. That's the beach. But they'll be along here, his men, if he's sent any ahead."

"Doesn't matter."

"What?"

"The beach isn't where we're going."

"It isn't? Where *are* we going?"

He held her eyes, her unblinking green eyes, as green as any of the foliage around them. "We're going back the way we came, to do what we came here to do – rid the world of Jake Lonestarr, and while we're at it save Double M."

She nodded. No argument. Good girl.

She asked, "How many men did you count back there?"

"Nine including Jake, Crow and Guerra."

She shivered. "How many will he bring with him when he comes after us?"

Sand spoke quickly, even as he looked all around him, ears perked for any suspicious rustle. "Oh, he's not coming after us. Not personally. He's back at the lodge waiting in case we try to rescue his hostage."

One blink. "He is?"

"He is. Jake knows I wouldn't leave Lord Marbury behind to his tender mercies. I doubt if he's sending more than half of his numbers in here. Of course there are likely others already spread through this damn jungle."

Bird sounds had started in since they'd paused. Lots of birds in Curacao. High-pitched calls like tiny warning sirens.

"You know," Stacey said, "when we make it out of here, you have some explaining to do."

"What – Kyla? I held my nose and had her. What else

do you need to know?"

She grinned, laughed. "You bastard."

"You knew that when you married me," he reminded her. "Now, to get us guns."

He led her off the path. When they were a good thirty meters into the underbrush, deep in its canopied shadows, he stopped. He'd found what he was looking for – a reasonably strong-looking sapling next to a fallen log.

"What's the plan?" she whispered.

"Jake figures we'll either overcome his men or they will kill us. Either prospect is likely to take a while. Well, we're not playing his dangerous game. We're sticking it out in this goddamn hellhole only long enough to get firearms."

"But if they're waiting for us in here..."

"Most will be deeper in, closer and closer to the beach. We wait for somebody from the lodge to come find us, or those already posted in this first area. We want guns, my dear. We want guns."

Taking off his blazer, then hanging it carefully over the branches of the sapling, he said, "We go back right away, and armed. *That* he may not be expecting."

She nodded toward the draped blazer. "Drawing them to us?"

"Hope to. From the path, this scarecrow may just be enough to fool somebody." He pulled off a sneaker, removed its lace, then slipped the shoe back on.

She frowned curiously. "Now what are you up to?"

"Yours is not to reason why. Yours is but to lay down behind that fallen log."

She eyed the lush green ground like he was asking her to hide in a quicksand bog, but she did as he asked.

Sand knelt on the soft ground and securely tied one end of the shoelace to a cuff button on his jacket, then draped the white lace behind enough greenery to make it disappear. With the other shoelace end in hand, he got down behind the log next to Stacey.

They waited.

Two voices came from the direction of the path, both speaking Dutch-accented English, not loud but easily discernible.

A rifle cracked, bird wings fluttered, and the blazer danced as a bullet tore through it. Sand yanked the shoelace and the jacket fell to the ground. At this distance, Sand hoped, the shooter would think he nailed his target.

Now the Sands just had to wait for the rifleman to come check on his kill.

"What do you think of *that* shot, Joshua?" a chuckling voice said, the words nearly masked by two men pushing through the foliage.

Next to him, Stacey emitted a small squeak, and Sand's first reaction was to see if the men coming toward them had heard her. Satisfied they hadn't, he turned his attention to her, and her very wide eyes directed him down.

A snake slithered around her ankle, like a living anklet, brown-and-black striped.

The two men were visible now, their attention directed toward the fallen coat. Sand reached down, snatched the snake behind the head and yanked it away. It tried to curl around his arm – it was a good foot and a half long – but he managed to shake the coiling off while keeping his grip.

Stacey's eyes were saucers, but she stayed quiet.

The two men were still a few meters away. Sand, with the snake in tow, crawled out from behind the log and, without being seen, flanked the two men.

He could see them now, one thin and tall, the other short and squat, both dressed like native Curacaoans in white shirts and dark slacks, both black. Not part of Lonestarr's house crew – Sand was probably coming into contact, finally, with some of Meier's vaunted security team. As they neared the fallen coat, he rushed them. They both turned toward him.

Sand flung the writhing snake into the face of the squat one, then launched himself, tackling the thin one at the waist, driving him to the ground, the man landing with a satisfying *whump*, letting out a *whoosh* as the air left his body.

Breaking a man's neck with a twist of the hands was tricky, but Sand had long since mastered it. That took care of the thin one. The squat one, screaming like an awful bird call, had batted away the snake, and was less concerned with any rational worry and more focused on scrambling on his ass the hell away from the reptile. That cost him. Picking up the thin man's rifle, Sand shot the squat one in the head while the squirming man was still on the ground, lending a splash of color to the jungle floor.

Stacey was on her feet. "You're a snake handler now?"

"Oh, I still hate snakes. But there are no poisonous ones in Curacao. Luckily, our late friend here didn't know that. Or just plain didn't care for them."

Sand collected the thin man's M1903 Springfield rifle, then knelt and went through his pockets, collecting two extra magazines for the weapon.

"Get the other one's gun," Sand said, sotto voce. "Check him for ammunition. Not much time now. The shots will bring more."

Stacey did so. Sand was detaching his shoelace from his blazer when she held up two extra mags triumphantly.

He tossed her the blazer. "Put this on – you'll have a couple pockets for ammo. The hole in the back will keep you cool."

"Very funny," she said with a smile. It was indeed humid and hot.

She slipped the jacket on, putting the magazines in the left-hand pocket. He was about to re-lace his shoe when footfalls coming up the path made themselves heard, and he motioned for her to get back down behind the log.

He picked a spot between two saplings, near one of the bodies, and tied his shoelace to the small trees, connecting them a few inches off the ground. With this half-assed tripwire in place, he joined Stacey behind the log.

Then, in a guttural voice, he called, "*Helpen! Hij heeft me neergeschoten.*"

Help, he shot me! in Netherlandic.

Stacey whispered, "You speak Dutch?"

"*Een beetje,*" he said.

Two more gunmen came running, neither being careful enough, one stumbling over Sand's tripwire, then tumbling onto the corpse. This stopped the other one, who turned when he heard something, which was Stacey and Sand popping up from behind their log. Stacey's rounds hit the standing one twice in the chest as Sand shot the fallen one, trying to get to his feet, in the head.

"We need to talk head shots," he told her.

"I like a bigger target."

"Time to move. But give me a second."

He stopped to again retrieve the lace and laced his sneaker before they took off into the jungle. They moved as fast as they could through the thick undergrowth, heading toward the lodge. A bullet thwacked into a tree next to Stacey.

"Head down!" he yelled at her. "Keep moving!"

Sand ran serpentine, hoping she would follow, and she

did, but it wasn't easy, encountering holes, stumps, fallen branches, damn near anything could lurk beneath a misleading placid layer of fallen leaves. They were bobbing and weaving, still moving, the thick jungle impeding their progress, but impeding their attackers as well.

Even as he plowed forward, Sand sought an advantage, an opportunity to flip positions with their pursuers; then as bullets zinged he heard Stacey grunt and she went down.

Sand stopped for a second, the two trading a look. She nodded and he ran on, slugs still whizzing past him. When the bullets stopped flying, he circled back. The two gunmen stood over Stacey. They were both white, one with brown hair, one blond; this pair was in camo and they spoke English with Texas accents. They were arguing, guns limp in their hands.

Removing his already loosened tie, wrapping the ends around either hand, Sand crept up behind them.

The blond one was saying, "Goddamnit, we gotta take her back to the boss! This ain't no time to screw around."

The brown-haired one said, "You kidding? It's *exactly* the time to screw around!" He was leering down at Stacey, in a heap on the ground, blood oozing from her arm where a bullet had nicked her.

Sand kicked the would-be rapist in the backside and sent him flying over Stacey as the blond gunman swung around and Sand kicked him in the groin. The gunman seemed to bow to Sand, who took the opportunity to wrap the tie around the man's neck, swing behind him, and strangle him, which took a good minute. Meanwhile, the first gunman got to his feet just long enough to have Stacey aim her rifle up at him and try a head shot for a change, adding more color to the surroundings.

Rising, the smoking weapon in her hands, Stacey said, "I was just starting to wonder about you, John."

"I got caught up in all this nature," he said, dropping his kill to the jungle floor. He wiped beads of sweat off his brow. "Are you all right?"

She glanced at her torn blood-spotted sleeve; against the black of the cat suit, it didn't show much. "I've hurt myself worse shaving my legs."

"Please don't spoil the mystery." He ripped a sleeve off his shirt and wrapped it around her arm, a bandage not a tourniquet. Bare-chested, Sand tossed the rest of his shirt on the ground next to the dead man, who now wore his tie, although sans a Windsor knot.

"You Tarzan?" she asked him.

"About time I got a Caribbean tan, Jane, don't you think?"

They were on the move again. They paused to rest for a moment at a gnarled tree.

Sand said, "We still have Lonestarr, Crow and Guerra to deal with."

She bobbed her head back, auburn hair flying. "There could be more behind us."

"Maybe. We'll stay sharp. But my guess is, any of them left were positioned down near the beach, in case we made it that far."

They crept to the edge of the jungle, keeping to the long shadows of the undergrowth. They stopped while still hidden, separated from the lodge by the well-kept front yard and the gravel apron with the Land Rovers.

Four men were out in front, waiting on this side of the barbecue pit and picnic tables. They were grouped a few feet apart – Crow at right, Guerra at left, and Lord Marbury in the middle with Lonestarr right behind him, his .45 revolver in his hostage's neck.

"Even from a distance, with these rifles," Sand told her, frowning, "we can't kill them all before Lonestarr shoots Double M."

"What do we do?"

Sand considered sneaking around back, coming through the lodge, and surprising Lonestarr and the two flunkies from behind; but if any others of Lonestarr's crew were still in the lodge – and that did not seem unlikely – the surprise would be on Sand.

"I know a way," he told her.

CHAPTER SEVENTEEN
SAND BLAST

Both Sand and Stacey were tucked behind trees on either side of at the path into the jungle, with the back yard of the lodge just inches away. Sand's bare chest was pearled with sweat, his chin dripping like a stubborn faucet. Even Stacey, so used to the Texas heat, was a victim to all the running and the wall of humidity, wiping perspiration from her pretty brow. They had come this far together, he told himself, and they would finish this thing together.

It would *not* finish them – they would finish *it.*

Standing in their staggered row, Crow in his plaid shirt and Guerra in his camo gear – on either side of Lonestarr using Marbury as a human shield – were waiting for what came next, each henchman with a hunting rifle in his hands and a holstered pistol on his hip. The captors were slowly scanning the jungle beyond the back yard, looking for Lonestarr's safari advance team to emerge either dragging the couple or the corpses thereof.

But perhaps other thoughts were beginning to dawn on Lonestarr and his henchmen, now that a flurry of gunfire had ended and none of Lonestarr's men were showing themselves.

The hunter of humans bellowed, *"Don't tell me you're still* standin', *Sand! You still* breathin', *Stacey darlin'? Well, if you want your precious duke or baron or whatever the hell he is...come and* bargain *for him! Never too late to negotiate in business!* You *should know that!"*

Double M, the snout of Lonestarr's .45 revolver dimpling his neck, stood perfectly straight, chin up, as if lacking only a briefcase and bumbershoot to be waiting for the next tube train. The man could stand a shave, Sand noted. But then Marbury had been a prisoner for some days, so that could be excused.

Before taking position at their respective trees, Sand had told Stacy, "Here's your chance to fine-tune your head shot. Take Jesus out. With luck he won't rise in two days."

"Poor taste, John."

"Then stop smiling. I'll take Crow out at the same time. Then we'll deal with Lonestarr – with both of them gone, he won't kill his hostage. It's all he'll have between us and him."

"But *then* what?"

He thumped his bare chest. "My turn for a head shot. It'll turn that bastard off like a light switch. His brain won't be sending signals anymore, meaning that trigger doesn't get squeezed."

"You sound confident."

"I am – unless I miss." He gave her a hard look. "When I nod, I'll whisper a three-count. Got it?"

"Got it."

Now, each behind his or her tree, Sand nodded.

She nodded back.

He whispered, "One..."

Guerra seemed to zero in on their position and said

something to Crow. *Had he heard that whisper?*

"Two..."

The two men took a step toward them.

"*Three!*"

The simultaneous rifle fire merged into one deafening roar, and the two men dropped at once, in perfect synchronization, leaving behind twin clouds of misty scarlet, though the flying particles of brain and blood were irregular, rising and falling like grotesque confetti.

It made Lonestarr jump, although Marbury stood tall, a condemned man whose firing squad had missed. His captor quickly recovered and threw an arm around Double M's throat and raised the snout of the .45 to the lord's head.

"*That changes* nothing!" Lonestarr screamed.

But of course it had changed everything.

"*You and the missus, you step out in the clearing! Right now! And we'll talk this out! Come to terms!*"

Sand stepped from behind his tree and out onto the path, leaving his rifle behind. "Change of plans," he whispered. "Wait for a clear head shot."

"What are you *doing,* John?"

"I'll distract him, cowgirl, and you take your best shot."

Before she could argue, he walked out onto the edge of the lawn, hands up.

"*I said* both of you! *Stacey, come on out and talk to your ol' Uncle Jake!*"

Sand yelled, "*She's wounded! She needs medical help!*"

"*How bad?*"

Sand was in Stacey's line of fire and knew it – and had to get out of it. But a sudden move might cost Marbury his life.

"*She's conscious!*" Sand began to slowly walk toward Lonestarr and his captive, at an angle, hoping to give Stacey a clear trajectory. "*But she can't walk! We'll deal!*"

Sand realized Lonestarr just wasn't presenting enough of himself for her to risk a shot. Marbury was a big enough man to block the lanky Texan, and the two men were equally tall. Damnit!

"*You stay put!*" Lonestarr shouted.

Stacey took the shot.

As its report echoed, Lonestarr screamed, his right ear gone, ripped off his head like a loose scab, the torn remains spritzing blood. It flustered the one-eared man enough to make him lower the gun. Marbury swiveled to face his captor and brought cuffed hands down as fists onto Lonestarr's right wrist, knocking the big revolver from his grasp. Then those cuffed hands came up and grabbed the man's skull in both hands, twisting swiftly, deftly, firmly, snapping the Texan's neck, producing a starter-gun crack.

Lonestarr's head drooped to one side, his eyes bulged, his tongue lolled, and he went down like a playing-card castle.

Sand ran over and Double M – wiping some blood off his still cuffed hands – said, "That bloody ear made a mess."

"Sorry you had to pitch in yourself, sir," Sand said.

"I'm a believer in group efforts, Triple Seven, which is something I doubt you'll ever grasp."

Stacey was running across the back yard with a rifle in one hand like an attacking Apache brave.

"I'm sorry!" she yelled as she came. "I'm sorry!"

When she alighted near the catawampus corpse of the man who killed her father, she said, "John! Lord Marbury! I am so sorry – I *missed!*"

"It served us well, just the same," Marbury said. "And had you erred in the other direction, we wouldn't be having this conversation. You could do me a favor, Mrs. Sand."

"Anything!"

"Check that scoundrel's pockets for the handcuff keys."

But Sand raised a hand and knelt and did that for her. He found them quick and easy and unlocked the cuffs.

"Don't tell my Boswell," Sand said to his wife and once-and-future boss, "that it was the two of you who took the villain down."

"I wouldn't worry," Double M said. "I'm sure you'll come off better in the fictional version."

Stacey's eyes were on Lonestarr, on the ground, his head twisted at an impossible angle.

"Finally dead," she said. She seemed to be thinking about shooting him again to make sure, but it so clearly wasn't necessary.

Sand searched the other corpses and was pleased to find his Walther in Crow's waistband. He retrieved the weapon, checked it. Fully loaded.

And perhaps he would need it, because coming out through the porch were half a dozen of Lonestarr's camo-clad Latinos who'd been standing guard in various fashions in the lodge. They lined up along the porch rail and looked down at the carnage and the three survivors. Each had a rifle. Each was aiming it at them.

Sand stepped forward. "You can shoot it out with us if you like, but your dead boss here won't be paying you for it."

The men traded looks all around.

Sand went on: "Or you can loot this place, and we can all go our separate ways."

Again the men traded looks all around. And then smiles. They filed back in, fast.

"Well-played," Marbury said, straightening his tie. "I

would suggest we take our leave."

Stacey asked, "No police?"

"No police. I'll be calling the Dutch Antilles counsel as soon as I can get back to civilization."

The keys were in the first Range Rover they checked. They all got in and, with Sand behind the wheel, drove to the one-lane road that would take them to the highway; they came upon the Jaguar, where it had been abandoned.

Sand found the keys in the ignition, but the two-seater would do them no good. It did provide him with his duffel from the trunk and his wife's purse from in front. With zero shame, he stripped out of his remaining clothes and, while the passengers in the Range Rover blinked at him, got into clean underwear, a fresh Polo, a gray blazer, and black slacks, staying only with the black sneakers. He left the ruined garb behind.

Sand took a deep breath, smiled, and got back in the Range Rover with them. He still smelled like the jungle, but nonetheless he felt alive again.

****

Sand drove with Stacey in the passenger seat and Lord Marbury in back, sitting forward like a big kid wondering how many more miles, Daddy.

"You really think this is advisable?" Marbury asked.

"You can stay in the car," Sand said. "I'll handle it."

Stacey asked, "Are you going to kill him?"

"Don't know. Been a lot of killing already."

"As in," Marbury said, "perhaps there's been enough bloodshed?"

"As in," Sand said, "what's one more dead bastard, more or less?"

The gate at the Meier estate was either still open or

open again. He pulled into the bricked circle drive and the big burnt-yellow villa loomed ahead. He drove past where all those expensive cars had been parked yesterday and stopped closer to the house, where a small yellow car, a DAF 600, was pulled up. He found one green front door unlocked and went in.

Sand took his re-confiscated Walther from his waistband and went into the high-ceilinged living room. It was empty, not just of people, but of...everything. No modern furniture. No abstract museum-quality paintings on the walls.

Well, there was one person – a woman in a navy blue blazer not unlike the one he'd turned into an impromptu scarecrow in the jungle. When she turned, the blazer had a crest that said CURACAO REALTY, and she was holding a clipboard. She was tall, brunette, forty-ish with cat's-eye glasses.

He was holding the Walther behind his back.

"I'm afraid we're not showing the house just yet," she said, pleasant but business-like. "You'll have to check with the office."

"Do you have a forwarding address for Mr. Meier?"

"Who?"

He backed out making apologetic noises.

In the Range Rover, he looked at his passengers. "Milan Meier has been a busy boy." He said to his wife, "While you and I were resting up at the lodge for our big day, he was pulling a vanishing act."

She asked, "Do you suppose we've seen the last of him?"

"Not bloody likely."

******

They discussed going to the hotel, but Stacey suggested Jaanchie's, the restaurant where she'd gone with Meier. Sand thought that was a fine idea. He'd worked up an appetite, and imagined they had, too.

Out front vari-colored birds flitted from sugar trough to sugar trough in a tree-shaded garden. Inside the old orange-and-white farmhouse were latticed windows, floral tablecloths, tile floors, and plenty of space between tables. Sand, who had been here several times on the oil refinery mission, recommended the iguana stew and the cactus soup. Stacey listened politely and ordered garlic shrimp with rice and peas.

They lingered for after-dinner coffee and Stacey excused herself and went off to the ladies' room.

"Alone at last," Sand said.

Marbury, leaning forward, asked, "GUILE headquarters?"

"It's still there, trashed but there. And you and I are the sole survivors. Well, Charlotte DuBois I dropped off at a hospital. She may have pulled through."

Sand gave him a brief rundown of events. An ashen Marbury listened silently, occasionally shaking his head. "My God." A hand cradled his forehead. "We have to start over."

"You have one man, if you still want him."

"I certainly do. Does your wife know about...?"

"GUILE? Only in the broadest of strokes. But she'll have questions, as the dust settles, and we're past keeping secrets. Understand, I need her blessing or I can't consider taking this on."

He raised his eyebrows. "We could use *her*, too, actually. A couple working together with an impeccable built-in cover? A genuine asset. And from what I've seen, she has formidable skills."

"Like shooting a man's ear off?" Sand huffed a laugh, then shrugged a nod. "Stacey was trained well by an ex-federale. You probably know she was there when we took Crow's brother Raven down."

"Yes. On your honeymoon."

"She was at my side in San Ignacio, too, and in the jungle today, more than held her own."

"So you like the idea."

Another laugh. "Hardly. But knowing her? If I want to be on call for your kind of fun and games, either she comes along or I'll be sleeping on the couch....Here she comes."

Stacey had freshened her make-up and, but for the makeshift bandage on her sleeve, looked band-box fresh.

She slipped into her chair. "What have you boys been talking about? This new spy agency of yours, Lord Marbury? Wouldn't need any female operatives, would you?"

They all smiled and laughed a little. *But was she joking?* Sand wondered.

"I was just telling John here," Double M said, "that he's right."

"Oh?"

"The Iguana stew is delicious."

ABOUT THE AUTHORS

—

MAX ALLAN COLLINS was named a Grand Master in 2017 by the Mystery Writers of America. He is a three-time winner of the Private Eye Writers of America "Shamus" award, receiving the PWA "Eye" for Life Achievement (2006) and their "Hammer" award for making a major contribution to the private eye genre with the Nathan Heller saga (2012).

His graphic novel *Road to Perdition* (1998) became the Academy Award-winning Tom Hanks film, followed by prose sequels and several graphic novels. His other comics credits include the syndicated strip "Dick Tracy"; "Batman"; and his own "Ms. Tree" and "Wild Dog."

His innovative Quarry novels were adapted as a 2016 TV series by Cinemax. His other suspense series include Eliot Ness, Krista Larson, Reeder and Rogers, and the "Disaster" novels. He has completed twelve "Mike Hammer" novels begun by the late Mickey Spillane; his audio novel, *Mike Hammer: The Little Death* with Stacy Keach, won a 2011 Audie.

For five years, he was sole licensing writer for TV's

*CSI: Crime Scene Investigation (*and its spin-offs*)*, writing best-selling novels, graphic novels, and video games. His tie-in books have appeared on the USA TODAY and *New York Times* bestseller lists, including *Saving Private Ryan, Air Force One,* and *American Gangster.*

Collins has written and directed four features and two documentaries, including the Lifetime movie "Mommy" (1996) and "Mike Hammer's Mickey Spillane" (1998); he scripted "The Expert," a 1995 HBO World Premiere and "The Last Lullaby" (2009) from his novel *The Last Quarry.* His Edgar-nominated play "Eliot Ness: An Untouchable Life" (2004) became a PBS special, and he co-authored (with A. Brad Schwartz) two non-fiction books on Ness, *Scarface and the Untouchable* (2018) and *Eliot Ness and the Mad Butcher* (2020).

Collins and his wife, writer Barbara Collins, live in Iowa; as "Barbara Allan," they have collaborated on six-teen novels, including the "Trash 'n' Treasures" mysteries, *Antiques Flee Market* (2008) winning the *Romantic Times* Best Humorous Mystery Novel award of 2009. Their son Nathan has translated numerous novels into English from Japanese, as well as video games and manga.

MATTHEW V. CLEMENS is a writer and teacher whose first book was a non-fiction true-crime title, *Dead Water: the Klindt Affair* (1995, with Pat Gipple). He has co-written numerous books with Max Allan Collins, the pair having collaborated on over thirty novels and numerous short stories, as well as the much-lauded non-fiction work, *The History of Mystery* (2001). They also contributed an essay to the Edgar-nominated *In Pursuit of Spenser* (2012).

In addition the duo has produced several comic books, four graphic novels, a computer game, and over a dozen mystery jigsaw puzzles for such famous TV properties as *CSI* (and its spin-offs), *NCIS, Buffy the Vampire Slayer, Hellboy,* and *The Mentalist,* as well as tie-in novels for *Bones, Dark Angel* and *Criminal Minds.* A number of the team's books made the USA TODAY bestseller list.

Matt also worked with Max on the bestselling "Reeder and Rogers" debut thriller, *Supreme Justice* (2014), and shared byline on its two sequels, *Fate of the Union* (2015) and *Executive Order* (2017). He has published a number of solo short stories and worked on numerous book projects with other authors, both non-fiction and fiction, including R. Karl Largent on several of the late author's bestselling techno-thrillers. He has also worked as a book doctor for numerous other authors.

Matt lives in Davenport, Iowa with his wife, Pam, a retired teacher.

CPSIA information can be obtained
at www.ICGtesting.com
Printed in the USA
LVHW090724210321
681997LV00073B/1703